PRAISE FOR

BELITTLED WOMEN

•••••

"With a little grit and a lot of wit and humor, Amanda Sellet dives deep into what it means for a teen to both live up to and strain against expectations, while navigating the challenges of forging one's own path in life. Jo's experiences manage to be delightfully outlandish yet perfectly authentic. *Belittled Women* is a pitch-perfect homage to the messy-yet-loving chaos of family life."

—MEGAN BANNEN,
author of *The Undertaking of Hart and Mercy*

•••••

"*Belittled Women* is not just for fans of *Little Women*—it's also for those of us who love a book featuring a rebellious, smart protagonist, a rustic, charming setting, and prose that makes us literally laugh out loud. Jo is a lovable and hilarious heroine, and readers will also fall in love with her family, her hometown, and her journey to figure out exactly who she is and what she wants."

—RAQUEL VASQUEZ GILLILAND,
author of the Pura Belpré Award winner
How Moon Fuentez Fell in Love with the Universe

"If Nora Roberts wrote a YA *Little Women* retelling, this would be it. Brimming with effortless banter set against a satisfying slow-burn romance, *Belittled Women* is the very definition of a romantic comedy. Hilarious from page one, Amanda Sellet draws us into Jo Porter's waking nightmare: the never-ending carousel of life in a literal *Little Women* reenactment at her mother's roadside Kansas attraction. Living under the weight of her alternate life portraying 'Book Jo' and her family's expectations, our Jo can't wait to bust free, but what's holding her back might be what's been holding her together all this time."

—SARAH HENNING,
author of *Throw Like a Girl* and *It's All in How You Fall*

"I loved this wry, witty, raucous take on *Little Women*. Sellet nails the absurdity, love, and occasional brawls of sisterhood. The Porters are a boisterous delight."

—JESSICA SPOTSWOOD,
coauthor of *Great or Nothing*

A story of three bickering sisters,
two cute boys, and one average Jo

BELITTLED WOMEN

Amanda Sellet

Clarion Books
An Imprint of HarperCollinsPublishers

Clarion Books is an imprint of HarperCollins Publishers.

Belittled Women
Copyright © 2022 by Amanda Sellet
All rights reserved. Printed in the United States of America. No part of this
book may be used or reproduced in any manner whatsoever without written
permission except in the case of brief quotations embodied in critical articles
and reviews. For information address HarperCollins Children's Books, a
division of HarperCollins Publishers, 195 Broadway, New York, NY 10007.
www.epicreads.com

ISBN 978-0-35-856735-6

Typography by Natalie Sousa
22 23 24 25 26 PC/LSCC 10 9 8 7 6 5 4 3 2 1
First Edition

For Claire, Leelanee, Beth, and Amy
Beloved sisters by birth, marriage, and a fateful
canoe trip down the Withlacoochee

And for Mom, my lifelong partner in laughter,
even at the fabric store

"I thought every story should have some sort of a moral, so I took care to have a few of my sinners repent."

– Jo March, fictional character,
Little Women

"New rule: The next person who quotes *Little Women* gets slapped."

– Jo Porter, actual human and
not-so-little woman

Contact: Abigail "Marmee" Porter, marmee@litlady.net

FOR IMMEDIATE RELEASE

Coming Soon: The Seventh Spectacular Season of
Little Women Live!

————••●••————

New Concord, KANSAS—Mark your calendars! The area's most literary attraction, *Little Women Live!*, kicks off a seventh spectacular season this June.

Our one-of-a-kind destination offers visitors a magical opportunity to see their favorite characters come to life in an intimate and family-friendly setting. Watch the March sisters grow up before your very eyes as our talented cast acts out classic scenes including: a Christmas with no presents! Amy bringing limes to school! Jo and Laurie getting into "scrapes"! And, of course, Beth's emotional farewell!

Brand new this year: Meg's wedding!

While here, take a seat in the parlor. Try your hand at making jam. Enjoy a picturesque stroll through our landscaped grounds. Discover your inner Little Woman! Bring your own costume or buy a pinafore and bonnet in the gift shop.

Ample parking, modern restrooms, dining at our quaint Tea Shoppe, and souvenir shopping at the Concord Mercantile are all part of your Living Literature Experience.

For group rates, school tours, or to inquire about holding your next special event at *Little Women Live!*, contact Abigail Porter (a.k.a. "Marmee").

"My child, the troubles and temptations of your life are beginning, and may be many."

–Little Women

CHAPTER ONE

It doesn't matter how fast you run, or how far. There are things in this life you can't escape.

Like your family.

At least not during track season.

If this had been a cross-country workout, my sister would be eating my dust right now. Unfortunately, it was spring, which meant circling the asphalt loop behind school like hamsters with delusions of NASCAR. It also gave Amy a chance to trail after me wailing, "Jo! Wait!" like she needed my help defusing a bomb.

When I sped up, she cut across the end of the field to catch me coming around the bend. By now the rest of the team had probably recognized that the freak in street clothes pinballing around the inside of the track was my sister, so there was no point pretending not to know her. Plus, Coach Solter blew her whistle, beckoning me with one finger. Fun time was over.

"Didn't you hear me calling?" Amy panted, when I jogged to a stop beside her.

"People in the next state heard you." I hadn't been ignoring her. Well, not the whole time. When I was running, my mind spun out into the future. Today I'd been imagining a college campus somewhere far, far away. Walking slowly across a grassy quadrangle. Autumn leaves. Lots of wool. I could almost smell the crispness of the air, until Amy bulldozed through the middle of my daydream.

"Why are you here?" I resisted the urge to yell. Coach probably thought all the drama signaled a legit emergency, as opposed to Amy's standard attention-seeking behavior.

My sister pressed a hand to her belly as she drew in a shaky breath. You could have made a sandwich during the pause that followed, because apparently no crisis was too urgent to keep her from grandstanding. "We need you at home, Jo."

"I have practice until four thirty."

"Whatever. You're not even on the team."

It was a cheap shot. The only reason I didn't run track was that I'd have to miss half the meets—including state championships—due to the demands of our family business. Though the word "business" was a stretch. Tragic obsession would be more accurate.

"Coach wants me here." A minimum of three weekly workouts was mandatory, so those of us who only ran cross-country didn't lose all our conditioning in the off-season. That was the official reason; unofficially, we were demonstrating our commitment, team spirit, and extreme dedication to the cause. All of which were crucial if I wanted a shot at being cross-country captain next fall. Not that Amy would care about that.

Coach pushed her sunglasses to the top of her head, clipboard balanced against one hip. She was already getting the distinctive ski-goggle tan line around her eyes. "Why didn't you tell me there was a problem at home, Jo?"

"It's not—" I pressed my lips together, doubting I could make her understand. "Everything was fine this morning. They were singing at breakfast."

"When the red, red robin goes bob-bob-bobbin' . . ." Amy began, falling silent when I glared at her.

"We need to be able to communicate." Coach squinted at me, and I caught the unspoken message: *if you want to be a leader.* And since I had yet to secure more than one provisional offer from a college team, there was a lot more riding on next year than another varsity letter.

Amy grabbed Coach by the arm, leaning in like she was paying her respects at a funeral. "Thank you for understanding," she said in a totally fake rasp. Straightening, she jerked her head at me. "Let's go."

"I have like three laps left—"

Coach shook her head. "Family is important, Jo. We'll see you next week."

"Such a beautiful message," Amy murmured. From her backpack she produced a crumpled piece of paper, which she handed to Coach with a smile. "Take one of these. I did the design myself."

Also known as "typing," if you weren't full of yourself. Although the blocky paragraphs were printed in simple black ink, certain phrases leaped off the page, sizzling behind my eyelids. *Family-friendly. Pinafore. Ample parking.* Because if you had to brag about the parking, didn't that say it all?

I tried to snatch it away, but the damage was done. Coach scanned the press release like there might be some hidden message, as opposed to the same tired promotional language we used every year.

"That time already, huh?"

"Not really. It's still March." For a few more days, anyway. If the clock wanted to stop right here, it would be okay with me.

"You know what they say. It's always March at our house." Amy sent Coach a hopeful look that with the slightest encouragement would turn into a wink.

"No one says that. Ever."

"I can send you a countdown widget," my sister told Coach Solter, as if I had myself on mute. "So you can *track* exactly how long it is until the big day."

Ha. Not the words I would have chosen to describe our annual pageant of humiliation. *Waking nightmare,* maybe. *A living hell.* And this year would be even worse.

"It's like watching the time tick down until Christmas," my sister blathered on.

"Or an asteroid on a collision course with Earth," I countered, not quite under my breath.

"The anticipation builds and builds." Amy squeezed her fists in a pantomime of excitement. "And then, bam! It's finally May."

"May Day," I said grimly, like the distress signal it was. *Mayday. Mayday.*

"We're so pleased to be able to offer an exclusive sneak preview for the local schoolchildren." Amy spoke like she was hosting a charity telethon. "Giving back to the community is hugely important to the entire *Little Women Live!* family."

"Did you take too much allergy medicine?" I tried to see if her pupils were dilated.

"All this"—she fluttered her fingers toward the track, ignoring me—"is such a valuable part of Jo's process." It sounded like she was throwing Coach a bone. Because three consecutive Class 4A state titles couldn't possibly compete with the personal validation of contributing to a third-rate tourist attraction.

"It's really not," I assured Coach.

"The Other Jo was always scampering about—"

I stepped on my sister's foot to shut her up. Her elbow caught me in the rib cage before I could dodge sideways.

Coach tucked the press release under the other papers on her clipboard. "You should hang one up in the locker room, Jo."

I made a noise that passed for agreement, even though what I really meant was *That would be tricky since my copies are at the bottom of the recycling bin outside the cafeteria.* By now they were probably drenched in Smurf-colored Powerade. Or worse.

"Thanks again," Amy said, like they'd just completed a professional transaction.

"I know school tours are a big deal." *For your sad, impoverished family.* Coach didn't say that part out loud; it was written in the sympathetic pinch of her expression.

My sister yanked me by the arm before I could disagree. We'd only gone a few steps when she let go, wiping her hand on the front of her shirt. "Is that sweat? Gross."

"I just ran four miles."

"I'm surprised you didn't flood the stadium."

That reminded me. "I think I left my water bottle by the bleachers." I gestured with my thumb. Amy glanced back at me, eyes widening.

"No way." This time she grabbed the hem of my T-shirt. "You're not going back there."

"It'll take me two seconds."

"That's not why," she hissed.

I was briefly distracted by a series of weird eyebrow contortions, like her face was using Morse code. "Are you glitching out right now?"

Although there was no one else within twenty feet of us, she got right up in my space. "David," Amy said through gritted teeth. "He's over there."

My shoulders lifted in a shrug I was only halfway to feeling. "So? The guys' team has practice too." I stole a quick glance in that direction, easily spotting David's lanky form among the knot of runners getting ready to hit the track. He was the tallest by several inches, but even without the extra height I would have recognized his posture: hands on hips and head down as he listened to someone else talk. It was a neat trick for someone his size to make himself so unobtrusive.

Amy smacked me on the shoulder. "Will you stop staring? He looks the same as always."

"He got new running shoes." In happier times, I would have known all about them: brand, model, how he was breaking them in. We might have even gone shopping together.

"Whatever, perv. Quit ogling. What if he looks over here?"

"I don't know. We'll wave at him, like normal people?"

"We can't do that." From the look on her face, you would have thought I'd suggested sawing off a limb.

"Why not? It would be way ruder to ignore him."

"News flash. David doesn't *want* to talk to you."

"And you know this how?"

"Because, unlike you, I'm capable of understanding delicate emotions." Amy placed a hand over her heart. She probably thought that was where feelings lived—the Hallmark version of human anatomy.

"What's your point?"

Her head tipped back as she heaved a sigh. "It's too painful for him to see us. A reminder of what he's lost."

I resisted the urge to glance at David. Not that I'd be able to read signs of devastation from this distance. Even up close he had a pretty good poker face. "I'm sure he's realized he's better off by now."

"Wow. Disloyal much? Meg is our *sister*."

"Which is how I know she was a terrible girlfriend."

Amy pressed her lips together. Even she couldn't pretend our space-case older sister was an ideal romantic partner.

"David's too nice for any of us," I continued.

"Except you, right?"

"I said *us,* dumbass. As in our whole family."

"There's no *me* in *team,* Jo." Amy glanced at Coach, like she was thinking of repeating this bit of sporty wisdom to her. "But that still doesn't mean he wants to be around *you.*"

"We were friends before. There's no reason that has to change." I'd been a little afraid to test this theory by actually talking to him, but I wasn't going to share that with Amy. "It's not like I'm the one who dumped him."

"He doesn't need you to run in circles with him, Jo. He has a whole team for that." She flung an arm in that direction, which of course made David look our way.

I froze, painfully aware we'd been busted. Had he gotten even taller, or were his shorts shorter than usual? Right as my brain sent a signal to my face that this would be a good time to smile instead of staring at his legs, Amy jumped in front of me.

"Nope." She held a hand in front of my face to block my view. "You are not going to charge over there like a wrecking ball and make him hang out with you. Let him grieve in peace."

"I wasn't going to *make* him do anything."

"That's right, because we're leaving. Mom needs us." She shoved me forward with both hands. I thought about turning around and slide-tackling her legs out from under her, but there was a chance Coach would see. Plus David probably thought we'd been talking about him and then deliberately given him the cold shoulder, which was like choking down a chili dog of awkwardness on top of the deluxe shameburger of Amy's earlier performance.

"Why exactly do we have to go home?"

"She'll tell us when we get there."

I gave a small yet eloquent huff.

"You're going to feel bad when it turns out to be something major."

"Somehow I'll survive."

As we stepped past the chain-link fence that bordered the track, Amy spotted a gaggle of her equally loud and show-offy sophomore friends, who of course she had to greet with squeals and hand-grabbing and hopping in place. It had probably been under ten minutes since they'd seen one another. I could have won the lottery and made less of a production.

Crossing my arms, I gave Amy a look.

"What?" She was faking it for her friends, pretending not to understand my silent warning. The one that said, *you are standing on thin ice.*

"I have to go," Amy told them, cutting her eyes at me. A chorus of "Bye-ee!" and kissy noises erupted. They hugged like it was a contact sport, swaying side to side. It was all very *notice me,* as evidenced by the way they kept stealing glances over one another's shoulders, hoping for an audience. I stared back, stony-faced.

"Could you *be* more of a downer?" Amy muttered as she joined me.

"You dragged me away from practice. I'm not going to stand there and watch *The Amy Show*."

"Sometimes I think that's my true medium." She stared dreamily into the distance, head cocked, before glancing at me to see if I was impressed.

"Acting fake in public?"

"It's not fake. I just *enhance* things. Make them more vivid. And beautiful."

"Then it's definitely not like your art." Our house was littered with Amy's failed experiments in everything from origami to bottled sand. When your own mother asks if you've considered paint-by-numbers, it's probably time to find a new hobby.

"At least I'm actually creating something." She stuck her tongue out. "Besides stanky puddles of sweat."

"Being dramatic is not an art. Nobody gasps that much unless they're being strangled. Which unfortunately hasn't happened."

Amy sucked in an outraged breath, not exactly disproving my point. "You wouldn't understand."

"The pathological need to be stared at? True."

"If anything, I'm more honest than other people because I express myself openly. Which is way better than trying to hide your feelings and then turning all sour and twisted on the inside." She side-eyed me while pretending to cough.

"Congratulations on being an exhibitionist." We'd reached the car, an ancient station wagon lacking any hint of vintage coolness. Amy thrust the keys at me without a word.

"Where's Meg?" I asked, wedging myself behind the steering wheel. The lever that moved the seat forward and back had broken several years earlier, leaving it permanently adjusted for a person with much shorter legs. "Did she get a ride?"

"Here," said a voice from behind me.

I jolted hard enough to hit my head on the roof of the car. "What the hell, Meg?"

She yawned hugely, then covered her mouth. "It was taking too long. Time goes way faster when you're sleeping."

I glanced between her and Amy. "How long have you been out here?"

"Since school got out," Amy snapped, like it was my fault.

"Why didn't you go home?"

This earned me an epic eye roll. "How were we supposed to do that?"

I tapped my chin, pretending to think. "I don't know, maybe with the car you were sitting in?"

"I don't have my license with me," Meg said sleepily.

That brought me up short. "Where is it?"

Pulling the elastic from around her messy bun, Meg fluffed her long hair before scratching her scalp with the pads of her fingers. "Manketti oil," she said, sniffing her hair. "Leonor Greyl Masque Quintessence."

Usually when Meg sounded like she was speaking in code, it had to do with one of her personal-care products, a subject of less than zero interest to me. "License?" I reminded her.

"It's in my wallet."

"Which is where?"

"My backpack."

I twisted to peer over the seat. There was the usual smattering of junk—candy wrappers, ten thousand hair bands (including the one she'd just dropped), a few pieces of paper stamped with muddy shoe prints—but no backpack. "Can you cut to the chase and tell me where you left your stuff?"

"In my locker." She blinked several times. "I'm pretty sure."

"This is why you need to get your license," I told Amy.

"Excuse you, I had a very traumatic experience."

I rolled my eyes at the latest installment in the Tragic Saga of Amy, Perpetual Victim. "You ran over the mailbox. It's not like you were in a plane crash."

"It was a head-on collision, Jo."

"I don't think that's what that means. Only one of you was moving, which you would have noticed if you'd been wearing your freaking glasses—"

"Number one," Amy interrupted, "it's called an *accident* for a reason. That means it wasn't my fault. And (b), glasses pinch my nose. It's agony!"

"So get contacts. And then maybe you'll make it out of the driveway next time."

"Maybe they shouldn't make driveways so narrow."

"They're about as wide as the road, though. That's the thing."

Amy made a scoffing sound. "The road is way wider."

"Yeah, but you only get one of the lanes. You know that, right?"

"Whatever. I see plenty."

"How many fingers am I holding up?" I raised the middle one on my right hand.

"Real mature, Jo." She stuck out her tongue. "Just drive us home. I'm hungry, I'm bored, and I have a new hairstyle I want to try."

Realization settled over me like a cold mist. "I thought Mom needed us."

Amy looked shifty, clicking the lock on the car door up and down. "She does. She texted."

"What did she say, exactly?" I glanced at Meg, who shrugged. Apparently, she'd misplaced her phone, too.

"That she had news. And she would tell us everything when we got home."

"That's it?" I gripped the steering wheel like I was going to rip it in half. "And you got me out of practice for that?"

"She used a lot of exclamation points!"

"Um, have you met our mother?" Mom shed excess punctuation like other people lost dead skin. I yanked the keys from the ignition. "I'm going back to practice."

Amy grabbed my wrist before I could escape. "You should be grateful." This was a frequent refrain around our house. *We should all be thankful for [insert random crappy thing]! Count your blessings!* "Running is the worst." Sticking a finger in her mouth, she pretended to gag.

It was fascinating how many people felt comfortable dumping on a major part of my life. *Oh, you're a runner? I can't stand running.* And then they'd explain in graphic detail how they'd once come really close to blowing out their shorts while jogging around the block. Yes, sometimes it felt like your lungs were saw blades and your thighs were actually on fire, but it was worth it to know you could push through the pain and come out the other side.

"You don't have to like it," I told Amy. "It's *my* thing." It wasn't like I went around to knitters saying, *Ugh, how do you not stab yourself with those needles to make it stop?*

"So you miss a day. Who cares? It's not like it's a competition."

"It literally is, though." I pictured Kiersten W., my chief rival for captain, finishing her run, then sticking around to bond with the team. She didn't need it as badly as I did. Her grades were good, running wasn't her only extracurricular, and she'd actually made it to the surprise workout Coach had held for college recruiters, during which I was following my mother around the fabric store because ugly plaids were on sale. Plus Kiersten's family could pay for college if they had to, since her parents worked real jobs.

Amy flicked me in the shoulder. "Can you not be difficult? Like, for once in your life?"

"Right. Because I'm the problem."

Shaking her head like I was too dense to understand, she pulled a lollipop out of her pocket. From the way the wrapper stuck as she peeled it off, I could tell this was one Amy had started earlier. Maybe the lint made it more delicious.

"Aren't you the least bit curious about what Mom's going to tell us?" she said between slurps.

"No." *Curious* wasn't the feeling. It was more of a numb state of dread, like if you're already standing in a cold rain and someone pulls out a squirt gun. *Here we go again.*

"Well, I think it's going to be amazing." Amy pointed the lollipop at our older sister. "Don't you?"

Meg gave a vague "hmmm." I suspected she'd tuned out a long time ago.

I stuck the key back in the ignition. "You want to bet?"

"Ha. It would be stealing your money."

"You have no idea, do you?"

Amy reached for her seat belt. "Just drive the stupid car, Jo. I want to go home already."

That made one of us.

"Why, you know I don't mind hard jobs much, and
there must always be one scrub in a family."

–Little Women

CHAPTER
TWO

In brochure language, our house was situated in "an
idyllic pastoral landscape."

That suggested rolling green hills dotted with wildflowers
and a few sheep, possibly with a babbling brook in the distance.
The reality was closer to a stretched-out suburb. The fences
were wire instead of wood, and the lots were bigger, but the
effect was similarly bland: flat expanses of patchy grass with
houses set back from a seldom-used county highway.

The weathered gray two-story hadn't always been our home.
I had vague memories of an apartment complex with a playground next door and a covered plastic slide that heated like an
oven in summer. But then our mother's great-aunt Helen died,
leaving Mom her house and a few acres of land. Where some
would have said, *Sweet, I'll sell it and bank the cash,* our mother

saw a sign from the universe. Time to move across the country and start a *Little Women* theme park!

Sometimes I wondered what it would be like if the family business were built around a different attraction—a giant ball of twine, maybe, or a fiberglass jackalope—instead of an old-fashioned book. Where exactly did we fall on the scale of sad tourist traps?

Most people have heard of *Little Women*. A lot of them sort of know the story, about a poor Civil War–era family with four daughters and lots of inspiring life lessons. It's a heartwarming and wholesome classic, *blah blah blah*, loosely based on the life of author Louisa May Alcott. For us, it was much more. A bedtime story, before we were old enough to read it ourselves. The soundtrack to every road trip, until we'd memorized the skips on each scratched-up disc of the audiobook. A constant at family movie nights. And of course there was the minor detail of being named after characters from the book. Sweet, domestic Meg; rambunctious Jo; tragic invalid Beth; and prissy narcissist Amy.

(Fun fact: our Amy's real name was Bethamy, which was Mom's way of covering her bases. Having an extra kid just to match the March family would have been extreme even by her standards of fandom.)

So yeah. All of us were aware that *Little Women* was our mother's forever fave. We knew the twists and turns of the plot, with its childhood dramas, picnics and ice-skating, sacrifices and sad times interspersed with worries about hair and clothes and Growing Up (which mostly meant getting married, like good little women). It was like living near the ocean: a constant baseline of wave sounds and salty air, so familiar you hardly noticed they were there.

Turning Mom's obsession into a semiprofessional tourist attraction was an escalation, but by our standards still in the neighborhood of normal. Or at least it seemed that way when we were young enough to be caught up in the adventure. Choosing fabric for costumes! Staying up late to talk over which scenes to do first! Imagining ourselves onstage! It was like an epic game of dress-up.

When we found out Dad wasn't coming because he wanted to keep his job as an adjunct philosophy professor, Mom explained that it was okay because in the story Mr. March is hardly ever around. That sort of tracked with our father's vague presence in the family, since he was generally too busy to be involved in our daily lives. It also meant I'd have to step up and be the co-adult, because Meg was the pretty one, Amy was the spoiled baby, and our mother might as well have been a Pinterest board in human form, all soft-focus daydreams with minimal follow-through. Which was how I became the kind of fourth-grader who clipped coupons.

Once the four of us settled into our new home, we started small. A few performances here and there for a handpicked audience, mostly bits from the first half of the book, when the March sisters are young. "You'll grow into the roles," Mom told us, meaning both chronologically and as performers.

In this, as in so much about me, she was dead wrong. As the years went by, I liked acting less and less. It was one thing to prance around in silly outfits when we were kids, but what passed for cute from a child was painful after a certain age—especially when I had to do it in front of my classmates.

Every year the fourth, seventh, and eleventh grades visited, plus a few slacker seniors who signed up for History of Environmental Studies because of its reputation as an easy science credit. Elementary kids read an abridged version, with most of the death removed. In middle school it was supposedly part of the American history curriculum, and in high school *Little Women* got bundled in with a bunch of other extremely boring writers from that era, like Thoreau and Hawthorne. Nature! Sin! Kill me now!

The first time my class visited, I was too young to care about anything except missing out on the bus ride. By seventh grade, school tours were like dancing with a sprained ankle.

Middle school is not the time you want to stand out. Every giggle from the audience sliced me like the cheap razor I'd just started using to shave my legs. Dorking out onstage with my whole family was like slapping a gift tag on my forehead that read *To Everyone, from Jo: Please Mock Me.*

The only thing that saved me from total loserdom was cross-country. I'd joined the team earlier that year, so at least part of my public persona didn't suck. That was the "me" I leaned into at school: Sporty Jo, as opposed to Embarrassing Reenactor-Family Jo.

Now the ax was about to fall again. After looming in the distance like the end-of-semester project you ignore until the week it's due, the dreaded event was here. Every junior at my school would soon be reminded that Jo Porter led a double life. Behind the semi-normal seventeen-year-old student athlete lurked a different Jo. The *Little Women* one.

It might have been easier if I'd found allies in my sisters, but nothing bothered Meg, who maxed out at about sixty-five percent consciousness, and Amy ate up the attention with a spoon. That left me on the outside, the problem child with the bad attitude—like one of the kids from *The Sound of Music* smashing a guitar and screaming, *Screw this—I hate folk songs!* in the middle of the cuckoo-clock number.

I thought they were nuts, they thought I was a jerk, and then we all strapped on our bonnets and pretended to be the happiest family in the history of books.

It seemed unjust that her few joys should be lessened, her burdens made heavier, and life get harder and harder as she toiled along.

−Little Women

CHAPTER THREE

The station wagon had barely stopped moving when Amy jumped out of her seat, not quite shutting the door behind her. She ran up the steps before I could call her back, Meg trailing at a slower pace.

Mom preferred us to park behind the house, where the car wouldn't destroy the olden-times illusion. Although not actually historic, Great-Aunt Helen's house was built in a traditional style, with a wraparound porch and a pointy roofline. Between the rattling windows, creaky floors, and front hallway lined with moderately hideous floral wallpaper, the mood was "antique" enough to fool most visitors. I didn't care how it looked, but it would have been nice to have a bedroom door that closed all the way without me having to throw my full body weight against it.

By the time I rolled up Meg's window, slammed Amy's door, and grabbed my backpack, a performance was underway in the kitchen.

"We would have been home sooner, if Jo had bothered to show up," Amy complained as she dropped into a chair at the small, round table where we ate most of our meals, the dining room being given over to Mom's sewing projects and stacks of junk mail.

"I told you I had practice," I reminded the room at large.

"She was off *running*." From her tone, you would have thought Amy had found me selling drugs on a playground. "On the bright side, I did give Coach Solter a press release, which Jo had totally forgotten to do."

Our mother smiled indulgently at Amy. "You know Jo needs to run. She has a lot of energy to burn off, so she doesn't get fractious." This was one of many things she believed about me because it was true of rough-and-tumble Jo March in the book.

"That's not why—"

My protest was drowned out by Amy's snort. "Doesn't seem to be helping."

"Amy," Mom said, like maybe she was going to tell her off, though I should have known better. "Nice work with the press release. Did you get the rest of them handed out?"

"Yep. Everyone was super excited."

I cough-snorted as I rummaged through the pantry in search of a snack.

"What?" Amy snapped.

I knew better than to say what I was really thinking, namely: *You're dreaming.* "Can there be one small part of my life that doesn't have anything to do with all this? Running is *my* thing. It's private and personal and I'd like to keep it that way."

"Please. We all know the real reason you started running. Speaking of getting into other people's *private* business." Amy side-eyed Meg, who was staring into the open refrigerator as though memorizing the contents.

It took me a second to realize what she was hinting at. Yes, I'd first gotten into running thanks to David, just like he'd gotten into yo-yo tricks because of me. But I'd kept at it for reasons of my own. Not that I was ready to announce my plan to get a cross-country scholarship, because I hadn't gotten around to discussing college with Mom. Especially the part where I wanted to go somewhere out of state — which would also mean quitting the show.

"You have no idea what you're talking about," I told Amy.

"For your information, I'm the assistant PR director. Mom put me in charge of school outreach. So suck it."

"Ooooh." I fluttered my fingers in Amy's face. "What is that, like assistant *to* the regional manager?"

"It's better than being 'captain' of the stupid cross-country team. You're not on a boat, okay? It's a bunch of dirty people running around like they're being chased. Woo-hoo."

"You'd know, being such an athlete."

"Excuse you, have you ever painted a mural? It's extremely physical."

"Have you?"

"Girls!" Our mother clapped her hands. "This is exactly what I wanted to talk to you about."

"Sailing?" I guessed. "Bad art? People who are about to get bitch-slapped?"

Mom exhaled through her nostrils. "Communication."

I turned to leave, tucking a box of graham crackers under my arm. "Sounds like Amy's department. Being the PR queen."

"Jo."

Reluctantly, I stopped.

"This is a family business. I want all of us—" Mom glanced over her shoulder, clearly expecting to see Meg. Once again, my older sister had vanished like a passing breeze, though not before leaving an open gallon of milk on the counter next to two boxes of cereal and a splash zone of milky dribbles.

"Well." Mom rubbed the frown line on her forehead. "I guess we'll fill her in later." She patted the back of a chair, beckoning me to sit beside her. "Let's start the meeting."

My left eyelid twitched. Why did we have to call it a meeting, like that made it businessy and official, when it was really just three of us sitting in our kitchen on a random afternoon?

"Fill her in on what?" I grumbled, sinking into my seat.

Mom laced her fingers together, resting her hands on the place mat in front of her. Her nails were short and unpainted, and she hadn't bothered with jewelry or makeup. When not in costume, Mom was like me, a jeans and T-shirt person. Except on the inside, where she lived in a Technicolor fantasyland full of rainbows and magical thinking. "As you know, I've been giving a lot of thought to expanding our performance season."

"What? No, I didn't know that." I set down the other half of the graham cracker that was currently turning to wet concrete in my throat.

"I did," Amy trilled.

"You're not talking about fall," I pressed, ignoring my sister. The timing was tight enough with cross-country, since Mom always wanted to keep the show running through Labor Day. As if anyone was that desperate to cap off their summer with a trip to *Little Women Live!*

"Much sooner than that." She tapped the table with one finger. "As in, this Saturday." The smile on her face said, *Ta-da!* Like I might have been bummed about the wait. "The beginning of a new month is such a hopeful time, don't you think?"

"It's April first."

Mom nodded. "There's a wonderful synchronicity to it. A preview event on April first, school tours the first of May, and then the regular season kickoff June first."

"Bada bing, bada boom." Amy brushed her hands together.

"But it's April Fool's. That's like holding your wedding on Friday the Thirteenth. People will think it's a joke." *Even more than they do already.*

"I don't see why." Mom blinked slowly at me, like I was out of focus. "That would be silly."

"Yeah, that's—" I blew a breath out the side of my mouth. You had to pick your battles in this family. "I already have plans."

"Sure you do." Amy rolled her eyes so hard I was surprised they didn't clank like bowling balls hitting the gutter.

"I'm signed up for a 5K." I pointed at the far wall of the kitchen, where a massive calendar displayed all our upcoming appointments. "I wrote it down."

"Why don't you do it Sunday?" Mom suggested.

"It's an event, Mom. With hundreds of people, including my whole cross-country team."

She sat up straighter, jaw tight. "I'm sorry, Jo, but we're having our own event, and I need you here."

"Why? Is one day really going to make that much of a difference?" I didn't have to mention the word *money*, because Mom would know what I meant. The bottom line was never far from my mind.

"It's a media preview." Each word was enunciated with extra crispness, like it was a spell you had to say just right to make it come true.

"What media? The local paper, circulation twelve? They'll run the same picture they always do, with a tiny caption, half of which will be misspelled." Another performance of *Little Women Live!* wasn't exactly news; they'd run out of fresh angles years ago.

"Leave that to me," Mom replied, smiling faintly.

"And me," Amy added, tapping herself on the chest.

It was impossible to tell whether the weird energy I was picking up meant they were faking it to seem interesting or they were keeping actual secrets. "You're not talking about that free mailer with the grocery ads that comes out Wednesdays?"

Mom leaned back in her chair, crossing one leg over her knee. "You'll have to wait and see."

"Yeah." Amy cracked open her seltzer, took a long swig, and ripped out a belch before wiping her mouth with her arm.

"You're a real princess," I told her.

"I know I am but what are you?" She coiled a strand of hair around her finger, considering it with pursed lips. "Speaking of which, I need a touch-up before the weekend."

"Seriously?" Between the yellow hair and the orange tint of her self-tanning lotion, she already looked like a human candy corn.

"News flash, some of us care about our appearance. It's called professionalism."

"It should be called 'if you bleach that mess any lighter it's going to shrivel up and fall off.'"

She made an exaggerated pouty face. "Yeah, I'll ask for *your* advice when I want to rock the PE teacher look."

"Ooooh, solid burn from a person who shampoos with Roundup."

Mom stretched an arm toward each of us, like we were going to join hands and sing. "That's enough."

"Enough peroxide," I muttered.

Amy threw up a hand in the universal sign for *See?*

Turning to our mother, I tried to summon my most reasonable voice. "Don't you ever get the feeling you're pushing a boulder uphill that's just going to slide down again?"

Mom frowned at me. "Actually, no, Jo. I can't say I've ever thought of my life's work that way."

"But it's like with the school tours. They've all seen the show a million times. Why keep doing it? What's the point?"

Amy's mouth fell open in outrage. "Are you trying to ruin my life?"

"Yes. I stay up at night dreaming of ways to torture you."

"I knew it!"

"Can't get anything past you." I gave an *oh darn* snap.

"Mom!" Amy pointed at me, bouncing in her seat. "She's doing it again."

"All right, Jo. That's enough sarcasm for today," Mom said.

"Why, are we rationing it now?"

"If only," she murmured.

I stared at our mother.

"What?" She tugged on the neck of her T-shirt, avoiding my accusatory gaze. "I was just illustrating the point."

"Which is?" I asked.

"No one likes to be teased." This platitude was accompanied by a Sunday-school-teacher smile.

Amy stuck her tongue out, which of course Mom said nothing about, because the only real crime in this family was being honest.

Closing my eyes, I rubbed the spot on my forehead where I would almost certainly develop stress wrinkles exactly like our mother's: three fine horizontal lines, as if she'd run the tines of a fork across her face.

"But we don't have a Beth yet," I reminded her.

"We can prop a broom in a corner and call it good." Amy kicked the floor like a toddler. "Beth is such a waste of space."

"Nice way to talk about our dead sister, you monster."

"I'll show you a dead sister!" Amy lunged at me, but Mom grabbed her by the shoulder.

"Jo's right," she said, and my heart lifted with a mix of hope and surprise. "We'll work around it for now. Focus on our strengths. Of which there are plenty." Mom winked at Amy, who gave a satisfied hair toss.

Outvoted, again. "So what scene are we supposed to do?"

"Something emotional," Mom said at once. "Primal."

"Yes!" Amy pumped her fist. "Go for the juggernaut."

"Um, try again, loser."

"You know what I mean, Jo-ker. We're going to open a vein. Let it bleed."

"Please tell me you're not talking about freaking Christmas."

"Language, Jo. And no. We'll save that for the schools." Mom stared dreamily into the distance. "I had something more intimate in mind."

"You wicked, wicked girl! I never can write it again, and I'll never forgive you as long as I live!"

–Little Women

CHAPTER FOUR

Never work with children or animals. Whoever said that about acting was one hundred percent correct — as I'd learned from sharing the stage with a sister who was both immature *and* barely housebroken.

"I still don't see why we can't have a real fire." Amy was sprawled across the threadbare armchair in our "parlor," a part of the house that had been repurposed as a performance space. "It would give the scene more intensity."

"Because I have to stick my hands in it." Though, knowing Amy, adding a twist where Jo goes to the burn ward would be more of an attraction than not. She'd been after Mom for ages to perform some of Alcott's other stories. Not the sequels, which might have made a tiny bit of sense, but the really sensational melodramas. Like we could magically pull an Italian villa and round-the-world boat chase out of the junk drawer.

It was one of the few Amy requests my mother had ever denied, probably because it was inconceivable to Mom that anyone could be sick of seeing the same old scenes. Like the one we were doing today, in which Jo discovers that Amy has maliciously set fire to the only copy of the manuscript Jo has been slaving over for months.

"What if I'm a pyromaniac?" Amy addressed the words to the brown ring on the ceiling, idly wrapping her pee-colored braid around her hand. "Maybe I can work that in. A psychological angle."

"You're a selfish brat. That's your motivation. It's not very complicated." I stretched my chin to one side and then the other, hoping to release some of the tension from my neck. Pretending to lose it all day was exhausting. I'd been trapped in this costume, and inside this room, since morning, thanks to the busload of book clubbers Mom had invited to join the day's "fun." The only thing keeping me sane was the thought of stripping off my tights and going for a run the second it was over. According to the clock on the mantel, we had about ten minutes left.

"Amy is way more layered than you could possibly understand," my sister said, pointing at me with the end of her braid.

"You mean like how she talks about herself in the third person?"

"If you ever did character work, you might understand my process."

"Maybe if I actually wanted to be an *actor*, I would."

"Sure." Amy ran her pinkie between her front teeth. "You're such a team player."

"This place sucks up enough of my life. I'm not giving it more." Did I enjoy or approve of our stupid family business? No. But I *always* showed up. There might be complaining involved, but at least I did the work. Unlike Meg, who smiled and pretended everything was golden, only to disappear when it was time for the heavy lifting.

"Thank you so much for your sacrifice, Queen Jo." Amy placed a hand over her heart. "It must be so *hard* getting handed the *lead* in a *professional* theater production. Boo-freaking-hoo."

There were so many things wrong with that statement it wasn't worth the effort of arguing. I turned to the fireplace and spread out the ashes and scraps of paper, ignoring the creaking springs and snap of elastic from Amy's direction. Finally I whipped around, ready to yell about jumping on the furniture, in time to watch her pull a power bar out of her tights.

"What?" She split the wrapper at one end. "I get low blood sugar."

"I doubt you'll go into a coma in the next five minutes."

"Unlike some people, I don't phone it in," she said through a mouthful of shelf-stable protein. "I give a hundred percent to every performance. I am always *on*."

"Then I guess you won't mind taking it to the next level."

"Please. I've been holding back so you don't look bad."

I cocked my head, listening to the unmistakable sound of approaching footsteps. "Try to keep up."

"I will improv circles around you." She shoved the empty wrapper under the waistband of her tights.

By the time the door swung inward, we had assumed our positions: Amy standing to one side of the hearth with her arms crossed in defiance while I loomed behind her, hands cupping my cheeks in a pantomime of shock.

A pair of women crept uncertainly across the threshold. People understood how to behave in a theater, but the fact that this was a house made it confusing. For all of us. After silently counting to ten, I took a deep breath, alerting everyone in the room that the wax-museum portion of the experience was over. There had been talk at one point about installing a big red button to "activate" a scene, but I drew the line at pretending to be animatronic.

"How could you do this to me, Amy?" My guttural yell made both women jump. Big dramatic moments weren't normally my strong suit, but I had no trouble tapping into the desire to pummel my younger sister. "I poured my heart and soul into those stories!"

"Get over it, loser." Amy made an L with her finger and thumb. "Take it from a *real* artist. Your book sucked."

Most of our performances weren't scripted, in the sense of using exact lines. Aside from a few iconic quotes, Mom was more concerned with capturing the "spirit of the book." That allowed a certain amount of interpretive leeway.

I dropped to my knees and scrabbled at the ashes in the fireplace, plucking out a blackened scrap. "*You* suck! One day I'll be famous, and you'll still be painting teacups."

Amy popped her hip. "At least my stuff is pretty."

"Unlike your nose."

"Shut up, Jo! Everyone knows you're the ugly one. And you're never going to get published writing crap like that. You should be thanking me."

My hand, which had been lovingly smoothing the partially incinerated paper, clenched into a fist. "How can you say that? I will never forgive you for this!"

"Ooooh," Amy taunted. "I'm so scared."

I stood, flexing my fingers. We circled each other slowly, arms hanging loose at our sides like a pair of gunslingers.

"You are such a little—" I choked on the rest when Amy smacked me in the head, hard enough to make my eyes water. "Wretch," I spat, though it came out sounding more like *writch,* thanks to the period-inappropriate word I'd come close to using.

"What are you going to do about it, Jo? I thought you were tough." She punctuated her words by poking me in the chest.

I slapped her arm away.

"That the best you got? Come at me, sis."

I grabbed the crispy yellow braid dangling over her shoulder and gave it a sharp tug.

"Hair-pulling, seriously?" Amy pushed her sleeves back. "Looks like somebody brought a knife to the gunfight."

Before I could react, she threw herself at me, leaping onto my back and wrapping an arm around my throat.

"What — are — you — doing," I ground out, twisting from side to side in an attempt to dislodge her. Amy clung like a koala, lace-up boots locked at the ankle in front of me.

"Give it up, Jo." She leaned back with all her weight, pulling me dangerously off balance. My gargled warning was too late. We crashed to the floor, the rag rug barely cushioning the impact.

An elbow to the gut forced Amy to let go. I flopped onto my back, trying to catch the breath that had been knocked out of me. Probably I should say something, get the scene back on track —

"Ungh!" I grunted as Amy landed on top of me. She was straddling my stomach, knees compressing my ribs.

"Say it," Amy growled.

"Say what?" I tried to buck her off.

"I'm the pretty one *and* the smart one." She bounced up and down on my midsection. "Everybody likes me best. Especially Laurie!" There was a wild light in her eyes as she looked around the room. I assumed she was mugging for the audience until she grabbed a throw pillow from the wingback chair.

"There can be only one." She raised the cushion above her head as though lightning bolts were about to shoot from the heavens and set the needlepoint on fire.

I scowled, sending her a silent message: *Tone it down, Drama Queen.*

"Goodbye, Jo."

"Wait," I started to say as the pillow descended toward my face. "*Mmmph.*" That was as close as I could get to rage-screaming my sister's name through a mouth full of scratchy fabric.

"What's that?" Amy taunted. "Afraid I'm going to mess up your 'one beauty'? I wouldn't worry. Your hair's not *that* great."

I tried to punch her, first with one arm and then the other, but Amy dodged every blow.

"Will you just die already?" she growled, twisting the pillow.

As my oxygen-starved brain caught on, I kicked my legs once, twice, and a third time, before my body went slack.

"Oh, Jo," my sister wailed, collapsing on top of me. "I didn't mean to kill you! Your book really was trash, though." Classic Amy: Even during someone else's death scene, she had to steal the spotlight.

After more fake sobbing and showily blowing her nose, Amy fell silent. One of the women offered a tentative clap, after which her friend joined in, the two of them managing a tepid round of applause.

"Excuse us," one of them whispered, like maybe they thought it was rude to leave without saying anything.

As they shuffled out of the room, I heard the other ask, "Was that part in the movie?"

"Yeah, don't you remember?" her friend replied. "One of the sisters definitely dies."

Their footsteps slowly receded. I felt Amy's laughter before I heard it.

"Get off." I rolled to the side, dumping her onto the floor. Then I whomped her in the head with the rock-solid pillow, the weave of which was gouged into my forehead. "What is wrong with you?"

She shrugged. "You said you wanted to amp it up."

I picked a strand of hair out of my mouth. "I didn't mean one of us should Hulk out."

"It's called being creative. That was amazing. 'I know one of the sisters dies.' Classic."

"Hard to believe Juilliard isn't blowing up your phone." I gently pressed a finger along the side of my nose, making sure my nostrils were still functional.

"You should be happy I didn't use the poker." She gestured at the brass tools hanging from a stand next to the fireplace. "That was my original plan."

"Why would Amy murder Jo? It makes no sense. If anyone's going to feel stabby, it's Jo."

"Jo, Jo, Jo. *Blehhhh*. She's so full of herself."

I shoved her in the shoulder. She kicked me in the shin. We were so busy slapping at each other's hands that neither of us registered the shadow falling across the doorway. It was the burst of a flash that finally tipped us off. Well, that and the huff of amusement, in a distinctly male register.

I hurried to pull my skirt down, kicking my sister when she stayed sprawled across the rug, staring at an unfamiliar guy with reddish-blond hair and horn-rimmed glasses. His faded black tee had a picture of a man's face on the front, with either a mohawk or a receding hairline, and an intense expression. Probably I was supposed to recognize whoever it was, but I was more interested in the person wearing the shirt. If the first glance said *nerd,* a closer inspection revealed full lips and rounded cheekbones, like the glasses were camouflage for his cuteness.

"Who are *you*?" Amy gave the question a flirty lift at the end.

She was out of elbowing range, so I settled for aggressively clearing my throat.

"I'm Hudson. Andrea's assistant." It sounded like that should mean something to us, but I had bigger concerns.

"How long have you been standing there?"

"I came in right before the—" He clutched his throat with both hands.

"She deserved it," Amy assured him, batting her lashes. "Jo was super mean to me."

"You burned her book," I retorted. "The *only* copy. It was handwritten."

Hudson shook his head. "I'm surprised you didn't suffocate *her.*"

"Thank you." I extended a hand in his direction. "He gets it."

My sister's expression turned sulky. "Jo can rewrite her stupid book. It's not like she has anything else to do."

"Whereas Amy's life is so full of meaning."

"This scene doesn't really do justice to my character," Amy informed our visitor. "She's way more polished and elegant than her sisters."

Said the girl who stored snacks in her underwear.

He pushed his glasses up his nose. "I prefer the more candid, backstage stuff anyway. Very Diane Arbus."

I made a mental note to google Diane Arbus as soon as I

was alone. It was obviously a reference to something sophisticated and a little edgy, and thus totally foreign to our cheeseball, wannabe-homespun world. Hudson looked like the kind of guy who hung out at painfully hip cafés in real cities. Places where no one ever smiled, or raised their voice, because they were so intellectual. Funny how you could tell something like that from a pair of jeans.

His phone buzzed, and he glanced at the screen. "The boss is waiting." Our eyes met and he ducked his head, a hint of pink staining his cheeks. "See you around, I guess."

"He's not as cute as I thought," Amy announced as his footsteps receded. "Doesn't hold a candle to Laurie."

I held a finger to my lips, relaxing slightly when the outer door closed behind him.

"That didn't stop you from hitting on him."

"At least I wasn't staring at his butt."

"I wasn't—" I decided to save my breath. Like the rest of my family, Amy lived in her own reality. Nothing I said was going to change her mind. Besides, whatever fluke had brought Hudson here, the odds of running into him again were basically nil. People didn't linger for days, immersing themselves in the magic kingdom of *Little Women Live!* You could maybe fill an hour—two if you walked really slowly.

"Five o'clock." Amy stretched her arms over her head. Frowning, she sniffed her armpit. "I need to change before the reception."

As she hopped to her feet, shaking out her skirt, I looked

down at the coarse plaid of my own dress. Somehow I'd forgotten about the costume. You got so used to it, you started to think, *Here I am, being myself,* when in reality you were dressed up in a fake 1860s dress sewn by your mom. That's what Hudson had seen: a seventeen-year-old with an unflattering hairstyle, wearing a cheap plaid sack.

"I'm going for a run," I announced. Not that I needed anyone's permission.

"Hello? What about meeting the press? Mom got fried chicken."

"No one's going to show up. It's a waste of time." *And money.*

"Laurie will be there." This was clearly my sister's trump card, as if everyone shared her obsession with our lone male costar. "And maybe Saggy Pants," she grudgingly added.

"Who?"

Amy jerked her chin at the door. "The guy who was just here. The one you were checking out. But that's fine. I'll say hello to your little friend."

"He wasn't that little."

"Five-nine, tops."

"Which is totally average." Not in our family, which tended more toward the Amazonian, but for the rest of the population.

"I'll take a closer look and let you know." She did a double eyebrow twitch. "He'll probably like me better anyway. I'm the fun one."

The clock on the mantel ticked in the silence. "There's no way he's here for the media whatever."

Amy examined her cuticles. "If you're sure."

"Mom's probably just going to make us do a bunch of team-building exercises."

"Guess it doesn't matter, since you won't be there." She was being suspiciously laid-back all of a sudden. It creeped me out.

"I already wasted a whole Saturday."

"Whatever. Don't let the door hit you on the way out."

For the life of me, I couldn't tell whether this was reverse psychology or another instance of sisterly sabotage.

"You don't care to make people like you,
to go into good society, and cultivate
your manners and tastes."

–*Little Women*

CHAPTER
FIVE

The difference between a staff dinner and a family
meal was that the former took place in the prefab building
that housed the café, right next to the matching gift shop. I'd
voted no when Mom had first presented the idea of taking out a
line of credit to expand, because we'd already spent a ton fixing
up the old barn that came with the property, but everyone else
loved the idea. (Final tally: 4–1. Mom claimed that since she
was the only parent on-site, she should have two votes, which
was fairly typical of my family's grasp of math.) So far the food
and souvenirs mostly paid for themselves because the profit
margin on candy was obscene, but it was only a matter of time
before the bottom fell out of the retro lollipop market, no matter what my mother claimed about the "sassafras renaissance."

I cut across the overgrown grass between our house and the

restaurant. The only people inside were my mother, Amy, and the heavily mustached guy who ran the local historical society. Apparently, their quarterly newsletter counted as "media."

Hudson of the cool jeans was nowhere in sight, not that I'd really expected otherwise. Maybe it wasn't too late to bail. Having seen the history guy eat through that mustache like a whale inhaling krill, I had no desire for a repeat.

"Jo!" my mother called, stopping me in my tracks. "You're here!"

Amy grunted at me before returning her attention to the buffet table. She'd changed out of her costume . . . into a different costume. Which was less disturbing than the way she was rooting through the massive aluminum pan of fried chicken with one hand, despite the prominently displayed tongs.

I was debating whether to run over and grab a few pieces before she could touch them all when a pair of beefy arms wrapped around me from behind.

"There you are," said the voice in my ear. And it was *right* in my ear, since the person pinning me against his chest was also nuzzling my neck.

My heel slammed down on his toes and I was abruptly released.

"Dang, Jo!" Laurie wheezed as I spun to face him. As usual, our leading man looked like he'd stepped out of a photo shoot, the sleeves of his immaculate polo shirt stretched tight around his biceps. "That hurt."

"Weird." I screwed up my face in mock confusion. "It's

almost like there were negative consequences to rubbing your-self all over me."

"I thought you'd be happy to see me."

"We go to the same school. I see you all the time."

He flashed his winning smile. "That's different."

This was true in the sense that I magically became invis-ible to him the second I walked through the doors of our high school. Probably he had trouble seeing me through his crowds of followers.

In *Little Women*, the neighbor and sometime love interest of Jo March is introduced as having black hair and brown skin, which back then probably translated to "vaguely Mediterranean-looking." Our Laurie fit the same general description, only he was Black, not half-Italian. Like the character he played, modern-day Laurie was charming and popular, thanks to his self-described "triple threat" status, his weapons being football, acting, and hotness, not necessarily in that order.

Unlike the *Little Women* version, our Laurie wasn't an aim-less playboy. He had serious acting ambitions, which explained his willingness to spend his summers with us, since there weren't many other theatrical gigs in town. And his real name wasn't Laurie — his parents were optometrists, not *Little Women* obsessives — but he'd decided the first summer he worked here to use his character's name offstage, too, as part of his "total immersion" in the role.

He held his arms wide. "Come on, JoJo. Bring it in. You know you want to."

"Because my self-esteem is just that low."

"You'd probably feel better about yourself if you showered," Laurie suggested, in a tone of sincere helpfulness.

"Thanks for the tip."

"Don't mention it."

Meg chose that moment to float into the dining area, ethereal even in yoga pants. She was wearing a crown of dried flowers. My older sister had spent the day in a comfortable chair, having her hair done for a fictional wedding, as opposed to being attacked by a berserker with a bad bleach job.

"She still single?" Laurie asked as Meg headed for the buffet.

"Are you seriously checking out my sister? Point-five seconds after you were all over me?"

"Just trying to read the room, Jo. Cast dynamics are important. And yeah, she's cute—" He broke off with a grunt when my elbow connected with his rib cage.

"Why are you so violent?"

"For your information, yes, she and David are still broken up. Which sucks." Although the problem wasn't so much the end of their relationship as the fact that the relationship had happened in the first place, in my humble opinion.

"She looks fine to me."

I raised my elbow; Laurie flinched.

"*Emotionally,* Jo. Geez."

Frowning, I watched Meg fill a plate with coleslaw and dinner rolls, a.k.a. the vegetarian menu. Laurie wasn't wrong. My sister seemed to have moved on as easily as water running downhill.

"It probably bothers us more than Meg," I admitted. David had always been a favorite around our house. Thoughtful, reliable, aware of other people — everything my older sister wasn't.

Laurie caressed his impressively defined deltoid. "I'm here if you need a shoulder to cry on."

"Tempting, but what I really need right now is food."

"It's not my cheat day," he sighed, peering over my shoulder at the buffet, "but I guess I can pull the skin off." Probably even Laurie knew he was going to eat every crispy fried mouthful. And lick his fingers afterward.

Once we'd served ourselves, he followed me to a table, prompting Amy to get up and join us.

"Why are you dressed like that?" she asked me as she pulled out a chair.

I looked down at the jeans and faded T-shirt I'd changed into before coming to dinner, on the off chance someone interesting showed up. "You mean, why am I wearing normal clothes from this century?"

"If you say so."

"Yeah, it's too bad I'm not hot off the rural Massachusetts runway, give or take a century."

"Guys! Please." Laurie held up both hands, like our bickering was too much for him. "What about me?"

"You're right," I said. "That was immature. I shouldn't sink to her level."

"No, what about my outfit? I wasn't sure about the color" — he ran a hand over the minty-green cotton encasing his stomach muscles — "but I think it's working for me."

"Totally," Amy agreed. She closed her lips around a gigantic mouthful of potato salad, then slowly dragged it off the fork. From the way she stared at Laurie the whole time, I guessed it was supposed to be seductive. *Watch me gobble this side salad, baby.*

He glanced at his plate, expression troubled. "Do you think they use full-fat mayo?"

"I think it's whatever you want it to be," she replied.

"Except that there's this concept known as reality, and it's full of these things called 'facts.'" I added air quotes around the last word, because it was better than flicking my sister in the forehead.

Amy wrinkled her nose. "What's your point?"

"The mayonnaise is either 'lite' or it isn't." It was hard to believe I had to say things like this out loud. Then again, it wasn't even the most absurd thing I'd argued about with my family that day. "You can't make it something else with the *power of positive thinking.*"

"Like you'd know anything about that," Amy muttered, earning an appreciative chortle from Laurie.

"I know, right?" He lifted his free hand for a fist bump. "Little Miss Glass Half-Empty over here."

"I'm not little. Or a miss."

"Uh, unless you got married, JoJo, you're totally a miss."

"She's definitely not a *hit.*" Amy pointed at Laurie.

"Oh, snap," he said, shaking out his hand.

"*I* would play Jo a lot more free-spirited."

"I am Jo," I reminded her.

Amy rolled her eyes. "Barely."

"I'm talking about myself. The real person. You can't be a better version of me than me, because I'm Jo. Period. Not somebody else's fictional alter ego."

"Exactly." Amy ripped her roll in two, gesturing at me with the bigger half. "Too much you. Not enough Jo March. Also known as the cool Jo."

Laurie helped himself to the other half of her roll. Anyone else who raided her plate would have lost a finger. "That's pretty harsh, Ames."

Good to know being me was an insult. Maybe I should take my plate back to the house and eat in my room. When I glanced at the buffet to make sure I hadn't missed dessert, the man from the historical society was ladling ranch dressing over his chicken.

"Can I have the rest of yours?" Laurie asked when I made an involuntary gagging noise, shoving my plate away.

Before I could reply, the front door opened. A woman I'd never seen before walked into the café. Her face was serious beneath the reddish pixie cut, and her clothes—a leather blazer and pristine white shirt—had an unfussy elegance so alien to the surroundings, she might as well have been wearing a space suit. I put her age at a decade or so older than my mother. Either that or the network of fine lines surrounding her eyes were the result of prolonged exposure to sun and wind, without a calico bonnet.

Mom hurried to meet her. The two of them exchanged a few words I couldn't hear as they crossed to the front of the room.

"Can I have your attention please?" Mom called out, waiting for everyone to look her way. The guy from the historical society paused in the act of shoving plastic silverware into his pocket. "As some of you know, I have exciting news."

Amy's nod was so over-the-top, she might as well have bounced up and down chanting, *I know! I know! Me me me!* It was probably something trivial like a new flavor of lemonade. Although that didn't explain the mystery woman.

"It's my pleasure to introduce Andrea Coster. You've probably seen her byline in major national magazines." A trace of doubt crossed our mother's face as her gaze fell on Meg, who wasn't exactly known for her keen interest in current events. "Ms. Coster is considering us for a possible feature story about family-run attractions."

The red-haired woman gave a microscopic nod.

"I hope you'll all help her get a feel for the very special environment we've created here." Mom smiled, but not quite broadly enough to disguise the hint of pleading. This wasn't news; it was the faint possibility of something newsworthy happening in the future, if we didn't screw up. "Let's have a round of applause for our very special guest."

A delayed and embarrassingly out-of-sync wave of clapping petered out after a few seconds.

"Call me Andrea," the woman said. My gaze snagged on her low-heeled boots, the camel-colored suede worn without looking ratty. I was glad my clearance Converse were hidden under the table. "I'll try not to get in your way."

I could tell my mother wanted more. A little gushing, or,

even better, our guest clutching her chest as she keeled over from the ecstasy of it all. "I'm sure I speak for all of us when I say what an honor it is to have you here." Mom glanced over her shoulder as the door creaked open. "And your assistant, of course."

The word *assistant* was still pinging around my brain when Hudson stepped up beside Andrea, lifting his hand in a self-conscious wave. My stomach roller-coastered as I mentally replayed our brief conversation. Not to mention his front-row seat for the brawl on the parlor floor.

"I love that this is a family affair on all sides," Mom continued, with a sweeping gesture that seemed to indicate a much larger audience than the one actually present. "Mother and daughters, and mother and son." And of course I saw it then: the unmistakable resemblance between Hudson and Andrea, and not just in attitude and style of clothing.

I caught Hudson's eye, and he flashed me a quick grin. Another wash of pink colored his cheeks as he stuck his hands in his pockets.

Laurie leaned in to me. "Why are you looking at him like that?"

"Like what?"

He batted his lashes, doing something duck-face-adjacent with his lips.

"I guarantee you my face is not doing that."

"You know what I mean. Like you know him. Or you're secretly laughing about something. Even though nobody said anything funny." Laurie bit his lip, obviously wondering whether he'd missed a joke. He would be an incredibly easy person to gaslight.

"We met him before." Amy didn't bother lowering her voice. "He's nowhere near as handsome as you."

The anxious wrinkle between Laurie's brows disappeared. "That's cool."

Amy frowned as I pushed my chair back. "Where are you going?"

"To say hello to our guests."

"Oh no you don't." She leaped to her feet. "Not without me."

"I guess I'll come too. She might want to ask me some questions." Laurie cupped a hand in front of his chin, sniffing his breath before flashing a thumbs-up.

As we approached the front of the restaurant, Mom's eyes met mine, tentative at first. I could almost hear the thought forming in her brain: *Even Jo is excited!*

She wasn't wrong, although I was pretty sure we had different reasons. Maybe this was the best Mom and I could hope for: being happy about separate things at the same time.

She had an instinctive sense of what was pleasing and proper, always said the right thing to the right person, did just what suited the time and place.

— Little Women

CHAPTER SIX

W hich one is Jo?" Andrea asked.

I raised my hand. Behind me, Amy blew a raspberry.

"Hello again," said Hudson.

"You've met?" His mother's tone was closer to *Explain yourself* than *What a thrilling coincidence!* (the way my mom would have said it).

"I caught the tail end of their act." His eyes met mine, glinting with amusement.

"Last show of the day," I said quickly. "Not really our best work."

Amy huffed. "Speak for yourself."

"Actually, I found it very . . . what's the term?" Hudson's face screwed up in thought.

"Pungent?" Amy suggested. "Loquacious? Impecunious?"

"No," he said slowly, while I scowled at my sister to let her know that *I* knew she had no idea what any of those words meant. "Visceral," he concluded, putting all of us out of our misery.

"Oh really?" Andrea glanced at me again. "I wasn't sure what to expect. Needlepoint by the fire or nudism and screaming your feelings."

Hudson made a choking sound as Amy lunged forward so she was half in front of me.

"Fruitlands," she chirped, like we were in a classroom and she was gunning for teacher's pet. "The commune where the real Alcotts lived—*and nearly died.*" She lowered her voice, movie trailer–style, before returning to what passed for normal in Amy's case. "Since they didn't know how to grow their own food and whatnot."

"A failed utopia. Hardly the first. Or the last," Andrea observed, surveying her surroundings. "Sorry we were late. Must have taken a wrong turn on the way from the airport."

"I can make you a special map," Amy volunteered. "Burnt edges, calligraphy. The whole shebang."

Instead of pretending not to hear this bizarre offer, Mom grabbed her arm. "We could use a tea bag to give the paper that parchment look."

"You do realize they're not pirates?" I said.

"I don't know, sounds like a pretty sweet life." Hudson patted his bicep. "Tattoos, piercings, parrots."

"Scurvy," Andrea added.

Amy thrust herself forward again, like one of those horror-movie villains who never really die. "I could paint a billboard."

I thought of suggesting she start by Sharpie-ing *I'M THE ARTISTIC ONE* on her forehead, since she was so desperate for everyone to know.

"Or I could carve a big sign," she went on.

"No power tools, dearest." Mom patted Amy's hand, as if to remind her that this would be the first body part to go if she ever got access to a table saw. "Are you hungry?" she asked our guests. "There's plenty of chicken."

"We ate on the road, but I'd kill for a glass of wine." Andrea squinted at the buffet. The closest equivalent was the carton of fruit punch.

"Why don't we head back to the house?" Mom suggested. "I'm sure Hudson would rather hang out with the young people."

"We can play checkers," I said, with obviously fake sincerity. Hudson looked down to hide his grin.

"I was hoping you'd give him a tour." Mom was still doing her Cheery McCheerful bit, but there was a hint of strain behind the smile.

I shrugged. "If he wants."

"Well, well, well," Amy said as the door closed behind our mother. "Jo volunteering? How interesting. I can't *imagine* why you suddenly decided to be helpful." She slowly pivoted until she was staring at Hudson.

I poked her in the side, forcing her to look at me. *Do you want to die?* I said with my eyes.

Like you could take me, she telepathically replied.

"If you want the real scoop, ask me," Amy told Hudson. "Jo has a lot of issues."

"You know what would be great right now?" Laurie interrupted. He paused to let us admire his dimples. "Dessert."

"It's probably from a mix," Amy grumbled as he led her away. This from someone who bought her "art" kits in the children's section at Michael's.

"So that whole thing with the . . ." Hudson made a throat-slitting gesture.

"WrestleMania?"

"It's not just for the show?"

"Eh, family stuff." I didn't want to get into the Jo-Amy relationship, on or off the page. "Sisters, am I right?"

Hudson shrugged. "I wouldn't know. It's just me and Andrea."

No sisters, no sappy nicknames, nonstop travel and adventure . . . he was basically living my dream. "I don't suppose you want to trade lives?"

He cocked his head, considering. "What's in it for me?"

"Um. It's like living inside a Renaissance festival, without the fun parts? You still get to dress up, though."

"Tempting."

"So do you actually want a tour?"

"If you're giving it."

Okay, then.

❧

"Is it a ghost tour?" he asked, as we stood outside the café in the gloomy twilight.

That would be a logical explanation for showing him around when the light of an already overcast day was fading fast, rendering everything even more gray and washed-out than normal. The real reason was that my mother had once again neglected to think through the practical details before hatching a plan.

"Ghosts would definitely liven things up." Though with my luck we'd be haunted by a spirit who wanted to talk about manners or canning your own vegetables.

"Seems like things are already pretty intense around here."

"That's *Little Women* in a nutshell. Hard-core. Gritty. In your face—like an olden-times soap opera."

"See? I was totally picking up on that vibe." He shifted his weight, looking at me instead of the hulking shadow of the barn. "Your boyfriend doesn't mind?"

"What?"

"You being alone with me." Hudson gestured at the café.

"Laurie is not my boyfriend. Except in the show. Well, sort of. I mean, he wants to be, but Jo shuts that down." I tried to read his expression, to make sure we were on the same page, but I didn't know him well enough to guess his thoughts. "In the book, obviously."

Apparently, real-life Laurie wasn't opposed to blurring those lines again. Not that Hudson needed to know about that one time a few summers ago Laurie and I had messed around, mostly out of boredom. There was a *lot* of downtime between visitors.

"I thought you were referring to yourself in the third person."

"I don't do that." *Unlike some people around here.* "Anyway, yes, it's fine. That we're out here."

"Good." Hudson sounded relieved. He hadn't been around long enough to realize Laurie was the least aggressive member of the cast.

"Yeah. It would be a real shame for you to miss out on this excitement. Like over there." I pointed toward the gift shop. "Our fully stocked store, ready to serve all your *Little Women–*themed souvenir needs. We're running a preseason special on extremely old candy."

"Sweet. I've been meaning to stock up."

We walked a few steps in that direction. Hudson picked his way across the grass, like maybe there was a ravine he'd need to sidestep.

I toyed with the idea of leading him around in circles to make it seem like a bigger operation. The truth was that from where we were standing, you could hit every building on the premises with a rock. You wouldn't even have to throw it that hard.

"So yeah, that's the gift shop. The café you know." I flapped a hand over my shoulder. "The menu's a little different during the season."

"Like what?"

"Theme stuff. From the book. The Christmas breakfast. Et cetera. And over there is the barn." I started in that direction, Hudson hurrying after me, like he was afraid of getting lost in the vast wilderness. When I stopped, he bumped into my back.

"Sorry."

"No problem." My heart was still racing a little, but I didn't think he could tell from my voice. "Like I said, that's the barn."

"Let me guess." This time when he touched my arm, it was deliberate. "The barn is where you keep the animals. And the big blocks of straw." His hands shaped a square in midair.

"Um, I hate to disappoint you"—*though you might as well get used to it*—"but this is not a farm. Also, if there were cows, you would smell them."

"Huh. So the reason you have a barn is—"

"It's our main performance space. For scenes we can't do at the house."

He was quiet for a moment, hopefully not imagining me in my costume. "You don't do the whole book, though."

"Ugh, no. We skip the boring parts." And the ones we couldn't afford. "No animals—unless you count Amy."

"Rim shot." He scuffed the grass with his shoe. "You know what this place reminds me of, with the big house and the empty fields?"

I shook my head, even though I was pretty sure the answer rhymed with *Piddle Vermin*.

"It's like one of those 'Whoops, stopped for gas in the wrong place' horror movies."

"Oh." I couldn't hide my relief. "I could see that."

"The doomsday cult, rusty agricultural tools, human sacrifice. Am I right?"

"Maybe we should add that to the show. Right between Christmas and Meg's wedding. We wouldn't even have to change costumes." I couldn't keep the sarcasm from turning a little sour. The longer I talked to Hudson, the more I wished he would hang around — and the less likely it seemed that Andrea would choose *us* for her story. "You've probably been to lots of really cool places. With your mom."

"Seems like those things should be mutually exclusive. How cool can it be if you're with your mother?"

"I feel that."

"So. Jo." Hudson angled himself toward me. "Is that short for something?"

"Nope. That's my full name. *Not* Josephine." A small difference from the book, but it mattered to me. "I'm just plain old Jo."

"Not exactly."

"Trust me. I'm like ninety-seven on the inside."

"Just *old* Jo then." This time he didn't try to hide his smile.

If someone had told me yesterday that I was going to meet a handsome stranger at our made-up media preview who would maybe sort of flirt with me on a random Saturday night, I would have laughed in their face. And yet here we were.

"Guess it depends who you ask." I tried to match his teasing tone. Annoyingly, a vision of Amy popped into my head.

"I prefer to go straight to the source."

I frowned. "You mean like for the article?"

"Definitely not thinking about my mom right now. Or her job."

I swallowed a sigh of relief. "Me neither."

Youth is seldom dyspeptic, and exercise
develops wholesome appetites.

– *Little Women*

CHAPTER
SEVEN

It was strange to wake up in a good mood. I wasn't
always grumpy, but this swooping, hopeful tingle in my
stomach was an unusual sensation. My birthday, actual Christmas (not the stage version), the morning after Labor Day, a.k.a.
our last performance of the season . . . that was pretty much it.

Now I could add "the afterglow of chatting up an interesting guy." Even if it was unlikely to happen again, because now
that Hudson and Andrea had seen for themselves what *Little
Women Live!* was all about, it was hard to imagine them coming
back for more.

At least I'd held my own last night, making Hudson laugh
and ask questions, despite the fact that my life was objectively
a billion times more boring than his. He'd gotten my number

before leaving, like I was someone worth keeping in touch with whether we wound up in Andrea's story or not. I counted that as a win.

My nose twitched, catching a hint of something sugary.

"Good morning," my mother sang when I stepped into the kitchen. She smiled over her shoulder before cracking an egg into the dented mixing bowl on the counter. The baking powder and measuring cups said pancakes, which meant Mom was in a good mood too.

"Thanks again for showing Hudson around." She reached for another egg and cracked it against the rim of the bowl with an expert whack.

"No problem." I could have told her it was surprisingly fun, the highlight of my month, et cetera, but I didn't want her to think this made up for all the times she'd asked me to do something that legitimately sucked.

"Andie was afraid he might be . . . challenging."

Judging by the nickname, Mom had already penciled Andrea in as a new BFF, like there was no doubt in her mind they'd be back. *Because dreaming is believing!*

I watched her measure out a tablespoon of oil. "Why?"

"Sounds like his work ethic may be a little underdeveloped."

"She told you he was lazy?" I wondered what Mom had said about *me*. Since it was apparently Bitch About Your Kids Night.

"No. More like . . . easily distracted. Not always focused on the task at hand." The shoulders of her fleece bathrobe rose in a shrug. "Very talented, though. She showed me some of his photography."

It must be nice to have a talent that fit right in with the career your parent had chosen for you.

"Anyway," she continued, setting the butter dish on the table, "he seemed happy to have people his own age around."

I shrugged, unsure whether she was thanking me or fishing for information.

"This could be really big for us, Jo."

A silent tug-of-war broke out between Mom's need for affirmation and my refusal to play along. Coverage in a national magazine would be a big deal—*if* it happened.

She glanced at the clock on the stove. "Are you hungry? We can wake up your sisters."

My stomach heaved at the thought of waiting for Meg and Amy to stagger downstairs, then cramming around the table with piles of pancakes and an ocean of syrup to talk about how everything was going to be perfect from here on out.

"I want to get in a run this morning." I grabbed a banana from the fruit bowl. "Since I missed the 5K."

Mom's smile wobbled. For once I wasn't being passive-aggressive. I really did want to run—and not just as a way to avoid Happy Family Time.

"Maybe I'll have some later," I mumbled as I slipped out the door.

⁓

The grass was still wet with dew, so I stuck to the dirt trail leading to the edge of our property, peeling the banana as I walked. The path wound past a muddy depression that changed from puddle to pond, depending on the season.

I wondered what Hudson was doing before hitting the road this morning. Going out for breakfast around here was a pretty bleak experience, unless you liked cinnamon rolls the size of your head. Mom's pancakes were way better, especially right off the griddle.

My steps slowed. Should I go back and make sure Amy didn't eat all the most perfectly golden-brown ones just to spite me, leaving only the pale and undercooked first round? Mom would be happy—until I ruined the mood by saying the wrong thing. If my family was a bowl of batter, I was the salt someone mistook for sugar, spoiling the whole batch.

I balled up the empty banana peel and lobbed it over-hand toward a scrubby cluster of cottonwood trees. A pale four-legged shape streaked to intercept it as it fell, snapping up the mottled peel before it hit the dirt. Fang, the neighbors' German shepherd, was a big sweetheart with a long pointy muzzle, named for his all-white color. *There's a book,* David had explained, when Fang first came to live at their house. *White Fang.*

It didn't hurt that Fang also had an impressive set of teeth, or that their last name was Vang-Gilligan. Fang Vang, as we called him, became a regular part of our games. That was back when I used to see David every day—before he became Meg's boyfriend, and then her ex.

Fang raced up to me with great joyful strides. After drop-ping the banana peel at my feet, he looked expectantly from it to me. His snowy coat was liberally spotted with grass and mud.

"What are you doing out here, buddy?" I bent to pluck the

dirty, slobbered-on peel from the ground. Fang ignored the question, his entire body focused on tracking the movement of my arm. "You want me to throw this? Is that what you want?" I dangled it in front of him. "You think you can get it, Fang Vang? Are you fast like lightning?"

I threw the ragged peel as far as it would go, which was not very far, considering it wasn't a particularly aerodynamic object. Fang made the best of it, nosing it a little farther before seizing the end in his teeth and giving it a sharp upward jerk.

"Did you break its spine? Yes, you did, killer. You showed that banana who's boss."

"Are you trying to corrupt my dog?"

I jumped at the sound of David's voice. Logically, it made sense for him to be nearby, since Fang didn't walk himself. On the other hand, we were definitely on our side of the drainage ditch that ran between our property and his, and David hadn't exactly been making frequent appearances in our neck of the woods since he and Meg had imploded.

If that was even the right word. It definitely wasn't an *explosion*, with tears and yelling and slammed doors, at least not at our house. Nor could I imagine David pitching a fit. He was too mellow. Plus, his parents cringed if someone laughed too loudly. I'd never felt more like a pony let loose inside a living room than on the rare occasions we hung out at his place.

"Hey." I tried to sound casual, like there wasn't a marching band chanting *BREAKUP* in the center of my brain. "I was just . . . throwing my banana peel." Because that explained it all.

A faint ridge formed between his brows. "Composting," he suggested, so seriously I knew he was joking.

"But more, you know, active."

"Cardio composting."

"I should start a YouTube channel."

"Ka-ching."

David's style of humor was as dry as a desert, but you always knew he wasn't making fun of *you*. Or at least not in a mean way. Right now, the fact that he was joking at all seemed like a subtle way of telling me either *I'm fine* or *We don't have to talk about it*. Possibly both. Which was okay by me. I got enough secondhand emotion at home.

"I hear you had an exciting day yesterday."

For a second I thought he was talking about Hudson, which would have been weird. David and I didn't usually gossip about our love lives — for obvious reasons.

"The reporter," he prompted.

Surely Mom hadn't already written a press release. But how else would David know, unless he and Meg were talking again? Maybe that was what he'd been trying to tell me. *It's cool, we're back together.* "How did you hear about that?"

"I ran into your mom at Price Saver."

"And she just ran up to you and blurted it out?"

He shook his head. "We were talking about something else."

Here it comes. The big emotional breakdown. He must have needed time to work around to it. I did my best to look understanding. Neutral. Calm.

"She offered me a job."

"What?" I screeched.

"A job," he repeated, like maybe the problem was my hearing.

"Here?" I pointed at the ground. "In the show? As in the *Little Women Live!* one?" It seemed important to give him as many outs as possible.

"It would mostly be behind the scenes. Landscaping and stuff."

"Oh." I pressed a hand to my heart, exhaling in relief. It wasn't as bad as it sounded.

"Just a very small part in the show."

"Aunt March?" I whispered.

David blinked at me.

"Sorry. She's been talking about finding an Aunt March for years. Which obviously would not be you." I studied his face, trying to imagine how it would look framed by a wig. Even if you ignored the bony jaw, there was the Adam's apple to consider—not to mention the shoulders. David wasn't beefy like Laurie, but his frame was still significantly broader than your average old lady. Plus, he was at least six-foot-three, which presented its own challenges.

"Wait, you're not playing my dad, are you?" Because that would mean he was also Meg's dad, which: shudder.

"I'm John Brooke."

So obvious and yet . . . so not. "Meg's *baby daddy*?"

"That's not how your mom presented it to me, but yeah."

"You told her no, right?"

The pause said it all.

"David!" I shoved him in the shoulder. "What's wrong with you?"

"I thought you knew! It was in the press release."

I reared back like he was contagious. "She mentioned you in the press release?"

"The wedding scene," he reminded me. "'Brand new this year.' How did you think they were going to do that without a groom?"

"First off, I never read our press releases. It's a coping mechanism. Second, since when are we queens of realism? If I'd thought about it, which I didn't, I would have assumed Mom was going to make one of us slap on a mustache, or say, 'Why, where is Mr. Brooke?' and then someone else would answer, 'I do believe he's gone to send an urgent telegram.'"

We had a long history of finding creative solutions for our small cast size. Our invisible maid, Hannah, was always announcing things in a voice no one else could hear—like a theatrical dog whistle.

"Listen, David. I say this as your friend." I stared him down, even though he had three or four inches on me. "It's not too late. Save yourself."

He shifted uncomfortably. "I'm pretty sure your mom is counting on me."

"She'll get over it."

He looked surprised, and maybe a little disappointed.

"I'm not trying to be a dick, but there's no reason for you to suffer." The *too* part went without saying.

"It won't be that bad."

"Oh, it'll be bad," I assured him, sensing weakness. "Badder than bad. The worst."

"You don't think I can do it?"

Putting both hands on his shoulders, I gave him a shake. "That is not the point. The cell door is open. Walk away while you still can! Don't let us drag you down." He started to smile, like I was exaggerating. "I'm serious. This is like if you lived next door to a family of mobsters, and one day the boss asks you to do a tiny little favor. *No big deal,* you think. *I can get out any time.* Next thing you know, you're driving around town with a trunk full of bodies."

He blinked at me. "Is . . . someone going to break my kneecaps?"

"You don't know what it's like." I stepped back, pressing a hand to my stomach.

"I've lived next door to you guys forever, Jo. I have a pretty good idea."

"It's not the same. It hasn't taken over your whole existence." Maybe I should have complained more. I really thought I'd been doing a solid job on that front.

"I'll be background scenery. People won't pay any attention to me." It sounded like he was trying to convince himself. "It's not like the show's called *Little Women and That Quiet Guy Who Tutors the Spoiled Neighbor.*"

"What about the school tours?"

"What about them?"

"Are you prepared to get up onstage in front of half our high school?"

"I'm graduating in a month. I'll probably never see most of those people again."

"There'll be reunions."

He raised his eyebrows.

Fang settled himself next to me, leaning against my leg like he knew I needed moral support. I bent to pet him, partly as an excuse not to look at David. "You're seriously going to do a *wedding* scene with Meg?"

"It's fine."

I raised my head long enough to scowl at him. "How is it fine?"

"It's not like we were married, Jo. We barely even dated. It was probably a bad idea—"

My snort cut him off. "Sorry." I swallowed the urge to add, *I could have told you that.* Fang nudged my hand with his head, reminding me I was falling down on the job. "So what happened?"

"You don't know?"

"Believe it or not, there wasn't a press release."

"Not that you would have read it anyway."

"True." I gave Fang a scratch between the ears. "All I know is you guys were going out—"

"Whatever that means."

"Um." I wasn't sure which part I was supposed to explain.

Fang dropped to the ground with a doggy sigh, resting his head on his paws like he'd heard it all before.

"She texted me at Christmas. When you were at your dad's."

We always flew out right before the twenty-fifth, when tickets were stupidly overpriced, so Mom could squeeze in a few special performances during the holiday season. The math didn't come close to adding up, which was typical Porter planning. I shook my head, refocusing on the subject at hand. "Meg dumped you by text?"

"It was more of a 'we need to talk.'"

"Ouch. Was that *on* Christmas?"

"Yeah. But I had my phone off, so I didn't see the message until the twenty-sixth."

"Unbelievable." If memory served, Meg had spent the holiday cheerfully starting the online return process for the gifts she "didn't really like." Apparently, that had included David.

"It's okay, Jo. Like I said, we weren't serious. At all." He looked sheepish. "I just thought . . . I don't know what I was thinking."

"Me neither." David was friendly with all three of us, but privately—until the Meg thing—I'd assumed he was closest to me. I was the one who'd dragged him into our lives, a crucial fourth player in whatever game we were into that month. Meg and Amy usually wandered off, leaving me and David to finish the tree fort or canine obstacle course or Snackfé, the short-lived restaurant we operated out of our kitchen. Maybe if our menu had consisted of more than peanut-butter crackers and room-temperature water, we would have had a shot.

Unlike Meg and David.

"Uh, thanks."

"Not because of *you*." Fang rolled over, showing me his belly. I crouched to give him a rub. "So what did she say?" I asked without looking up. "When you had your 'talk.'"

"You know Meg."

"Eh. Kind of."

"I asked her if everything was okay, and she did that thing where you can't tell if she's sighing or yawning?"

"Uh-huh."

"And then she goes, 'Can we just not?'"

"Not . . . talk?"

"That's what I thought at first, so I was like, 'Okay,' and I shut up. Trying to respect her boundaries. And then she started making designs on the table with salt—"

I held up a hand. "Where were you?"

"Taco John's." He opened his mouth, then closed it again. "Is that important?"

"I just wondered whose salt she was wasting." And who was going to get stuck cleaning up afterward, since it definitely wouldn't have been Meg.

"Oh." He took a deep breath. "Then Meg said, 'It's such a hassle.'"

It took me a second to catch on. "You mean 'it' as in the two of you? Your 'relationship'?"

"Yes." He imitated my finger spasms. "Our air-quotes 'relationship.'"

"Dude."

"I know." He wasn't smiling, and yet I got the feeling David appreciated the absurdity of getting dumped over a greasy basket of Potato Olés. Or maybe *appreciate* wasn't the right word. Still, it didn't seem like his heart was broken. We'd played enough Uno together for me to know when David was bluffing.

"And this was right after Christmas?" I wasn't sure how I'd missed that development, because I distinctly remembered feeling queasy about the prospect of Valentine's Day. The explosion of candy and teddy bears and hearts was always pretty sickening. David getting sloppy over my sister was not high on my list of Things I Want to See.

He shook his head. "It took a few weeks — to find a good time. Scheduling conflicts."

"You were too busy?" Maybe he'd joined a club I didn't know about. Either that or David had been postponing the inevitable, because the only "conflicts" on my older sister's schedule were slathering herself in retinol and napping.

"It was Meg."

"She left you hanging?" I had so many questions. Did they see each other at all, apart from David giving her rides to school? Were they still . . . romantic during that time? On second thought, I didn't want to know. "And that was it? The end?"

"Basically. Except for asking me to give her the prom tickets."

"Uh, what? Is that like splitting up your assets after the divorce? She gets the prom tickets, you get the weird lamp? We're talking about somebody who pre-dumped you by text and then blew you off for like a month." During which time David and I could have been friends again, if I hadn't been keeping my distance from their supposed coupledom. That probably wasn't the main bummer for *him*, but still. "I wouldn't have given her a fingernail clipping."

"Like from your stash or a new one?"

"You know what I mean. It's ridiculous. Why should Meg get to keep tickets you bought?"

"She said she figured I wouldn't need them."

It was very David to have bought the tickets months in advance. And it was very Meg to selfishly demand them for herself while casually dissing her ex. Did she even have another date lined up, now that the dance was only a few weeks away, or was she going to flake on the whole thing and let the tickets go to waste? It didn't feel like something I could ask David.

Standing, I brushed the grass off the back of my thighs. "You want to go for a run?"

"I have to measure the pond."

"That pond?" I jerked a thumb at the mud pit.

"Your mom wants to put in a bridge."

I squeezed my eyes shut. "Do I even want to know?"

"It's a beautification project. To encourage people to 'stroll the grounds.'"

"She's back on her apple-orchard trip, isn't she?" Mom had this fantasy of recreating the part in *Little Women* where everyone is grown up and married and they picnic among the apple trees with the next generation of cursed children. It was only slightly less impractical than her idea of filling the rest of our property with an entire village of literary reenactors — like things were going so well it was only logical to expand.

I could feel my teeth grinding. Time to run. "Okay if I take Fang with me?"

David looked torn. Maybe I was rushing things, pushing too hard for a return to normal. Patience didn't come naturally to me, but for David I was willing to try.

"It's fine," I mumbled.

At the same instant, he said, "Can we swing by my house so I can change?"

I grinned at him. *Aw, yes.* Moving on.

"I'm afraid I couldn't like him without
a spice of human naughtiness."

–*Little Women*

CHAPTER EIGHT

The whine of the handheld vacuum sucking up dead bugs and dust balls muffled the ding of the bell over the gift-shop door. A week had passed since the so-called media preview, bringing us ever closer to May. Little by little, we were getting ready for the season, though when it came to dirty jobs like this one, "we" mostly meant me.

I thought about crawling out from under the display table to see who'd walked in, but it was most likely Amy raiding the candy. Or Meg, since the store was the one part of the business that interested her. She liked to say she was rearranging the jewelry displays and then spend an hour trying things on. That was what Mom referred to as *everyone helping in their own way.*

"Bad time?" asked a voice that did not belong to either of my sisters.

I crab-crawled backwards so fast the back of my head probably had splinters from scraping the underside of the table. "Um, hey. Hudson?"

It sounded like I was iffy on his name, when the real mystery was what he was doing here. Mom hadn't breathed a word about a return visit. If she had, I might have showered after my morning run.

He held out a hand, but I didn't take it. My palms were sticky with grime, and I wasn't convinced he had the strength to lift me without injuring himself.

"You're back." I scrambled to my feet. "Obviously."

"Not an astral projection," he agreed, gaze straying to my legs. Hopefully he was checking out the muscles, not whatever filth I'd picked up under the table.

"Just passing through?" I tried to sound casual, but I could tell from the twitch of his lips that Hudson saw through me.

"Nope."

My heart did a somersault. I should have been hearing cash-register sound effects, but I was mostly thinking about the guy standing in front of me in another faded concert T-shirt, with the clunky glasses that did nothing to hide his laughing eyes. "Really?"

"There was stiff competition from the clogging dynasty, but you edged them out."

"Put that in your wooden shoes, losers."

Hudson leaned closer, like he was about to share a secret. "I don't want to say it was my influence, because Andrea doesn't give a shit what I think, but you definitely had my vote."

"Thanks. I think?"

"Don't mention it. You can pay me in old candy."

He grinned at me before turning in a slow circle. "Pretty rad you have your own store. This would have been my dream as a kid."

"It's no Dollar General, but we try." I watched Hudson spin a rack of embossed leather bookmarks. "How long will you be here?"

"Sick of me already? That hurts." He pretended to trace the track of a tear down his cheek.

"I don't know how long this kind of thing takes. We've been written up before, but it was more like 'Top Ten Things to Do If Your Car Breaks Down on This One Stretch of Highway.' And we were number nine."

"I don't know if we can top that kind of hard-hitting journalism, but we'll hang around for a few weeks at least. Sounds like there's a big event May first we absolutely cannot miss?"

"Oh. Yeah." I made an executive decision not to think about Hudson witnessing the school tours, because the alternative was to collapse in a heap of boneless flesh and humiliation.

"Your mom and my mom are working out the details right now."

"Like what?"

"You have to be nice to me. It's in the contract."

"Well, forget it, then."

He threw a grin over his shoulder before wandering to a wall-mounted display of books. Or, rather, book.

"It's mostly waivers and releases. Letting us take pictures. That kind of thing." His head scanned back and forth like he was at a tennis match. "That's a lot of *Little Women*."

"Especially considering everyone who comes here has already read it." I pulled a dust rag from my waistband and half-heartedly brushed off a few spines.

Hudson plucked a book from the shelf and turned it over to read the back. "Is it just different covers? For people who want to collect them all?"

"Mostly. There's a shorter version for kids. Less death."

"But the strangling scene is my favorite."

"Yeah, well. That was a one-time-only special."

"Lucky me." Hudson moved to the section catering to our younger clientele. From the barrel we had repurposed as a display, he grabbed a pink calico bonnet and set it on top of his head like a maraschino cherry. "How do I look?"

"Fetching. All you need is the matching parasol." Only the most loaded visitors shelled out for dress-up gear, so the clothes tended to hang around until they were too faded and limp to sell.

The door to the storeroom opened and Meg emerged, blowing on the top of a soda can.

"Do you have the candle catalog?" She took a sip of warm Dr. Pip, the least popular of our off-brand beverages. "The Sweet 'n' Glow one, not Summer Scentsations."

It always took a few seconds to adjust to Shopping Meg, who was approximately two thousand times more focused than Regular Meg. And yet even in this rare moment of being tuned in, she had no clue that I was the last person on the planet who would care about overpriced blobs of wax.

When I shook my head, she glanced at the counter, knuckling aside a padded envelope. Sighing, she turned to go.

"That's it?"

Meg shrugged. "I don't see it."

She slipped out of sight, sucking on her lukewarm soda. Hopefully I'd never be buried under an avalanche and need to rely on my sister to lead the search party.

Hudson leaned out from behind a display. "Is this what I think it is?" His arm swung forward to reveal a doll with yarn braids, stitched-on eyes, and a green plaid dress. Grinning, he held the cloth face next to mine. "The likeness is uncanny. Except for the outfit." He snuck another look at my legs. "I can't believe you have your own doll."

"It's not *my* doll."

"You know what I mean." He lifted the skirt to peek underneath.

"Uh, creepy much?"

"I thought it might be a puppet."

"Ha. They wish." The image was a little too close to the truth for comfort.

Hudson handed me the Jo March doll. "Hold this a second."

"What? Why?" I was still sputtering when he took out his phone and snapped a picture.

He glanced at the screen, smiling at what he saw. "Nice."

"I bet."

"What's behind the glass?" He lifted his chin at a display case mounted on the wall.

"You know how in the book Amy's supposed to be artistic? This is IRL Amy's attempt to 'embody all aspects of her character.' She hasn't really found her medium yet, so she keeps experimenting."

He bent to squint at one of the objects behind the protective panel. "Is that a Pokémon?"

"From her 'sculpture' phase."

"Michelangelo better watch his back." He edged a few inches to the side, pointing at a rumpled sheet of paper. "Self-portrait?"

"I think it's actually supposed to be Taylor Swift."

"Watercolors are tricky."

"Apparently. FYI, her new thing is flower arranging, so don't set down your water glass unless you want to find a bunch of dried plants in it."

He moved off, leaving me to wonder if I'd come across too harsh. It wasn't that I cared how Amy spent her spare time, or whether her art sucked, except when I was supposed to pretend it didn't. What bugged me was that she acted like borrowing her personality from a book made her a better daughter. As if you could measure love by the number of times you hung out at the paint-your-own-ceramics place.

"What's this?" Hudson had stepped around a shoulder-height divider into the far corner of the store. "Oh. Oh wow." Even before the flash went off, I knew what he'd found.

"Those are really old." I joined him in front of the framed array of eight-by-ten photographs that lined the back of the store. It was a Wall of Shame, preserving the costumed version of our childhood. Way more pictures existed of Young Me onstage than off, in case anyone wasn't clear on Mom's priorities.

"But Jo. The memories." He put a hand to his heart while pretending to admire an image of me with my hands clasped, like I was praying for someone to fix my criminally short bangs. "So precious."

I grunted. He was rubbing up against a subject I preferred to drop. And then bury in a deep hole. With a haunted subdivision built on top.

"How old are you here?"

"Ten or eleven, maybe?" Like I didn't know. The bangs were a dead giveaway. In fifth grade there had been a minor outbreak of bobs among the girls in my class. When I asked if I could chop my hair off too, Mom explained that Jo needed long hair, because of the famous part in the story where she sells it when her father gets sick. She offered bangs as a compromise.

In hindsight, that was the line in the sand—or, rather, across my forehead. The beginning of the end.

"Did you do that to yourself?"

"Believe it or not, my mother paid someone."

"What's this one?" He pointed to the picture two frames over. "I'm guessing from the tinsel it must be Christmas?"

I sighed from the bottom of my soul. "Every friggin' year."

"That's pretty much how holidays work."

"We do that scene for the school tours," I clarified. "Even though they're in May."

"Right." He squinted at the photo. "Who's the rando? Did somebody rush the stage?"

"You mean Beth?" I pointed at that year's version, Ruby Xie. She'd been one of my favorite fake sisters. Not too sappy, mostly punching the clock with us because as summer jobs went, pretending to be sick was easier than peddling fast food.

"What happened to her?"

"She graduated, so we hired somebody else the next summer. The circle of life. Or death, in this case." I pointed out a few of the other Beths we'd employed in the past, including the memorable summer my cousin Jasper had filled in for a week while that season's Beth went to a music festival in Tennessee.

"Who's your Beth this year?"

"We'll find out Tuesday." I hesitated, not sure how deep of a dive he and Andrea were planning. "Are you coming to auditions?"

"Will you be there?"

"No choice."

"Okay, then. Sign me up."

"If you're sure you can handle that much excitement."

"Is it like a cattle call? Hundreds of hopefuls lining up with their headshots?"

"I think the most we ever had was seven. Which is a lot when you consider what they're signing on for."

"Pink bonnets?"

"Ritual humiliation." Though at least our Beths, like Laurie, didn't have the added layer of *Meet my bizarro family, to whom I am genetically related!* I stretched a hand to the nearest photo, covering my face with the pad of my thumb. "Imagine your face here. Now picture your entire social circle staring as you make speeches about being virtuous and sweet."

"I figured it was mostly tourists. Do people give you crap?"

"Not to my face." It would almost be better if they *did* tease me. That would mean it was okay to laugh, instead of being too horrified to mention my not-so-secret shame. "But I can feel them looking at me."

"And that's bad?"

"I just want to be the one who gets to decide what people see. Of me."

Hudson lifted a faux quill pen from the display on the counter and pressed the ballpoint against his palm. "Defining your own brand is crucial."

It sounded a little like something Laurie would say, though I was sure Hudson meant it in a more intellectual way. "Or getting to decide if you even want to have a brand."

He returned the pen to the canister. "As opposed to what?"

"Being normal. Anonymous."

He held up his phone. I blinked as the flash went off in my eyes.

"Excuse you."

"Sorry. It's just—photography helps me see things. You know?"

I shrugged, because I wasn't sure I did know, but Hudson didn't look up from his phone.

"Nope," he said, still studying the screen. "Doesn't track."

I moved to stand beside him, wondering what Hudson

saw in a picture of me with a display of *Little Women* coloring books peeking from behind my shoulder. "Our fine selection of souvenirs?"

"You blending in with the crowd."

"Because I'm so weird?"

"I'm saying this is not a girl who disappears." Slipping his phone back in his pocket, Hudson smiled at the flesh-and-blood me.

It was like another flash going off, this one inside my brain. I wasn't used to compliments, unless you counted the back-handed ones from my mom. *Good job not antagonizing your sister today, Jo. So nice to see you in a dress for a change!*

"It would be cool if I could, though. Cut ties and vanish. Later, haters." I pictured an empty spot in the middle of the stage, maybe a puff of colored smoke.

"Yeah." It was almost a sigh, his voice softening with surprise. He studied my face like he'd discovered something new there. "Let me know if you figure out that trick."

"Jo March, you are perverse enough
to provoke a saint!"

–Little Women

CHAPTER NINE

On Tuesday afternoon, I was loitering near the door of the café when Amy raced around the corner. At the sight of me, she slowed to a stroll.

"Look who showed up on time for once. I wonder why?" The words were accompanied by a squinting, lip-tapping panto-mime worthy of a silent movie.

"I have to be here. I don't know if you know this, but that's what *mandatory* means." I'd actually gotten here half an hour early to meet Hudson, after he texted to ask if I wanted to hang out before auditions. Not that I was going to share that with Amy.

Laurie arrived next, and draped an arm around each of our shoulders. "My ladies. Sometimes I don't know which of you I like more."

"She's not going to share," Amy informed him as he reached for the box of granola bars I was holding. "So you're better off picking me."

Dropping his hand to my waist, Laurie tugged me back against his side. "No snacks for your Laurie?" He fluttered his lashes.

"Something in your eye?" I asked sweetly.

"I bet she's saving them for *him*." Amy nodded at Hudson, who was crossing the gravel driveway. "Which he obviously needs the calories."

"Aha! I see how it is." Laurie winked at me but didn't let go. "You're afraid little lover boy will be jealous."

"No. And also, no."

"You can't use a double negative, JoJo. Even I know that."

"That's not . . ." I gave up. "Maybe your cologne is too strong for me."

He held his shirt away from his chest, inhaling deeply. "Really? I like it."

Amy loudly sniffed his shoulder. "Oh yeah."

"Hey." Hudson studied our odd trio for a moment before smiling at me. I smacked Laurie's hand away from the box of granola bars. I was distracted, not blind.

"Hi." Hopefully Hudson could tell from my sigh that I hadn't invited these two clowns. "You ready for the excitement?"

Amy huffed. "It's not that big of a deal."

"Actually, Amy, it's a life-or-*Beth* situation." I did a fair imitation of my sister in unsolicited-monologue mode, which was about where my acting ability maxed out.

Hudson snickered, but Amy's face pruned with annoyance.

"That's funny." Laurie shook his head. "Usually Amy's the one who's like, 'I love this so much,' and Jo's all 'Ugh, I hate it here.'" He spoke in a screechy falsetto for Amy, hands splayed on either side of his face, while I sounded like a constipated stoner.

"So Jo's the cynical one." Hudson made a note on his phone. "Tell me more."

Amy threw her shoulders back, like she'd been waiting for her cue. "Jo March is mostly a self-insert Louisa May Alcott, with a slightly happier ending. Although not artistically, since her creativity is totally stifled."

"I was talking about this Jo, actually." He indicated me with his thumb.

"It's not that complicated. Bad mood, no style, running. Boom. The story of Jo."

I bared my teeth at her. "Amy's even easier, because her top three are all peroxide."

"I forgot to say 'no sense of humor.'" She nodded at his phone. "Add that to the list."

Hudson attempted a redirect. "What's Jo like at school?"

"Oh, Jo's not popular like me and Meg."

"You're kidding, right?" Just when I thought I knew all my sister's delusions by heart, she busted out a new one. Amy had a gaggle of friends, but they were mostly legends in their own minds. Meg's crowd was more of the rich 'n' lazy set. They didn't star in plays or play sports or wear crowns at homecoming, but if there had been a yacht club in our landlocked town, my older sister's crew would have been charter members. Our family was obviously not on the same level financially, but somehow my sister's pretty face and inertia had granted her access to the boat-shoes scene.

"FYI, in real life Laurie was never hung up on Jo," Amy informed Hudson, waving at me. "Don't believe the hype."

"It was pretty casual." Laurie winked at him, bro to bro. "Not that I'm the type to kiss and tell."

"Can we talk about something interesting now?" Amy whined, one thousand percent referring to herself.

"You're from New York, right?" Laurie leaned past me to address Hudson, like I was an inconvenient wooden post. "The Big Apple." Hudson nodded. "Ask me how many times I've seen *Phantom*."

"How many times have you seen *Phantom*?"

"Seven." Laurie let that sit for a few beats. "And counting."

Hudson absorbed this important data with a slow nod before turning to me. "What about you?"

"Hard pass. No phantoms, no opera."

The corners of his mouth tipped up. "I mean, have you been to New York?"

"Uh, no." Was it supposed to be a universal rite of passage, like riding a bike? Also, did we look like we had that kind of cash?

"You should go. I could show you around."

He sounded playful, but also like he meant it, which . . . I'd have to unpack later, without an audience. Laurie executed a precise single-brow lift, an expression I'd watched him practice in an endless succession of selfies.

Amy squirmed with impatience. "This is almost as boring as watching a roomful of Beths."

"It must be a little weird, having a new sister every year," Hudson said.

"At least we get to pick a Beth. As opposed to being stuck with someone from birth." She wrinkled her nose. "Know what I mean, Faux Jo?"

"Sure, Shamy." I ran a finger under my lower eyelid. The middle finger, to be precise.

"Ah, sisterhood," Mom said loudly, opening the café door from inside.

Andrea peered from behind her. "What are we talking about?"

"You know how it is with Jo and Amy. So much good-natured ribbing." Mom threw in a hand wave, like that made it more convincing.

"Life imitating art?" Andrea suggested.

"Yes." Mom beamed at her. "Exactly."

"Speaking of blurred lines," Hudson said, "doesn't the name thing get confusing? Someone says 'Jo' and it's like, which one?"

"Just say JoJo," Laurie offered. "That's what I do."

"No, you don't." I stared into his eyes. The power of suggestion.

"And there have been, what, seven or eight different Beths?" Hudson went on.

"But Beth doesn't matter," Amy reminded everyone. "Her character is basically a prop on Jo's emotional journey, and who needs more of that?" She pretended to snore.

"You know, I think that's a wonderful idea, Hudson."

We all stared at my mother with varying degrees of *Huh?*

"To help our visitors, let's all try to express ourselves more clearly over the next few weeks, whether we're speaking to or about each other."

"Okay." I lifted my chin at Amy. "You annoy the crap out of me. How was that?"

"I meant that we should use proper names, Jo."

"Sorry. You annoy the crap out of me, *Amy*."

"'You annoy the you-know-what out of me, Amy Porter' would be better," Mom admonished. "The point is to distinguish between the workaday you and your character."

"Like Dr. Jekyll and Mr. Hyde," Laurie suggested awesomely.

"Or we could simply say Book Jo instead of, you know, *Jo*." Mom gestured at me like this were the most natural thing in the world, even though I'd been trying for years to convince my family to draw a hard line between That Book and our real lives.

"Ooh," Amy jumped in, not above using my name to draw attention to herself, "it could be BJ for short."

Mom winced. "No, dear."

"What about you?" Andrea leaned closer to Laurie, who automatically shifted to display the three-quarters profile he considered his best angle. "Interesting they don't call you by your given name."

"I don't mind," he said.

"No?" she pressed, like maybe he hadn't thought it through.

Laurie shook his head. "I can rock a girl's name. It's cool."

"Some might consider it erasing the identity of the only cast member of color." It wasn't clear from Andrea's tone whether she counted herself among the *some* or was playing devil's advocate.

It was true that *Little Women Live!* was a predominantly white production of a very white book. Mom hired less homogeneous Beths whenever possible, but we were limited by the pastiness of the local population—and the fact that most of the roles were permanently taken. It would be hard to diversify the cast unless she started bumping off her daughters.

Maybe I should volunteer?

"Some people call me LB when I'm not in character," Laurie offered. "If it makes you feel better."

"It's a football thing," I told Hudson. "His real name is Leo."

"LB as in *pound* it." Laurie raised his fist, and Amy fell over herself in the rush to tap his knuckles. "And because I bench major LBs, if you know what I mean." *Pounds,* he mouthed, adding a bicep flex in case we still didn't get it.

"Also those are your initials," I reminded him.

"That too. But the *L* could stand for Laurie." He winked at us. "The one in the book."

"Shouldn't it be BL?" Hudson asked. "For Book Laurie?"

Amy scowled at him. "As someone who has *studied* the text,

I think it's close enough. And you can all start calling me BA, as in *Bad Ass*." She elbowed Laurie, who gave a belated nod of appreciation.

"Except the whole point is you're not BA. You're just Amy." It was like working in a head-trauma ward.

"Who's on first," Andrea murmured.

"What about you?" I asked my mother.

"Me?"

"What will we call you?" It was no secret that Mom loved when people conflated her with Marmee, the saintly maternal figure from *Little Women*.

"That shouldn't be an issue." Her smile was serene, like she'd just sipped a cup of chamomile tea after an hour of predawn yoga. "Marmee keeps herself in the background. She's all about letting her girls take center stage."

I didn't intend to roll my eyes. It was an involuntary reaction, like a sneeze.

"You know what your nickname should be, Jo?" Amy didn't wait to be asked. "The Weekly Volcano. Because you're always about to *blow*."

"That's not really appropriate," Mom began, but my little sister was on a roll.

"I know *you* know what I'm talking about." Amy tipped her head toward Andrea, like they were fellow scientists in a disaster movie, surrounded by clueless civilians. "In the book, Jo submits some of her TV-MA stories to a newspaper called the *Weekly Volcano*, but then this old boring guy guilt-trips her about writing racy romance. Which is sort of what happened to the real Louisa May. Personally, I think it's a bummer she doesn't get more attention for her sensation stories, which totally slap. I'm talking about Alcott," she clarified. "And also Book Jo. But not *this* Jo. She's no writer. We don't let her anywhere near our press materials."

"Keep going," I deadpanned. "It gets funnier the more you explain."

Mom made a show of checking her watch. "Why don't we head inside?"

"Aren't we missing a sister?" Hudson asked.

"Meg will join us as soon as she can," Mom assured him. Translation: sometime between tomorrow and never.

"Don't you mean BM?" Amy wondered aloud. "Our BM doesn't follow a regular schedule, but it's always a relief when she finally gets here."

Andrea looked amused.

"You're still doing it wrong," I told her. "But also, we don't need a code name for Meg. If she's doing something, it's the one from the book. If she's comatose or doesn't bother showing up, we're talking about the actual Meg."

Amy mimed a head explosion, complete with sonic boom. Maybe I'd taken the bitchiness too far, but the double standard in our family when it came to Meg made me want to punch something.

"Jo's just jealous," Amy informed everyone as we trooped into the café. "Because of David."

"Who's David?" Hudson asked, with what sounded like more than journalistic interest.

The head tip, the hand curl, the inhale like she was about to deep-sea dive: this was Amy's version of stepping up to a podium and tapping the mike. "If you ask me, David is the real Laurie of this story."

Laurie gasped like she'd sucker-punched him.

"Not as a performer. You own that role," my sister purred, before turning to Hudson with a chilling smile. "You should ask Jo about David. She's the one who's obsessed with him."

I sent her a look that threatened violent retribution, but Amy was too caught up in the scene playing out in her head to notice.

"Jo used to follow David around like a puppy, only not small or cute. Even though he has a real dog who's way cooler." She paused, possibly recognizing she'd stopped making sense. "Too bad for her he chose Meg instead."

"And now I cry myself to sleep every night." I slow-clapped. "Great story."

"Girls," Mom scolded, like we were equally guilty. "Let's focus. It's time to meet our Beth."

"You mean NB?" Amy suggested, in her most sickeningly sweet voice. "For New Beth?"

"That could work," Mom said vaguely, gesturing us to our seats.

"Or NBD," my sister went on. "Since she's No Big Deal."

It was the kind of editorializing that would have earned

me an expression of Deep Disappointment, with a side of Sad Feelings. Since this was Amy, Mom merely touched a finger to her lips, like she was telling her to use her library voice. "Is everyone ready?"

"To Beth or not to Beth, that is the question," I said, mostly to myself.

"Don't write that down," Amy told Hudson, who was grinning at me. "It's not funny."

"Beth number one," our mother called, before her real daughters could start slapping each other. "You're on."

"Is Beth the rosy one, who stays at home a good
deal, and sometimes goes out with a little basket?"

—*Little Women*

CHAPTER TEN

Most would-be Beths followed a standard formula. A faint cough, some handkerchief choreography, a hurricane of piteous sighs. Speaking above a whisper was unheard of, though they got plenty loud when it was time to fake cry. The only prop we provided was a bare wooden chair, which the Beths struggled to slump across like a deathbed. More rarely a would-be Beth might stagger in and announce she was back from visiting the poor, sad Hummel children and "suddenly... I feel... so strange... cold... and damp... so tired..."

And *crash*. Down she went.

Other aspiring Beths took the "scarlet fever" part literally, wearing so much blush it looked like they were seconds from heatstroke.

This year we got a "Mama! I see a bright light!" right out

of the gate, followed by a girl who choked so hard at the sight of Laurie that I thought we were going to have to Heimlich her. The next one came out in barely there dancewear, a marked contrast to the usual floor-length nightgowns, and proceeded to writhe her way through a modern-dance routine full of reaching arms and falling to her knees.

"Well." Mom made a note on the audition form. "She seems very flexible."

"I wonder if she does tap?" Andrea murmured.

The fourth wannabe Beth was notable mainly for her accent.

"Why is she pretending to be British?" Amy hissed.

"Oim a chimney sweep, oi am," Laurie put in, sounding like he'd watched *Mary Poppins* one too many times.

There was a long silence after Cockney Beth left the stage, presumably to go have tea and crumpets with the queen.

"Are we done?" I asked hopefully.

"There should be one more." Frowning, Mom sifted through the stack of audition forms. "Ah," she said, setting down the paperwork as the door opened. "Here we go."

The fifth Beth brought her own props, carrying in a cardboard box painted to look like a wooden trunk. After kicking the chair out of the way, she sat on the floor with her fake toy chest between her legs.

"Don't worry, dolly." She gently lifted a headless plastic baby from the box. "I'll fix you."

Her voice was higher than expected from someone built like a WNBA forward, but it didn't tremble, or turn all breathy and phlegmy. Points for originality. She set down the doll body, pulled a threaded needle from a pincushion, and held it between her teeth while she dug a teddy-bear head from her box.

"The doll hospital," I explained to Hudson, in case he hadn't recognized what was a fairly obscure bit in the book. "Beth likes to fix sad, broken things."

As she began sewing the fuzzy bear face onto the human-oid body, he held up his phone to take a picture, positioning it in front of him like a shield.

"Interesting," Andrea murmured, scribbling in her notebook.

Amy stuck out her tongue. "Too bad she can't fix herself."

Laurie pointed at her. "Irony."

"I love my family," Beth sang. "I keep them with me always."

We all stared in fascination as she rocked the bear-headed baby in her arms.

"Good night, Marmee," she whispered, kissing the fuzzy forehead before placing it back in the box. "Hello, Jo," she greeted the next creation, a glassy-eyed baby-doll head that had been grafted onto the body of a Transformer. "You're so fierce."

Amy snorted.

"Oh, look, it's Amy." Beth barely raised her voice as she held up a decapitated Raggedy Ann. She rummaged in the box until she came up with a Barbie head. "Empty inside," she sighed, squinting into the neck. "Oh well."

"Mom!" Amy smacked the table with both hands.

"I like her," I said, as Beth crooned another creepy lullaby.

Laurie sniffed loudly, like he was holding back tears, provoking a scowl from Amy. "It's just so sad," he whispered. I knew he was sensitive, but you'd think some of the sting of watching Beth bite it would have worn off by now. It was practically an everyday occurrence in these parts. He wiped his nose with the back of his hand. "Can't somebody get this kid a new toy?"

Beth arranged her dolls in the box and closed the flaps. "Good night, little family," she sang in her eerie soprano, making the hairs on the back of my neck stand up. "All together, safe and sound, forever." She raised her head to stare at us as she trilled the last line. "None of you will ever leave me."

"Is she going to kill us?" Hudson asked me.

"That would be a twist."

"She's not interesting." Amy jabbed a hand at Beth, who had collapsed over her box in what looked like child's pose. "Can't you see she's manipulating you all?" She crossed her arms, refusing to clap as Beth stood and brushed off her skirt before taking a bow.

When she had taken her toys and gone home, Mom turned to us with a blissed-out smile. "At least the choice is simple this year."

"I have no idea what you're talking about," Amy lied.

"The dolls! And her death rattle!" Mom said, like that would jog her memory. "So affecting!"

"But she didn't do the death scene." Amy looked at me to make sure I didn't know something she didn't.

"Not today, of course," Mom agreed. "I saw it before. At Price Saver."

I was still trying to imagine how this might have played out — deli counter? Frozen-food aisle? — when Laurie asked, "Is she a cashier?"

Because that would explain it. *Is this romaine? And by the way, do you want to watch my Dying Beth act?*

"Possibly. I do know she was carrying a bag of oranges. It fell during the whole . . ." Mom fluttered her fingers, like we could all fill in the blank. Hudson cut his eyes at me.

"Can you maybe finish that thought, Mom?"

"When she showed me how she would play Beth's farewell. Right there at the cart return. With a lone orange rolling across the asphalt." She stretched out an arm, fingers slowly uncurling.

"That's nothing!" With a grunt, Amy hauled herself across the table, spinning to face us. "You want edgy? You want twisted?"

"No." It was the easiest question I'd ever had to answer.

"Um," said Laurie, trying to balance out my snark. "Sometimes?"

That was all the encouragement she needed. "It's over for you hoes now." She clapped her hands like cymbals. "Picture this. I'm young, hot, and winsome. Not that different from what's in front of you."

I sighed like I was blowing out birthday candles.

"Only I'm also timid and demure, so you can tell just by looking at me that I have a tragic backstory. Classic governess arc." Amy pressed the back of her hand to her forehead. "O woe is me! Though I am virtuous and sweet, I have fallen on hard times!" Dropping the act, she circled a hand in the air. "Your hearts melt, I work my way under your skin, et cetera."

"Like a *Silence of the Lambs* thing?" Laurie guessed.

She held a finger to her lips. "Next thing you know, *everyone* is in love with me. I'm just that good."

"Is she doing her affirmations?" I asked, earning a helpless shrug from our mother.

"As I was saying" — Amy raised her voice to drown out the commentary — "no one can resist my charms, especially when I sing like a nightingale in my lilting Scottish brogue."

"Please don't." I covered my ears, just in case.

"But then!" Amy swept an arm backwards and forward, like she was clearing cobwebs out of her way.

"Uh-oh," Laurie intoned, genuinely caught up in the performance.

"I go to my room at night, where no one can see. First I take off my hairpiece." Amy mimed ripping off her bangs. "Then I spit out my false teeth." With a liquid *pluh* she coughed into her cupped hand. "I wash off the makeup that makes me look young and girlish." She flicked her fingers at either cheek. Straightening, she stared at her unwilling audience for an uncomfortably long moment. "Guess what."

"What?" Laurie asked, like he was afraid not to.

"It turns out I've been fooling you all. I'm not a sweet young maiden wronged by a cruel world; I'm a homely thirty-year-old actress with a drinking problem!" She mimed glugging from an invisible flask.

Mom's mouth worked like she wanted to protest but had lost the ability to make words. Amy hurried on.

"Before the haters can expose my secret, I marry their rich old uncle. Title, estate, and a husband who probably won't be around much longer — they're all mine, because all I do is win." She dropped into a bow.

We sat in weirded-out silence until Amy raised her head to scowl at us, at which point Laurie clapped.

"Mom," I stage-whispered. "I think she finally cracked."

"That was not from the book," Hudson confirmed, glancing at me. I didn't blame him for the confusion. It felt like the air had been pumped full of hallucinogens.

"Hello?" Amy's pout was visible from space. "Am I the only one who knows how to do interlibrary loans? *Behind a Mask.* Ring any bells? It's one of Alcott's best stories. Totally effed-up and awesome. Exactly the kind of thing Jo March wanted to write, before Professor Un-Bhaer-able crapped on her dreams."

"Good for you, doing background research!" You could tell that what Mom really meant was *That's enough.*

Sighing, my sister subsided. I knew the reprieve was temporary. One day she'd find a way to force "the spicy side" of Louisa May down all our throats; it was just a matter of wearing Mom down. Because what Amy really needed was an excuse to over-act even more.

"Excuse me," said Doll Hospital Beth, who had slipped back

through the door like a shadow. She waited until every eye was trained in her direction. A slight teeter to the left, a wobble to the right, and then *crash!* A sudden collapse into a boneless heap. The open eyes were a particularly effective touch. If this was how she'd dropped in the Price Saver parking lot, I had to admire her commitment.

Amy looked outraged even before Laurie leaped to his feet, clapping and whistling.

"And scene," Andrea quipped, closing her notebook.

Jo's ambition was to do something very
splendid; what it was she had no idea, as
yet, but left it for time to tell her.

—Little Women

CHAPTER ELEVEN

Amy was still babbling about how dying was easy but living well was the real victory, when Andrea caught my eye.

"Do you have a minute?" she asked.

I suggested we chat outside, since the atmosphere in the café was a little stifling from all the emoting.

"Are you involved in the food side of operations?" Andrea asked as I led the way through the kitchen to avoid being waylaid by stray members of my family or random Beths. Hudson followed, either to help or (as I preferred to believe) because he enjoyed my company.

"Not really." If we were going by the book, Meg should have been the kitchen wench in the family, but unlike Amy with her art mania, my older sister didn't feel compelled to dabble in food prep just because her fictional alter ego was a happy homemaker.

"Good. Once they get you in the kitchen, you're trapped."

"Not a problem at our house," Hudson joked. "We mostly use the oven for storage."

Andrea stopped. "Why are you here?"

I watched a bug crawl across the grass, veering off before it reached my shoe. Other people's family tension was none of my business, so I should probably keep my mouth shut.

"I was just leaving." He nodded at me in parting, jaw stiff. Even though I couldn't imagine dealing with that level of maternal harshness on a regular basis—in public or in private—a small part of me envied Hudson the freedom to blow off work.

"We can sit over there." I pointed to a wooden picnic table under the canopy of an oak tree, on the far side of the driveway.

"This place reminds me of parts of Eastern Europe," she said as she settled onto the weathered gray slats of the bench. Today's outfit was a chambray shirt and cargo pants, like she was on a suburban safari. "It's like stepping into the past."

"Yeah." *In more ways than one.*

Andrea studied me with eyes that were greener than her son's, even in the dappled light of late afternoon. "I'm not taking you away from anything?"

It was weird to be asked; my family assumed I was available 24/7. The thought of homework crossed my mind, but if someone like Andrea had time to talk to me, what was I going to say? *Nope, sorry, I'm busy filling in this worksheet.*

"It's fine."

"How do you like working with your mother?"

So much for easing into the tough stuff. "I guess . . . it has its moments?"

"You don't have to make it pretty, Jo. I'm not in the market for platitudes."

I nodded like I understood. Andrea was a different kind of adult than I was used to. Less stuffy, but more intimidating.

She shifted to rest both elbows on the table, a movement that apparently signaled a change in tack. "Let's talk about you."

"Okay." Compared to discussing my mom, that sounded simple.

The fingers of her left hand lightly drummed the table. "You're Jo March."

I winced, which was apparently enough of a *yes* for Andrea.

"What does that mean to you?"

Spending half my life pretending to be someone else. Living in a constant state of embarrassment. Not even being allowed to cut my freaking hair. I shoved those thoughts down.

"Livin' the dream." I meant it as a nonanswer, too much of a cliché to give anything away, but Andrea pounced.

"Whose dream?"

"Everyone who wants to be Jo March. The superfans." With a stab of dread, I realized I might be talking to one. "Uh, are you like, you know—"

"One of those little girls who grew up with ink-stained fingers, dreaming of scribbling books of her own? I had a Jo March phase, yes. But I got over it. As soon as you dig into Alcott's life, the attraction fades. As I suspect you know."

You interest me, her expression said. Maybe because I wasn't wearing a costume, or saying someone else's lines, it felt like she was seeing the *real* me, not Jo March.

"What you do," she continued, chipping at the edge of the table with her thumbnail, "it's not really interrogating the book, is it? I don't sense a lot of critical distance. The quaint home, your idyllic childhood, everyone pitching in. It's all fairly on the nose."

"I wouldn't say we're *that* old-fashioned." We all used our mother's maiden name, for one thing. That was pretty different by local standards, though I wasn't sure it would impress Andrea. I could have told her about Mom's post-Dad dating history, but it seemed childish to brag about the fact that my Mommy once had a girlfriend.

"Not in the sense of being twee." Reaching across the table, she touched the back of my wrist. "What interests me is how you reconcile the book's themes with your life as a modern young woman."

"You mean do I dream of being a happy housewife?"

"Is that the message of *Little Women?*"

I had no idea if this was her interview mode or the way everyone talked in big cities. "I think that's part of it."

"What about the rage?"

"Um." That definitely wasn't the first word people usually brought up when they were talking about *Little Women.*

"Don't you feel it simmering under the surface every time Jo gets her wings clipped, or has to give up her dreams to help her family?" She held up her hand, fingers wrapped into a fist. "And yet Alcott can't let herself go there. There's no scream of defiance, no attempt to escape. She lets them suffocate her flame."

My heart stuttered. Who were we really talking about — Louisa May? Jo March? Andrea? Or was this about me? I tried the word *rage* on for size, shaping it on my tongue.

"It must chafe," Andrea prompted.

I'd only ever thought of that word in the context of friction rashes on my inner thighs from running. This didn't sound like a problem Vaseline could solve. "I guess?"

She waited, like I might rise to the occasion. "What about your sisters?"

"For sure. They make me feel extremely ragey."

Her mouth quirked. "I meant how do they relate to all of this — the source material?"

"Oh. Right. Um." I hoped my blush wasn't visible. "Amy can't get enough. She'll probably be doing this when she's sixty. And Meg is barely here even when she's here. Like you have to hold a mirror to her face to make sure she's breathing. She won't make any waves."

"*They* don't long for more?"

The words were like a swing, lifting me up and away from my family. Amazing how Andrea had seen what was going on with me in minutes, when my own mother didn't have a clue. "Definitely not."

"How much do you know about Margaret Fuller?"

I shook my head, not wanting to admit I knew diddly about Margaret Whatsit.

"She was a trailblazer. Scholar, journalist, world traveler—an independent woman in an era when that was almost impossible to achieve. A neglected feminist icon." She studied me, as if to gauge my reaction. "Alcott knew her."

"Were they . . . friends?" That was probably a stupid thing to ask, but it was too late to come up with a less juvenile question.

"I imagine Louisa admired her. Possibly more. They were all a little in love with her."

"'They'?"

"The New England literati. Hawthorne, Emerson, Thoreau. Rumor has it several of them based fictional characters on Margaret Fuller. She was something of a muse—though never *just* that. Meanwhile Alcott was stuck at home, slaving away to support her family."

I waited for her to go on, drive home the comparison, but Andrea seemed to expect me to fill in the blanks on my own. What was I supposed to say? *You're right—her life sucked.* Or maybe: *This Margaret chick sure sounds a lot like you!*

"I'll be honest with you, Jo." Andrea paused, and I braced myself. It hadn't seemed like she was holding back before. "I expected more of the transcendentalism to come through."

Even though I sort of knew what she was talking about—the nature freaks who ran in the same circles as Louisa May Alcott—I felt the same stab of paralyzing doubt that hit every time someone brought up an *ism.* Communism, socialism, capitalism: each one was like a lake with hidden rocks. You get it on a surface level, but underneath, it's hella complicated.

"What a wasted opportunity to focus on environmental issues," she continued. "It's a bit naïve to pretend we're still living in a pastoral paradise."

"Um." I definitely agreed about the not-a-paradise part but wasn't sure what else to say. *We totally recycle, yo.* It wasn't like Andrea had rolled up in a Tesla, wearing hemp shoes. "I guess we could do more."

She threaded her fingers together, gazing at me over her linked hands. "What about you? Is Jo Porter an aspiring writer, like her namesake?"

"No way." Writing was the last career I could ever choose, even if I wanted to do it. It would be like telling my mom, *You win! I am a carbon copy of Jo March.*

The problem was that I didn't have an alternative. *I want to be cross-country captain* was such a high school answer. Andrea wouldn't care about youth sports. "Um, I'd like to go to college."

She shrugged this off like it was obvious, barely worth mentioning. "And then?"

"I don't know." Was I really supposed to have all the answers when most of my life was a chorus of *not this*?

Andrea leaned across the table. "Go on. Make your point."

"I just want room to breathe. So I can figure it out." *It* as in *everything.*

"You know I grew up in a small town?"

I shook my head.

"Couldn't wait to get out." Her lips curved at the memory,

though it wasn't a happy smile. "Filled my first passport before I was twenty-three."

"That's incredible." Six years from now, what would I have accomplished? Somehow I doubted the list would include traveling around the world.

"It was what I wanted, so I made it happen." She tucked her barely there hair behind her ears. No long, horsey ponytail to get in the way of Andrea's globe-trotting adventures. "I suspect it's the same for you. Everyone wants you to play the role they've written, instead of choosing your own path."

My mouth opened, but something held me back. It was one thing to make pissy comments, but straight-up admitting *I hate it here*? I wasn't sure I could come back from that.

"She didn't want to write it, you know." Andrea's expression softened, as if she sensed my struggle. "It was her publisher's idea—an inspirational story for young girls. Do you know what Alcott called *Little Women*?"

"Wasn't it the four girls' names?"

"No. Her working title was *The Pathetic Family*."

"Oh." Mom had never mentioned that fun fact.

Andrea watched the branches of a redbud tree sway. "In my experience, Jo, the world is as big—or as small—as you make it."

She tried not to be envious or discontented,
but it was very natural that the young girl
should long for pretty things, gay friends,
accomplishments, and a happy life.

–*Little Women*

CHAPTER TWELVE

The conversation with Andrea kept poking into my thoughts long after she left and I sat through an evening of spaghetti and dodging questions about my "interview." If that was what it had been.

It was like eating popcorn and then spending days picking shards of kernel out of your gums. There were parts of our talk I was still digesting, and I wanted to have answers before Andrea approached me again. Assuming she hadn't written me off as a boring teenager with nothing intelligent to say.

So yeah, I had some processing to do. Little things like *Who am I?* and *What am I passionate about?* The first opportunity for quality thinking came Wednesday afternoon. New Beth was being fitted for her costume, which meant I could stay after school for track practice. It was a distance workout, so double bonus. There weren't enough miles between here and the edge of town to figure it all out, but an hour of pounding the pavement should at least shake loose a few clues.

While most of my teammates opted for a route that would take them along the access road by the highway where they could buy a Powerade from the gas station, I headed for the park.

"Jo. Wait up."

I slowed but didn't stop, glancing back over my shoulder as David caught up to me.

"Okay if I run with you?"

I jerked my head in a yes. Even though I'd deliberately set a bruising pace to keep other people from joining me, David wasn't other people. I was glad he'd sought me out. It was further evidence that things between us had officially thawed, or cooled off, or settled — some state of matter.

"You okay?" he asked.

"Fine."

There was a David-like lag, during which I probably would have been able to hear the thoughts churning in his brain if my breath hadn't been whooshing in and out so loudly. "I thought maybe you were having a crisis."

"Why do you say that?"

"You're kind of hauling ass right now."

"I have a lot on my mind," I said, taking the pace down a notch.

We split up to jog around a woman pushing a double

stroller. "School tours?" he asked as we met up again, feet hitting the sidewalk in sync.

"No." I tightened my ponytail. "But thanks for reminding me of the worst day of the year."

"Did something happen at auditions?"

"Nah. New Beth is awesome. She's giving Amy fits."

"And of course you hate to see Amy suffer."

"It's killing me on the inside." I would have happily left it at that, but David was still waiting for me to fess up. "It's more of a personal thing."

"Oh. Sorry." His shoulders hitched up toward his ears, like he was trying to disappear.

"You think I'm talking about my period, don't you?"

"No?"

I might have laughed at David's squirming, but I didn't have the oxygen to spare. "It's just." *Pound, pound, pound.* "The future."

He waited for me to go on. Which was tricky, since I was basically one giant question mark. I flapped an elbow at him. "What about you?"

"Me?"

"Do you have a plan? Big picture."

"Uh, not really. I mean, I know *some* things."

"Like?"

"I don't want to be a billionaire industrialist polluting the environment and exploiting the poor."

"Me neither."

"There you go." He grinned at me.

"I think my life plan needs to be a little more detailed than that."

"Really? I thought we still had time to figure it out. Since we're not even old enough to buy beer."

"Greta Thunberg was a teenager when she gave that speech to the UN."

"That was amazing," he conceded.

At one point I'd suspected David of harboring a crush on Greta Thunberg—until he went for Meg, who was the least activist person I knew.

"It's really two separate problems." He held up two fingers like a peace sign while we waited for a break in traffic. "What do you want to do with your life, and what can you tell everyone else so they'll leave you alone?"

"How about 'I'm joining a cult'?" I suggested as we jogged across the street to the park. "Oh wait! I'm already in one."

A partially paved path wound through the trees and around the grassy areas, far enough from the playground that we wouldn't have to dodge little kids. Street sounds gave way to the chirping of birds as we started the loop.

"You like being outside," David said. "And doing physical stuff. Maybe you can look for jobs where you get to be active, in nature."

"So . . . lumberjack?"

"Worth it for the wardrobe."

I tried to imagine telling Andrea I'd chosen a direction in life based on my deep love of flannel. Doing something ecological did appeal to me. I probably would have signed up for the environmental science class next year if it didn't attract so many idiots in search of an easy C. Case in point: half of Meg's friend group was taking it this semester.

"Do you think I'm a loser?" Even though I was deliberately not looking at him, I heard the change in rhythm as David's steps faltered. "Am I going to be forty years old and still stuck here, acting out scenes from *Little Women* with my sisters?"

"That's . . . pretty hard to imagine."

I grunted, lunging sideways to avoid a fallen branch. "Did you know Andrea filled up a whole passport by the time she was twenty-three? I don't even know how many countries that is." It wasn't like I'd ever seen a passport in person, much less held one of my own.

"Andrea?"

"The one who's writing the article."

David lifted the neck of his T-shirt to blot the sweat from his upper lip. "Pretty easy to do when someone else is footing the bill. Doesn't she come from money?"

"Why do you say that?"

"Just an attitude, I guess."

"You met her?"

"Your mom introduced us. When I stopped by your house to update her on the bridge."

"Nice of you to humor her." He looked like he wanted to say more, but I wasn't interested in discussing my mother's land-scaping fantasies. "So you met Andrea."

"Briefly."

"And, what, she fired off one of those money guns and that's why you think she's loaded?"

He shook his head, but I could see the telltale crinkle at the corner of his eye. David thought I was funny. "She just seemed confident. Like someone who always gets what she wants. And doesn't have to worry about paying for it."

I thought of Andrea's boots, her leather bag, the watch that was probably a status brand. If she was rich, then so was Hudson, though it wasn't like he made constant references to his second home in Tuscany with the infinity pool or carried a big wad of bills in his pocket. Part of me wanted to ask David if he'd met Hudson, too, but it would have been like dropping a barbell in the middle of the conversation. Zero percent subtle.

"Maybe it's because she's accomplished so much," I suggested. "And she's kind of famous."

"Did she tell you that herself? 'I'm kind of a big deal'?"

I tried to shove him, but he leaped out of the way.

"I'm serious. She's had a big life, out in the world. Like Margaret Fuller."

There was a patch of mud in the path ahead. David fell behind me for a few strides until the ground was dry again. "Should I know who that is?"

"She was like Louisa May Alcott, but better. They lived at the same time, in the same places, knew the same people. Only instead of getting stuck at home and being her family's cash cow, Margaret Fuller was this independent career woman who moved to Italy and shacked up with a hot young nobleman.

Why couldn't my mom have modeled her life on someone like *that*?"

"Is that the dream?" He glanced at me sidelong. "A hot guy with an accent?"

"Don't forget the castle."

"Fair. Although Alcott's the one people still talk about." Even panting with exertion, David sounded calm and reasonable. "Just because she didn't move to Italy and shack up with Count Ravioli doesn't mean her life sucked. I thought she ended up famous and rich."

"If you overlook the mercury poisoning and chronic pain and all her hair falling out."

David frowned at my ponytail, which was thick and heavy and making my head sweat like a sprinkler, though hopefully he couldn't see that part. "Is that something you're worried about?"

"No, I'm worried I'll never figure out what I want because everyone expects me to stay here and keep doing the same thing forever. Like Louisa May Alcott. But with hair. Not that I'm obsessed with my hair." No matter what Amy said.

A short spur of sidewalk branched off ahead, ending at a picnic shelter and drinking fountain. David tipped his head in silent inquiry, then veered off at my nod. The water was warm, emerging in a sluggish trickle. After I'd bent over to drink for what felt like ten minutes, I cupped my hand to splash my face. David waited until I'd finished wiping the drips off my nose and mouth to speak.

"Have you talked to your mom?"

I grabbed my ankle and pulled it up behind me as if I had an urgent need to stretch my quad, when in fact I was stalling for time.

"Do you need help?" David looked from my face to my leg, and then away again like he'd gotten caught doing something wrong.

"I'm fine."

"We can do the partner stretch. If you want." He wiped his forehead on the back of his hand, not meeting my eyes.

"Now that you're lubed up?"

His cheeks flushed a deeper red as he rubbed his arm against his slightly less damp T-shirt. The mechanics of the two-person quad stretch we'd learned at practice involved lying on the ground while your partner braced one hand on your hip and used the other to grab your ankle and gently tug it toward your butt. The idea was that the one with the spasming quad could focus all their energy on relaxing tense muscles.

Because that was definitely going to happen if David straddled me, gripping my ass like a steering wheel. Just imagining it made my knee wobble so badly I almost tipped over and had to grab his shoulder for balance. He put a hand at my waist to steady me.

"Sorry," we said at the same time.

"Why are you sorry? I'm the one who almost took you down." I smoothed his shirt, hoping I hadn't permanently twisted the neckline out of shape.

"Yeah, but I made it weird."

"'Hey, baby, let me stretch your quad'? Guys yell that at

me all the time from passing cars. Anyway, I'm the one who brought up lube."

David choked, covering his mouth with his wrist, and I took a step back, glad I'd made him laugh, and relieved we'd changed the subject. I knew he was trying to help, with my quad and my emotional troubles, but there was no point talking to anyone in my family. They were terrible listeners, too full of their own agendas to take in anything new. Not like David. You could spill your guts to him without worrying he'd freak or urge you to look on the bright side. Besides, Mom knew how I felt, and I knew she didn't want to hear any more about it. Especially now, while she was desperate to impress Andrea with our performance as the perfect family.

I glanced at my watch. "Should we get going?"

It wasn't really a question. I launched myself back toward the path, knowing David would follow.

"No, thank you, sir; you're very charming, but you've no more stability than a weathercock."

—Little Women

CHAPTER THIRTEEN

When I got to the barn for rehearsal the following afternoon, I made sure to leave an empty seat beside me for Hudson. Two seconds later, Amy dropped into the chair.

"Waiting for Professor Bhae?" she sang in my ear.

I held my hand in front of her face. "I have no idea what you're talking about."

"It's soooo obvious. Number one, he's from New York. Number two, he's not as hot as Laurie. Number three, he looks kind of judgy. Hello, Professor Bhae—like Bhaer plus bae. Get it? The one Book Jo marries?"

"I'm familiar with the plot."

"Then you do know what I'm talking about."

"Nope." That was my blanket response to all attempts to shoehorn my real life into a *Little Women* parallel, but I also wanted to shut down this particular conversation before Hudson walked into the barn.

"I don't know, Jo. There are some similarities." Mom sat down at the other end of the table. "The New York thing, the worldly older man —"

"Hudson is like a year older, not two decades," I reminded her.

"Oh, *Hudson*," Amy moaned, writhing like she needed an exorcism, "please scold me. Tell me what I'm doing wrong with my life. Be my big German daddy-o."

Naturally, the door opened at that moment.

Andrea sized the scene up in a flash. "Are we talking about l'affaire Bhaer?" she asked, slinging her bag onto the rough floor. "Alcott really stuck it to her readers with that one, didn't she?"

"I never thought of it like that." Mom's expression was polite, but I recognized her tone as one that meant *Someday you'll realize how wrong you are.*

"You don't think she was giving the finger to all the Jo-and-Laurie shippers?"

Hudson caught my eye, mouthing, *Shippers?* He gave a full-body cringe, and I had to look down to avoid giving away the game.

"Personally," Andrea continued, "I suspect she was playing out her daddy issues. The professor was clearly a stand-in for her feckless father. Noble ideals but no life skills."

"I think Professor Bhaer gives Jo good advice," Mom said as Andrea settled beside her. "It leads her to write something honest and true — a work of lasting importance, not just disposable entertainment."

"Debatable," I coughed, covering my mouth with my fist.

"He's the wo-orst," Amy groaned at the same time. We glared at each other, annoyed to find ourselves on the same side of an argument. "I've said it before and I'll say it again: Alcott was robbed. She should be just as famous for her hot gothics. That's the real tragedy of *Little Women,* if you ask me."

"You know people die in that book, right?"

Amy shook her head, like I was the unreasonable one.

"You assume she *wanted* to write those lurid stories," Mom put in. "With all the murder and poison and chases."

Andrea leaned forward. "You disagree?"

"I think she was twisting herself into the shape she thought the world wanted. Pretending to be sophisticated and racy. That wasn't the real Louisa May."

"Interesting." Andrea propped her chin in her hand. "What makes you say that?"

"Because *Little Women* is her best work. And when you discover your own authentic voice, you start to make real art. Whether it's fashionable or not."

How convenient for my mother if it was all meant to be and, instead of being oppressed, Jo was actually *liberated* by the demands of her family.

"But doesn't it feel like something is lost? That restless spirit and wild, passionate imagination? She could have been so much more." Andrea didn't look at me, but I felt the words land on my skin like drops of rain.

Amy tossed her hair so forcefully I had to duck to avoid losing an eye. Of course she assumed Andrea was describing *her*.

"You can't have it all," Mom said, like that settled the argument. Her smile was vaguely patronizing, as if she'd been humoring Andrea by letting her spout nonsense. It was a look I knew well.

But didn't *Andrea* have it all? Her family was right there, doing something on his phone. I glanced at my mother, taking in the long, unstyled hair and plain T-shirt. Between the two of them, she definitely looked more like a "mom." On the other hand, her "work" was an inescapable part of our lives. Which made me wonder: Did Mom think she'd chosen the career or the family?

The door flew open. Laurie posed on the threshold, backlit. When no one made a huge fuss over his arrival, his brow furrowed. "Why so serious, people?"

"We're talking about how Jo ends up with someone old and crusty." Amy patted the table, inviting Laurie to sit next to her.

"That is sad," he agreed, settling his massive water bottle in front of him. Hydration was the foundation of Laurie's fitness regimen, a fact he'd shared with me so many times I'd threatened to have T-shirts made.

"But it's also for the best," my sister continued, "since Amy and Laurie are couple goals." She smiled at Laurie, but his attention was diverted by the arrival of New Beth.

"Bethie Beth," Laurie rumbled, holding out his hand for a fist bump.

"What up, LB?" She knocked knuckles with him hard enough to make Laurie shake off the impact.

"Damn, girl."

"What is this?" Amy demanded, waving a finger between them.

"Turns out we have a lot in common." Laurie beamed at Amy, expecting her to be equally thrilled. "Not being actual members of the fam and all."

"Maybe you should have yourself emancipated," I suggested, fake smiling at Amy. "Then you can be a free agent too."

Mom cleared her throat. "Welcome to our newest Beth. We're so glad you're here."

Amy raised her hand, waiting until our mother acknowledged her like we were in kindergarten. "We're all here."

"Except Meg," I pointed out.

"And I was here before anyone." Amy thumped herself in the chest, continuing her one-woman argument.

Mom glanced at her clipboard. "Laurie and Jo, why don't we start with the proposal scene? I want to pair it with Meg's wedding, like a one-two punch."

"I'm ready." Laurie clapped his hands. "Let's do this."

My stomach turned over. Doing a serious scene in front of Hudson and Andrea felt like a lose-lose proposition. Try to give a "good" performance and I'd look like a huge dork. If I half-assed it, they would assume I sucked. "Maybe we should warm up with something less . . . emotional?"

"Let's be spontaneous." Mom pointed me to the front of the room. "No need to overthink."

"Jo has a tendency to get robotic," Amy translated for the benefit of our guests.

Laurie leaped into position, posing like that sculpture *The Thinker:* hunched forward, chin propped on one hand. I could tell he'd thought about how his shoulder and back muscles would appear from that angle.

I approached him warily. This wasn't our usual blocking. When I got within a few steps, Laurie shot up from his chair, spinning to wrap his arms around me. It felt more like a football tackle than a romantic embrace.

"Let go," I gritted out.

"Nice," Mom narrated. "I like the edge of panic. For years you've been dreading this moment, trying to run, trying to hide, but there's no escaping now."

"I don't want to let go of you, Jo." Laurie smoldered down at me. I cut my eyes at Mom, waiting for her to steer us back toward historical accuracy, but she flicked her fingers, signaling me to continue.

"Jo," said Laurie, cupping a hand around the back of my head and smashing my face into his chest. He spoke the next words into my hair. "My sweet little JoJo." My protest was swallowed by his shirt. "Jo," he said again, shoving me back far enough to stare into my eyes. "You know how I feel about you."

I twisted my torso to one side, but his arms barely budged. It turned out those biceps weren't just for show. "You feel a close bond of platonic friendship?" I suggested. "Almost like a sibling? Since we practically grew up together."

"No." He released one hand to rake it through his hair before quickly grabbing hold of me again. "It's more than that. A lot more. Jo" — he paused to bat his lashes — "I think I love you."

"You *think*?" I maneuvered my fingers so I could pinch his side.

He bit off a yelp. "I mean, I *know*. I definitely love you. You're the only girl for me."

"For now," Amy said darkly, reminding all of us that Laurie would eventually ditch Book Jo to marry her annoying little sister. I tuned her out.

"Here's the thing, Laurie. We're just too similar. Both of us are passionate. Boyish. Dark-haired."

"But Jo," he said, shaking me. "I love you."

"You mentioned that."

He threw his head back. "Don't you care?"

"I do care," I snapped, feeling a spark of genuine anger. Not from the manhandling, which was more like being jumped on by a Labradoodle, but because I was sick of being treated like the un-fun one, who spoiled everything by not playing along. I took a deep breath.

"You know, I wouldn't mind being rich."

Laurie's brows drew together. "You . . . what?"

Andrea's huff of amusement briefly distracted me, but I rallied, staring wistfully into the distance. "You have that big house and the fancy clothes. Books and art and gardens. Spare pianos. You don't have to spend your evenings knitting or darning or dusting. Plus I've always wanted to travel. Preferably to Europe, with first-class accommodations."

"Then — you will marry me?" Laurie shot a nervous look at my mother.

"Hmmm." I tapped my chin with one finger. "Would it be worth it?"

"I like that," Mom called. "Draw out the suspense. Will she or won't she?"

With a guttural growl, Laurie fell to his knees, gripping the front of his T-shirt with both fists. The sound of tearing fabric made me jump.

Silence descended as we absorbed the fact that Laurie had ripped his shirt in half. This was followed by another quiet moment during which everyone admired his abs.

Beth cupped her hands around her mouth. "Do you even lift, bro?"

Laurie winked at her.

I sank down beside him, one hand fanned across his chest.

"Enjoy it while you can," Amy catcalled.

"Do it for feminism," Andrea chimed in.

He tried to yank me against him, so I let my fingernails press ever so slightly into his pec. "Don't make me knee you in the crotch," I whispered. Patting his chest one more time, I drew back. "I'm too much of a sourpuss for you, Laurie. I'd make you unhappy."

"Hold up." Making a T with his hands, Laurie turned to my mother. "Can she say that in front of children?"

"It means I'm grumpy," I told him.

"Shocker," Amy muttered.

Laurie closed his eyes, lips moving in some kind of centering exercise. "Come here, you bitter kitty," he growled, throwing himself back into the scene.

He made a grab for me, but I scooted out of reach, crawling under one of the tables. When I emerged on the other side, Laurie had gone into full vein-popping werewolf mode, howling at the ceiling.

"Joooooooooo! Joooooooooo!"

He collapsed forward, palms on the floor. Amy gave him a standing ovation, while everyone but Andrea (who was taking notes) and Hudson (who was taking pictures) chimed in with less frenzied applause.

Andrea clicked the end of her pen before turning to Mom. "Was he doing Brando in *Streetcar*?"

Laurie sat up, beaming at her. "Yes! We watched the movie in class." He brushed a piece of sawdust off his abdomen. "I get a lot of inspiration from other artists."

"The only thing missing was the monsoon," Andrea deadpanned.

Amy grabbed Mom's sleeve. "Can we get a rain machine? That would be *epic*."

Our mother squeezed her hand, a patented nonanswer. "Maybe we can stage the proposal on the bridge. That would be romantic."

"There is no bridge," I reminded her. And if my mother thought I was going to stand in the mucky stock pond and grapple with Laurie, she needed to let go of that dream right now.

"You have to have vision, Jo." Mom glanced around the barn, and I was tempted to ask if she had a *vision* of her oldest daughter showing up for rehearsal anytime soon, but she was already turning to Andrea. "Shall we take a brief intermission? Laurie probably wants to find a new shirt."

"I have one in my gym bag," he confirmed.

"Wonderful. In the meantime," she asked Andrea, "is there anything you'd like to see?"

Andrea threaded her fingers together, resting them on her knee. "Dazzle me."

Mom's lips pursed as she thought it over. "Well, we do have a new line of paper dolls."

Hudson wagged his brows at me. I looked down, not sure what — or who — we were supposed to be laughing at.

"Work is wholesome, and there is plenty for
every one; it keeps us from *ennui* and mischief."

– Little Women

CHAPTER FOURTEEN

After limping through another day of school-plus-
rehearsal, followed by a Saturday marathon of work-
shopping scenes, I woke Sunday to a silent house. *Sweet freedom.*
Grabbing my breakfast to go, I slipped out the kitchen door,
eager to put some distance between myself and the rest of the
family.

The weather was still warm, in that tricky way spring had of
promising there would never be another cold day, even though
it was only mid-April, and we always got another burst of rainy
chill before summer brought the heat. Maybe this was a confusing season for everyone, the up-and-down of *yay, sunshine*
and *ugh, mud*. The in-between feeling was even stronger this
year, thanks to our special guests. Time was passing so quickly,
every day scratching out another square on the calendar of

their time here. And yet I wasn't sure we were moving forward at all, at least not in the ways that mattered to me. Andrea's research appeared to be chugging along, if the number of notes she dictated into her phone was any indication, but no one was answering *my* questions. Such as: Was Hudson flirting with intent, or just being friendly? He seemed interested, but what if it was only because I was the least frightening person here?

If it wasn't wishful thinking, what then? I'd date a guy passing through town so that twenty years from now I could brag about that one time I was cool by association? It wasn't like I needed a man to rescue me, or that romance was my top priority. What I couldn't shake was the sense that Hudson and Andrea had the keys to a bigger world. They could show me how to take the first step toward a more exciting life, far from this familiar patch of land and the taste of cherry Pop-Tarts straight from the pouch.

As I walked, a faint percussive noise caught my ear. It came from the direction of the pond. David was crouched near the edge, toolbox at his side. Stretched in front of him like the spine of a whale were two long, arched pieces of wood.

"No way." I stared down at the curved beams resting parallel on the grass. "Is that what I think it is?"

"If you're thinking 'bridge,' then yes."

"You really are building it."

"I told you I was."

I nodded, swallowing a flicker of dismay along with a mouthful of crumbs. It wasn't that I'd doubted David. *He* was one of the least flaky people I knew, though that wasn't saying much. What bugged me was that I'd been wrong. My mother wasn't full of it; the bridge was happening.

David sat back on his heels. "What are you doing right now?"

"Avoiding people. Thinking dark thoughts." I shrugged. "The usual."

He gestured at the pile of wood. "Want to help?"

"You need more negative energy?"

He swung a hammer back and forth like a pendulum. "You get to hit stuff."

"Well, since you put it that way." I knelt beside him. "Where do I start?"

∾

Bridge-building turned out to be an absorbing process, especially if you didn't want splintered palms or bruised fingers. I paid no attention to the passing of time, so it surprised me when David opened a small blue-and-white cooler and handed me a peanut butter sandwich.

"I can't take your lunch."

"I packed extra." He held up a second sandwich, like the planner he was.

"Thanks." I disposed of mine in a few bites. "I was hungry."

He shrugged like it was nothing, but in my experience, you could always tell when someone didn't bring their A game to sandwich-making: condiments not spread all the way to the edges, dried-out crust, skimpy fillings. David's PB&J had a generous layer of crunchy peanut butter with a good ratio of strawberry jam, and the bread didn't squish to a sticky paste in your mouth. It was like how when I went to his house, David didn't just splash tap water into a cup. He took the time to fill my favorite glass with ice and filtered water from the fridge. He was as careful with the little things as he was with the big ones —like this bridge.

By afternoon, we'd both worked up a sweat. When David stripped off his T-shirt to wipe his face, I decided it was okay (as a fellow athlete) to notice that he had a classic runner's body, lean without being scrawny. A little hairier than Laurie's, but I suspected Laurie of waxing.

"What do you think?" David asked, setting down his hammer.

"Um." How was I supposed to answer that? *Lookin' tight, buddy.*

"Come on, it's awesome. That thing is solid. I'd let my grand-mother walk across it."

Ah. We were talking about the bridge. "Totally awesome. Really . . . strong."

We surveyed our work, the even line of pale wooden slats stretching almost to the end of the support beams. It was unex-pectedly satisfying to see something I'd had a hand in making take shape.

"You know what's weird?" I said, thinking out loud. He shook his head. "How they didn't believe women could handle this kind of physical labor, but they totally let them work in army field hospitals. Alcott saw some gnarly business when she was a nurse. It was all, 'Hey, lady, pass me the saw; I'm going to hack that soldier's leg off.'"

David's mouth pinched.

"Lots of amputations back then. Gangrene and whatnot." In my mind, gangrene was a vague medical condition involving moldy flesh. I wasn't stupid enough to google it.

"Have I mentioned how glad I am we don't live in the past?"

"Don't we?" I followed this with a stare I'd seen Andrea use, as if she were examining you under a microscope. It would have been more impressive if a droplet of sweat hadn't plopped off the end of my nose, staining the wood at my feet.

David unscrewed the cap of the iced-tea jug he'd repurposed as a water bottle and took a long drink. "I'm a little worried about that. The show. I've never really performed in front of people."

"More of a private dancer?" I joked.

He gave me a token smile, but didn't stop rolling the cap between his fingers.

I racked my brains for something reassuring to say that wouldn't be a lie. "At least you're not in the Christmas scene. That's the actual worst."

"Geez, Jo. What are you, a communist?"

I ripped out a few blades of grass and tossed them at David. "You know what I mean. It's so *sappy*. Like that blueberry syrup they have at IHOP. Way too sweet, and totally fake. And now Hudson and Andrea will be here to watch the whole thing go down, which is basically the cherry on top of my personal nightmare sundae."

He frowned like he was having trouble keeping up. "Do they hate Christmas too?"

"It's just embarrassing." I brushed away a fly that was trying to land on my knee. "The fewer witnesses the better. And they probably go to real shows, with professional actors, so this is going to look even more Podunk to them."

"In a few weeks they'll be gone. You never have to see them again."

I knew David was trying to be nice, so I didn't tell him that that was a bigger downer than Christmas. "Let's talk more about our bridge."

"Subject change."

"You know what I like best about this bridge? It's so bridge-like. It is what it is."

"A bridge."

"Exactly. No pretense or identity crisis."

The actual construction had been accomplished on dry land, which meant we now had a medium-length span of wood rising above a patch of scrubby grass. But I'd hammered the crap out of my share of boards, and they were all lined up, neat and orderly, which was not something you could say about most areas of my life.

"Maybe you should add carpentry to your list of possible careers."

Huh. It always surprised me when someone paid attention while I talked, much less remembered the details later. "Can we see how it looks?"

David glanced from me to the pond. "I wasn't going to put in the piers until tomorrow."

"Come on. What's the point of a bridge on dry land?"

He frowned, but I knew I had him. "I guess we can try."

While I held on to the nearer end, David pulled the other side of the bridge in a slow semicircle. We shuffled sideways until we were facing each other across the pond.

"Here?" I asked, straightening from my crouch.

"What do you think?"

"Perfect." The bridge was more or less centered, unsecured ends resting on the grass. Aside from the greenish-yellow newness of the wood, it almost looked like it belonged there. I placed one foot on the nearest board. "Should we test it out?"

"What? No."

"Oh, come on. Don't you have any faith in our awesomeness?"

"This is the first time either of us has ever done this. And I still have to sand it, and stain it, and anchor the ends."

"Looks done to me. Hashtag nailed-it." I placed my weight more firmly on my end of the bridge.

"Wait!" David held up a hand. "Let me go first."

I stepped back onto the grass. "Okay, Mr. Man. I hope that Y chromosome doesn't weigh you down too much."

He moved cautiously onto the other end of the bridge, eyes glued to his feet. You could have driven a truck through the pause before his next step.

"It's not a tightrope," I called, watching him place the heel of one foot in front of the toes of the other.

"There's no railing."

"It's like four feet wide. You could ride a Big Wheel over that thing."

He raised his head long enough to fix me with a stern look. "Jo. Promise me you won't."

"David," I said, copying his tone. "I don't have a Big Wheel."

When he returned his attention to the snail-like progress of his feet, I stepped onto my side of the bridge.

"What are you doing?" He threw both arms out for balance, though the boards had barely moved.

Flexing my knees, I bounced up and down. "See? Rock solid."

"Okay, that's probably enough."

"Enough what?" I hopped forward, swinging my arms. David started to back away. "Where are you going?"

"I don't think both of us should be in the middle at the same time. That's the weakest point."

"You do realize there are going to be busloads of ten-year-olds pounding across this thing?" I took a deliberate step closer.

"Yeah, but they're small."

"Is that a comment about my size?"

"What? No!" He sounded genuinely alarmed, especially when I bounced twice in rapid succession. "Okay, listen." David held up both hands in a *stay back* gesture. "Jo."

"David."

"You're in one of those moods, aren't you?"

That brought me up short. "What moods? And don't even think about using the word *tomboy*."

"Meg said you get fidgety sometimes — maybe that wasn't it. Some *F* word."

"But not *the F* word?"

He waved this off, brows drawing together in concentration. "I'm thinking."

"Was it *funky*? *Fresh*? *Flexible*?"

"I think it was *feisty*, actually."

"Please. A stalactite is feisty compared to Meg."

"Geology trash talk. Nice."

I stared at the murky water sitting stagnant a few feet below. "Did Meg say anything else about me?"

"I don't know. Probably. It would be weird if she didn't. You guys are sisters." He tried to play this off with a shrug, but the blush told a different story. That meant it was something worse than my alleged feistiness, another of those Jo March characteristics everyone assumed I shared. He glanced over his shoulder. "Should we go back?"

"I think we need to do more quality control."

"Really?"

"Yeah, because I'm feisty like that."

He closed his eyes in resignation. "What did you have in mind?"

"More jumping," I said, demonstrating. He gave a half-hearted knee bend.

"You have to get crazy," I told him, flapping my arms. "Think of your fourth-grade self. Channel that alley-dog energy."

"In fourth grade I was into model planes."

"Okay?"

"It takes a steady hand. No sudden moves."

"What about sports?" He was still shirtless, so his physical fitness was right there at the front of my mind. "You must have played soccer or something."

"I wanted to learn golf, but my parents said it was too expensive."

I stared at him. "That's the saddest thing I've ever heard. And I don't mean the money."

"I thought it would be like mini golf! With windmills and stuff."

"Wow. This is a real eye-opener. It's a good thing we moved here to shake you out of your routine."

"Yeah." He smiled at me, and there wasn't an ounce of sarcasm in it. Sometimes I worried we were too much for David, even before the Meg situation. Both sides of his huge extended family were noisy and heavily into group socializing, which apparently drove his parents' decision to raise one quiet son on the outskirts of a smallish town, where they were less likely to be ambushed by a constant parade of in-laws, cousins, and aunts and uncles.

And then we showed up and sucked David into our loud and messy home life. I almost felt sorry for him.

"Do you want to fight for it?" I asked, uncomfortable as always with the touchy-feely stuff. "Winner takes the bridge."

"Jo. Do you have any idea how many YouTube videos I had to watch? Have you ever even *tried* to steer one of those metal carts around Home Depot? I have shin bruises that will never go away. This bridge is *mine*."

"I guess you better defend your territory then. Unless you

want to walk away and spare yourself the humiliation, Golf Boy?"

"I'm not walking away. You walk away."

"Maybe I will." I half turned before spinning back and lunging at him. What I hadn't counted on was the bare-skin-plus-sweat factor, which made grabbing him around the midsection a lot trickier. When I tried to shove him backwards, my arms slipped. Lowering my head, I adjusted my hold. My cheek was now stuck to his ribs like a postage stamp. "Just give up."

He administered several strategic pokes along my sides. "You give up."

"Never," I laughed, because of course he'd found one of my many ticklish spots. This wasn't our first wrestling match, though it had been long enough that both of our bodies had changed a lot—except for the ticklish places, apparently.

I stuck my leg between his, positioning my foot behind his ankle as I tried to shove him off balance. He retaliated by lifting me up and swinging me around behind him. Those long arms were stronger than they looked.

He raised both fists above his head. "Yes! I am the champion."

"Nice try." It would have sounded tougher if I hadn't been out of breath. "But I'm still standing."

David executed a careful turn so that we were once again facing each other. "Maybe we should call it a draw."

My mouth opened to tell him where he could shove that idea, only to let out a grunt of surprise when he latched on to my arm with both hands. I was so convinced he was about to push me away that I threw myself at him, trying to make a preemptive strike. Unfortunately, by then he'd already yanked me forward. Our combined force sent me crashing into David like a bowling ball.

I tried to brace my feet against the boards, but it was too late. His eyes widened as I tipped over the edge. Maybe if our arms hadn't been exhausted from all the hauling and hammering, we would have managed to hold each other up. As it was, his attempt to keep me on the bridge sent him tumbling over the edge with me.

"Ugh!" I sprang to my feet, flinging tepid pond water off my face. "Gross. I'm touching slime. Slime is touching me." The water barely reached my thighs, but that didn't make it less repulsive. I lifted one foot after the other, trying to get as much of me out of the water as possible.

"Are you okay?" David asked, narrowly avoiding an accidental kick to the rib cage.

I waved both arms at him, spraying droplets of pond water. "I am standing in *muck*, David. It's *oozing.* We're both covered in pond scum that's probably crawling with *bacteria.* How could I be okay?"

"I think the flesh-eating ones have to get in through your mouth. Or maybe your eyes?"

"Not helping." I rubbed frantically at my face.

"Here." He leaned toward me. I figured he was offering a piggyback ride, but when he bent to scoop my legs out of the muck I wound up shimmying up his front. It was the closest I'd ever come to accidentally pantsing someone. Somehow I ended up with my thighs around David's waist, my feet sticking out behind him like we were ballroom dancers doing a lift. He gripped my sides with both hands to keep me from sliding down.

"Okay." I exhaled heavily. "I'm out of the water."

He cough-laughed. "I don't see this as a long-term solution."

His voice sounded a little strained, so I loosened my hold on his neck.

"Thanks." He took a sloshing step forward. Our epic belly flop had tipped the bridge onto its side. Rather than trying to right it with me in his arms, David carried me all the way to the edge of the pond.

"It looks even more disgusting now," I observed, peering over his shoulder. The water was fringed in rotting plant life and stinking mud. "Like it has gangrene."

"Not helping," he grunted, staggering onto the bank. I jumped down, careful not to take his shorts with me.

"Phew. That's a relief." I was about to thank David for the rescue when I noticed his shorts were still hanging dangerously low. He jerked back when I reached for his waistband. "Relax. I'm not going to give you a wedgie."

He looked skeptical. "You threw me off a bridge."

"Sorry." I bit my lip. "I hope it's okay."

"Your bloodthirstiness?"

I punched him in the arm. "The *bridge*."

Together we pulled the whole dripping structure clear of the water, inspecting the wood for damage.

"It's fine," he assured me. "Or it will be, once we fix the ends in place. And add a railing."

"Probably a good idea." I sat down to strip off my shoes and socks. "Can you hose me down with bleach?"

"Totally. If I had a hose. Or bleach."

After debating whether it would be more traumatizing to take my T-shirt off, thus risking face contact, or leave it on, I yanked it over my head in one quick motion. It landed on the grass with a moist *plop*.

"Here." From his backpack David produced a faded blue towel.

"I'm wearing a sports bra. You can't see anything."

"I thought you might want to dry off." He sounded all casual about it, like I was the one being silly, but I noticed he wasn't looking at me.

"I don't want to contaminate your towel," I said, taking it from him anyway.

"It's okay. I know how to use a washing machine." David rested his elbows on his knees. "This is a side of you I've never seen."

I covered my belly button with my thumb. "Yes, I have an outie."

"I know." It might have been the sun, but his cheekbones looked a little pink. "I'm talking about your pond-water phobia."

"I have a very healthy fear of toxic sludge, thank you very much."

"Uh-huh."

He reached out to pick something from my hair.

I squeezed my eyes shut. "Tell me it's not a leech — or worse."

There was a beat of silence. "What would be worse than a leech?"

"I don't know. A piranha? Electric eels?"

"I'm guessing marine biology isn't on your future-jobs list?"

I stuck my tongue out.

"It was a piece of grass. I think."

I opened my eyes to see him flick something off his fingers. "I'm a swamp monster. I should crawl back to my lair."

Before I could slither away, a voice called out from the other side of the pond. "Was I supposed to bring my suit?"

A sudden chill cut through the heat of the afternoon. I thought Hudson was waving, until I realized he was holding up his phone for a picture. It was almost enough to send me diving back into the muck.

"They're here for dinner," I told David, feeling more self-conscious than when I'd whipped off my shirt. "Must be later than I thought."

If there was an etiquette rule that covered whether to invite your sister's ex who is also your good friend and sometimes semi-naked wrestling partner to a meal with the guy you've been chatting up and his mom, while you are both covered in pond gunk, I didn't know what it was. The wind shifted, letting me know I smelled as bad as I looked.

"What is it?" David asked. "Besides the hygiene thing. You're frowning."

"I was supposed to help cook. Mom's probably mad."

He peeled a strip of vegetation off my shoulder, barely touching the skin underneath. "You can bring the salad."

What could be harder for a restless, ambitious girl than to give up her own hopes, plans, and desires, and cheerfully live for others?

–*Little Women*

CHAPTER FIFTEEN

I thought that went well." Mom was up to her elbows in suds, scrubbing the pots and pans while I loaded the bowls and plates into the dishwasher.

I made a vague noise of agreement, because I was familiar with Mom's need for postgame analysis. Maybe if Dad had been around, she would have talked this stuff over with him. Assuming he didn't disappear as soon as our guests left, like Amy and Meg.

"The food was good," she said, feeding me a cue.

"Uh-huh." I could tell from my mother's hopeful silence that she wanted more. "The cornbread was very moist."

"New recipe. Buttermilk and honey." She relayed the secret ingredients with a flourish, like it was the final clue in a frenzied treasure hunt.

Privately I wondered if chili might have seemed peasanty to Andrea and Hudson. Both of them had eaten what they were served, though Hudson had paid way more attention to me than he had to the food. I had a sneaking suspicion it had to do with the scene at the pond. Either it was the cheap thrill of seeing me in a sports bra (unlike David, Hudson had had no trouble staring at my exposed midriff, which had forced me to suck in my stomach all the way home), or my stock had gone up because he thought another guy was interested. It would have been a clever move on my part, if I were the kind of person who liked to play games. And was willing to risk parasites eating her brain to impress a dude. I touched my hairline, wondering if I should shower again before bed.

"You got some sun today," Mom observed.

I didn't think it was a criticism, because Book Jo was frequently described as the dark one, and not just in terms of her soul. Compared to Hudson's skim-milk complexion, my skin looked like overbaked piecrust, though I was still several shades lighter than Amy, thanks to her self-tanner addiction. Which reminded me: "Why am I the only one helping?"

"Amy's studying for an exam."

"What about Meg?"

She finished rinsing the chili pot and upended it on the drying rack next to the sink before replying. "Meg's having a hard time right now. She needs our support."

I wasn't sure whether that translated to "doing her share of the housework" or "not yelling at her for being lazy." Knowing

Mom, and myself, and how things usually went down around here, it was both.

"What's wrong with her?"

Mom dried her hands on the dish towel hanging from the handle of the stove. "There was the breakup with David."

I was shaking my head before she finished. "They were barely even dating. And the breakup, if that's what you want to call it, was Meg's idea."

"It's still a disappointment." Mom sighed as she wadded up the towel and tossed it down the basement stairs. "Change is hard. On top of everything else."

"Like what?"

"Normal teenage things." Mom's back was to me as she returned spices to the cupboard, so I couldn't read her expression.

"Drugs?"

"Your sister is not on drugs," Mom huffed. "Meg's always been like that."

I would have enjoyed the low-key maternal burn if another idea hadn't sent my stomach plummeting. "She's not pregnant, is she?"

"No!" Mom turned around, jar of paprika in hand. "Where are you getting these ideas?"

"You said it was a normal teenage thing." I might also have been thinking about Book Meg's story arc, where she goes from daughter to mother in the blink of an eye, but I wasn't going to admit that part.

"Emphasis on *normal*. Not something from an after-school special."

"Is that code for 'smoking weed in the parking lot' or, you know . . ." I waved my hand, really hoping she wasn't about to educate me on the sex slang of her youth.

"They were TV movies. Like a PSA, only dramatized. Cautionary tales, to make kids think twice before playing with matches or riding their bikes on the train tracks."

"Sounds riveting." And like it might explain my mother's strange idea of what constituted entertainment. "So what *is* Meg's problem?"

Mom pulled out a chair and sat down at the kitchen table, patting the spot next to hers. Reluctantly, I joined her.

"It's not a disease or anything?" Because then I'd feel like a jerk.

"Meg's having trouble finding her way." Mom placed her hand on mine, squeezing lightly. "I wish the two of you were closer."

"Me and Meg?"

She nodded, and I knew she was thinking of the sisterly bond between Book Meg and Book Jo. Which if you asked me was intense to the point of freakiness, at least on Jo's side, since she basically wants Meg to stay home and play house with her instead of getting married. Typical of Mom to read those codependent undertones as pure and heartwarming.

"You've always had a strong sense of self. Meg could use more grounding right now. A solid foundation."

As recently as thirty seconds ago, I would have sworn my

mother considered me complainer in chief, the problem child, her number one most frustrating daughter. It was flattering to be described as a good influence, although it would have been nicer if Mom had noticed that Meg wasn't the only one struggling.

"Did you have a nice day with David?" she asked.

I nodded warily in case this was a segue into talking about the bridge. Maybe I should bring up the provocative use of canned garbanzos in the chili.

"It was like old times." Mom paused for a nostalgic sigh. "You used to come in after a hard day's play looking like you'd been buried alive. Twigs in your hair, streaks of mud and heaven only knows what else—"

"I get it."

"The two of you were constantly getting into scrapes." Her blatant attempt to reframe my childhood as a page from *Little Women* made my teeth grind. "Sweet little David."

"He's not little anymore, Mom."

"You finally noticed? I wondered when that would happen."

"I've always paid attention to David." Like how sometimes he wanted you to talk for him and other times you had to wait for him to find his words. His deep hatred of watermelon-flavored candy. The contrast between his stick-straight hair and curly eyelashes. The list went on. Just today I'd discovered the wishbone-shaped indentation between his bicep and the rest of his arm. People assumed I didn't realize David was a cute guy, as if that must be the reason we'd never crossed any lines. But I was also the kind of person who saved her good trick-or-treat candy until the *next* Halloween, to make sure I wasn't left with nothing. Besides, it wasn't like he'd ever asked *me* out. "Unlike *some* people, I've never taken him for granted."

Mom smiled like she knew something I didn't. "You have a very special bond. It's nice to see you being gentle with someone."

The *for a change* was strongly implied. "Are you calling me a bitch?"

"Language, Jo. I'm saying David brings out your softer side. It may be buried deep, but it's there. A kernel of sweetness."

A warning light flashed in my brain. We were milliseconds away from words like *tenderhearted* and *womanly* being deployed.

"How come we don't do more environmental stuff?" I asked before my mother could urge me to be more nurturing or whatever. "Like with the transcendentalists." *Instead of reinforcing tired gender stereotypes.*

"It would be wonderful to have our own Emerson and Thoreau, wouldn't it?" Mom pursed her lips. "Maybe I should put out feelers to a few community theaters? Or we could ask David to build a tar-paper shack. He could sit in a canoe and sketch."

"On the *pond*?" My face screwed up in disgust. The scent memory was way too fresh.

"This is a lovely natural setting," she retorted. "You blossomed when we moved here, you know." When I looked at her blankly, my mother nodded. "I think it was the easy access to the outdoors. And then meeting David, of course. He always seemed to know how to talk to you." Her voice took on a wistful tinge, like she was waiting for me to share the secret of Handling Jo.

Like a normal person. That's how David treats me. Or at least weird in my own way. As opposed to bringing up Louisa May Alcott every five seconds.

"I take it he had other plans tonight?" Mom asked.

"I don't know."

She ran a finger under her chin, considering me. "It might have been awkward to invite him."

It sounded more like a hypothesis than a question. I shrugged, assuming we were talking about Meg.

"Entertaining two beaux is always complicated."

I flinched so hard it felt like I'd cracked a rib. It was difficult to say which was more embarrassing: that my mother had noticed the vibe between me and Hudson, or her suggestion that David was more than a friend. Not even speaking of the word *beaux*.

"It isn't in your nature to be a flirt," Mom continued. "Unlike Amy."

"Pretty sure you're thinking of Book Amy. Our Amy has the social skills of a wild boar."

I waited for the inevitable *don't be mean* scolding, but Mom didn't bat an eyelash. "The thing to remember, Jo, is not to trade something of lasting value for the lure of newness."

Although I was pretty sure she'd used the same line to discourage excessive back-to-school shopping, this was much cringier territory.

"I'm not—can we not turn this into a teachable moment? It was just chili and cornbread, not a valuable moral lesson."

She blinked hard. Lines of hurt radiated from the corners of her mouth.

It didn't matter that I'd stayed to help or tried to say positive things. The final score was always the same: Jo bad, Mom sad.

"To be loved and chosen by a good man is the best and sweetest thing which can happen to a woman."

-Little Women

CHAPTER SIXTEEN

A week passed.

We watched New Beth bite it. We built an arsenal of flower crowns, because you could never have too many. Mom read us uncomfortable sex metaphors from *Little Women* about tender buds and unfurling petals. Meg made nonsensical remarks about whatever she was basting herself in that day. I witnessed David and Meg's fake wedding and was nearly trampled to death by Amy and Beth's competitive contra dancing. Amy monologued about the perils of getting tricked into a phony marriage by a dissolute nobleman whose other wives were locked in his crumbling European castle, which was apparently a recurring issue in Alcott's other fiction and therefore extremely relevant to modern life. I missed too many practices and had to squeeze in extra runs before school.

It was your average mid-April at *Little Women Live!*, especially after Hudson and Andrea ditched us to visit a big-cat sanctuary in Nebraska. I knew the animal-rescue family was their next stop after they finished here, but it still felt like a judgment. We must not have been keeping them sufficiently entertained. How could we compete with cats of any size?

The two days they were away felt like a depressing preview of life after they left us for good, even though Hudson texted all the time, starting with a picture of the gas-station sandwich he ate on the road. This was followed by a video of a jaguar after they arrived.

Reminds me of you

Did he mean the caged part? Pacing back and forth? My seldom shaved legs?

Murdery eyes, the next message explained. **Not the smell.**

That made me feel slightly better. (Possible new slogan: *Little Women Live! At least we don't reek of cat pee!*)

Thursday night, I was half asleep when my phone buzzed with a series of new texts.

Halp

Might do a mattress side

The correction came a second later:

Matricide

Duck you autocorrect

I knew the feeling. **Good times?**

He sent back a skull emoji. Then:

I'm bored

Why are these states so big?

Are you driving? I typed back. There might not be other cars on the road this time of night, but you still had to keep an eye out for deer.

Ha

Like she'd let me

Can we go out this weekend?

That woke me up. I was still trying to figure out whether he was asking me on a date or just wanted to hang when the next string of texts arrived.

Please, Jo

I need this

Save me

The warm fuzzies shot straight to my brain, but I forced myself to remain calm. **Where?**

Away from moms

I sent him a thumbs-up, then stayed awake for ages in case he texted again.

⁓

Lack of sleep didn't help my mood on Friday, especially as the hours stacked up without word from Hudson. Maybe he hadn't meant *go out* the way it sounded. Or he was allergic to making specific plans. Or he'd lost his phone.

Attempting to rationalize his behavior made me feel like even more of a loser.

When I walked into the parking lot after school, I sensed the gravitational shift of Something Happening, like we were all marbles on a game board being tipped in the same direction. After weaving past a few clumps of people pretending not to gawk, I realized they were staring at our station wagon. Or, more specifically, at Hudson leaning against the passenger door, the sun picking out glints of copper in his hair. The T-shirt, the glasses, the jeans . . . he looked even more not-from-around-here than usual.

There was a carbonated feeling in my chest. If I could have chosen any reputation to have at school, it would have been "really good runner." Well, maybe "really good runner who is not a *Little Women* stan." That didn't mean I was immune to the status boost of a cute stranger showing up to meet me in the parking lot. *That's right, people. There's a lot more to me than my embarrassing family*—

Oh. Meg was there too. Which meant no one would assume he was waiting for me.

My older sister was sitting in the back seat with the door open, looking pretty and slightly less bored than usual. In an instant, a whole new scenario sprang into my mind: *Hudson suddenly becomes intrigued by Meg because that's how it always goes when you think someone likes you better.*

Once, I argued with myself. *That happened one time.* Was this how brains worked? A single bad experience and for the rest of your life you expected the pattern to repeat itself? How annoying.

"Hey," Hudson called. "There you are." His smile did not say, *I forgot all about you because your sister is hotter.*

"What are you doing here?"

"I walked over." He gestured vaguely in the direction of the motel where he and Andrea were staying. "Did you forget? Our big night?"

"I told him about the party at Grant McKinley's," Meg said, like it was something we'd discussed.

"I'm in." Hudson playfully nudged me with his elbow. "Underwear on the ceiling fan, sports car in the pool, pizza on the turntable. Bring it on."

Meg blinked at him, expressionless.

I couldn't tell if he was making fun of our town, high school parties in general, or himself for knowing nothing about the local scene. Such as it was.

"You guys are going to a party?" Amy screeched, popping out from behind the car. "I want to go to a party."

And I wanted to go on an actual date. "Life is full of disappointments."

"Maybe for you, Bitter Betty." Amy turned to Meg for support. Our older sister slid me a look that said, *Fix this.* Because of course she wanted me to be the bad guy.

"You're too young," I told Amy.

She stamped her foot. "You'll regret this, Jo. I'm going to stay home and burn something of yours."

"No, you won't, because this isn't *Little Women.*" I really needed to have that on a laminated sign.

"I might." She spun to face Hudson. "Remember the scene we did your first day, where I totally dominated Jo? That was because she wouldn't let me go with her to a show, since I was supposedly too young, even though everyone knows Amy is precocious. So I had to teach her a lesson by torching her manuscript."

"He doesn't have amnesia," I growled. Amy gave a pointed sniff before throwing herself into the back seat.

"Okay." Hudson drew out the second syllable, swinging his arms. "Should I just come home with you?"

A couple of extra hours to hang out, without an audience? I opened my mouth to say yes, but Meg got there first.

"No." She didn't look at him. "You can pick us up at eight."

"Oh. Okay." He shoved his hands in his pockets. "Guess I'll walk back to the motel."

"It's like a block," Amy muttered as he turned to go.

"What was that?" I glared at Meg in the rearview mirror.

"His rental car is way cooler than our stupid station wagon."

"Duh," Amy chimed in.

Maybe I'd misjudged them both. It wasn't laziness that kept my sisters from driving. The problem was that their egos didn't fit behind the wheel of our crappy car.

Her heart felt very heavy as she stood by
herself, while the others laughed, chattered,
and flew about like gauzy butterflies.

—Little Women

CHAPTER
SEVENTEEN

At eight forty-five, also known as fifteen minutes before the time I generally liked to be in bed with my laptop and the lights off, to discourage visits from my family, Hudson showed up. Meg gave directions to Grant's house with the ease of someone who'd been there many times before, an impression that was confirmed when she strolled through the front door without knocking. Two girls I thought of as Ashley and Not Ashley, because they were the same height, styled their hair in identical beachy waves, and appeared to share both a closet and a social calendar, were waiting inside. They latched on to my sister, whispering as the three of them headed for a tiled staircase with a wrought-iron railing.

Hudson smiled at me, and I tried to shake off the mild sense of *What am I doing here?* and get my head in the game. It was fine. We were still hanging out, at night, away from our mothers. Somewhere ahead there was laughter and guttural chanting, which … sounded like a party. Or a prison riot, depending on your perspective.

I led the way down the hall. It wasn't one of those *call the cops* disasters where bodies are packed so tight that property destruction is inevitable. But it wasn't just Meg's friends, either. The football team had shown up, though a quick glance around the kitchen suggested it was mostly varsity starters — including Laurie.

"Huds!" Laurie's shouted greeting sent every eye in our direction.

Hudson leaned closer to me, like he might need protection. "Is that … a gallon of chocolate milk?"

"Yep."

"Bold choice."

"Laurie's all about bone density." I would have been willing to bet that (a) most of the people in this room preferred the taste of chocolate milk to whatever cheap beer they were swilling and (b) Laurie could be sipping a glass of MiraLAX and people would still think he was cool.

"What up?" Laurie spread his arms wide, still holding his bottle of TruMoo, before wrapping Hudson in an embrace. "Come on, man. You gotta meet my squad."

I got a barely detectable chin thrust before Laurie led my date away. Hudson's shrug said, *What can I do?*

Well. Time to recalibrate my vision for the evening. I must

have read too much into our late-night texts. It made sense Hudson would ask me to take him out, like a tour guide. I was the closest thing he had to a friend around here.

I wandered through the rest of the first floor, nodding at people but not stopping to talk. Most of them seemed to be having a good time, or at least doing an okay job of faking it. Spotting a set of sliding glass doors, I headed for the backyard, where at least I could be alone in peace. Like most houses in the neighborhood, this one bordered a golf course. A man-made pond marked the edge of the property. There was even a small deck with patio furniture, in case you wanted to stare at a body of water the size of a kiddie pool. Or maybe the entertainment was watching people drive past in golf carts?

I was halfway across the lawn before I realized one of the Adirondack chairs was occupied. The person turned, probably at the sound of my shoes shuffling through the grass, and I spotted a faint yellow glow. Surprise washed over me, followed by relief.

"Uh, David? Did you bring a book light to a party?"

"I also have a book. If that makes it less weird."

"Depends on the book. Like if you're out here reading *The Serial Killer's Guide to Small Talk*, then no."

He switched the light off, but not before I caught the flicker of a smile. "I prefer the sequel, *How to Get Rid of a Body in Five Easy Steps*. Do you want to sit?"

"Why not?" I made a move toward the unoccupied chair.

"That one's broken. Jacob McCready thought it was a

bouncy castle." David started to stand. "Take this one. I'll sit on the ground."

"Excuse you, my butt is not that big." It took a couple of tries and some lower body contortions (to the point that we probably looked like two people who had never used a chair before), but I eventually managed to wedge myself in beside him. That didn't solve the problem of where to put our arms. We seemed to have at least one too many.

"Here." He worked his left arm free and threaded it behind my neck. "Is this okay?"

"Sure." It was maybe not the best idea I'd ever had to sandwich myself against my sister's ex when I was supposed to be at this party with another guy, but it was too late now. We'd probably need to grease ourselves to get free. "This would have worked better when we were kids."

"You could have stacked four of me in here. And a bag of chips."

I smiled at the memory of scrawny David and the many, many quarters I'd won off him at arm wrestling. "Remember when you had that massive growth spurt and I started calling you Spaghetti Arms, because I'm such a sensitive person?"

"It felt like my bones were going to crack." He shuddered. "Six inches in one summer."

"They seem normal now." I gave his forearm an experimental squeeze.

"Hopefully? I haven't x-rayed myself."

"You have more padding, so it's hard to tell." I prodded the leg of his jeans. "They used to be closer to the surface."

"I'm not sure that's how bodies work."

We were sitting so close I felt the laughter he was trying to contain. "You know what I mean."

In the silence, I became increasingly aware that the side of my boob was smooshed against his rib cage. "So what are you doing here?" I asked super casually.

"At the party, or in the backyard?"

"I don't know, Professor Plum. Either. Both."

"Short version? I lost the push-up challenge at practice."

"And your punishment was to show up here?"

"I'm Nathan's driver."

"Ah. He's in there getting wrecked, and you get to babysit?"

"I told him I wasn't cleaning up puke." David frowned at the barely there sleeves of my top. "Aren't you cold?"

"How could I be cold when I'm wearing you like a skin suit?"

"Or Luke Skywalker inside the tauntaun."

"Okay, but obviously I'm Han Solo, so, you know."

"I have to be Luke?"

I couldn't really shrug, but he must have felt the slight motion of my shoulder. I'd always been the bossy one in our games, down to feeding him his lines. My theory was that David secretly liked not having to decide everything for himself. Looking back, I had a twinge of *AITA?*

"You can be Han," I sighed. "If you want."

He pressed his palm to my forehead. "You don't feel feverish."

"Ha-ha." I shoved his arm off me. "I can be nice."

"Spoken like a true Solo."

My attempt to punch him in the gut accomplished very little beyond giving me a feel for the tautness of his abdominal muscles. "You should eat more junk food."

"Why? Is there a vending machine inside?"

"If only. I don't think people come to these things for the food."

"Why are you here?"

"Hudson wanted to check it out." My head filled with things I needed to not say, like *It was supposed to be a date* and *Meg's here too.*

David glanced behind us, like he was expecting Hudson to appear.

"He's off with Laurie and those guys." I tried to sound like I didn't care.

"Did they put a sign on their tree house? 'No Girls Allowed'?"

"They're probably doing something stupid."

"Like getting wrecked?"

"What else is there to do?" Show up, show off, drink too much, make out with people you may or may not ever want to speak to again . . . that was pretty much it, in my experience. The party scene.

"Hence the book." He lifted a warped paperback from the armrest. The cover featured some kind of ice fortress.

"Always thinking ahead."

"I figured it would be less awkward this way."

I tapped my chin, pretending to think it over. "Reading your nerd book alone at a party?"

"I knew Meg would be here, and I didn't want it to look like I was following her, considering."

I thought of myself as a better-than-average mind reader when it came to David, but I was drawing a blank. "Considering what? Your non-relationship has been over since Christmas. You're allowed to show your face in public."

"I think this was part of the problem." He waved the book at himself, indicating what—his face? The stretched-out sweatshirt? Literacy? "For Meg and me. She didn't come right out and say it, but that's the impression I got."

"What impression?"

"That I was bringing her down. I don't fit in with her friends. Not 'cool' enough."

"What does that even mean? Who decides what's 'cool'?"

"I think it's one of those situations where if you don't know the answer, it's already too late."

"Like if you have to ask how much something costs, you probably can't afford it?"

"Basically."

"That sucks." What I really meant was *She sucks.* "I'm sorry."

"That your hip bone is puncturing my spleen?"

"Didn't realize you were such a delicate flower." I lifted my legs and plopped them across his lap. "Happy now?"

An owl hooted in the distance, and the pond grasses rustled in the evening breeze. "Yeah," he said quietly.

I took a deep breath, feeling my side expand against David's. The chill was starting to nip at the exposed bits of my skin, but it was still nicer than being inside.

"How's your existential crisis going?" He wrapped a warm hand around my bare upper arm and began rubbing lightly.

"Back-burnered for now." I used his shoulder to shove the hair out of my face. "I'll schedule another freak-out for after I survive the school tours. *If* I survive the school tours."

My shiver was only partly because of the temperature, but David contorted his shoulders to pull off his sweatshirt, one arm at a time. He draped it over us like a blanket.

"Better?"

"Mmmph," I said into his sleeve.

Whether it was the cold or the long week or the social stress of not partying at this stupid party, exhaustion hit me like a train. Once or twice the back door opened and noise spilled out into the night, but no one ever lingered, or came looking for us. We could have been on a canoe, drifting in the middle of a lake.

Weird that I was here with David, feeling the curves and angles of his familiar/not-familiar body, when I'd imagined tonight bringing me closer to Hudson, in every way. Not that you could cram seven years' worth of knowing someone into a few hours.

I felt the weight of time pressing down on me like a physical object. There was either too little of it, or way too much. Would I still be here in seven years? If I left, would this part of my life be lost? Were there people who stayed close for decades, until they were old, or did you have to find all new friends when you grew up, no matter what?

"Jo?"

I looked down at my hands, which were kneading David's

forearm like it was a piece of wet laundry. "Sorry." I smoothed his arm hair. "Just thinking."

"What about?"

"Time, I guess. Change. Death."

"Existential crisis, part deux?"

"This is why I go to bed early. Less time to freak yourself out." I yawned, settling more securely against him. "You can read your book if you want."

His cheek came to rest on top of my head. "I'm good."

"What *shall* I do with him?" sighed
Jo, finding that emotions were more
unmanageable than she expected.

– *Little Women*

CHAPTER EIGHTEEN

Jo."

"No." If this was morning, I wasn't interested.

"Jo."

I grunted but kept my eyes shut.

My whole body tipped from side to side, like I was sharing an air mattress and the person next to me had rolled over.

"What?" When I realized it was David, I was glad I hadn't come up punching.

"Hudson."

I jerked my head to look back at the house, tweaking my neck. The porch was empty. "Where?"

"He went back inside. But I think he was looking for you."

"Why didn't you wake me up?"

"Um. I thought you might want to—"

"Fix my hair?" I tried to comb it out with my fingers, but gave up when they snagged on a knot.

"No." David squirmed, like he was too embarrassed to say. The movement reminded me how many points of contact there were between our bodies. Even through two layers of denim, the butt-to-thigh friction did not feel as innocent as it should, considering our long friendship. Not to mention the part where he was my sister's ex.

"Crap. Sorry. I didn't mean to—" *Wrap myself around you like a vine.* "Invade your space."

"It's okay, Jo." The arm curved around my back squeezed lightly. I assumed it was a *there, there; get-off-me-now* kind of thing, except he didn't let go.

Maybe my brain was still foggy from sleep, but I had a sudden sense of balancing on the edge of something, like I could tip one way or the other. What if I didn't get up and find Hudson? Staying with David now would be leaning into new territory.

As in the territory of his arms and chest.

Did I want to take that chance? Did he? How could I be sure this wasn't one more thing I'd bossed him into? Maybe David was just being his friendly neighbor self, keeping me from freezing to death. And was I ready to give up on Hudson after half a night out?

I rubbed my sore neck, dislodging the sweatshirt we were sharing. It was warm and soft and all I wanted was to cuddle up and go back to sleep, but I handed it to David like a big girl.

He pushed it back at me. "Keep it. I'm a lot furrier than you are."

Not wanting to argue with him about which of us had more body hair, or why I had actually shaved my legs for once, I peeled myself off him and stood. My silenced phone was sitting on the arm of the chair. The absence of notifications suggested Hudson hadn't been trying *that* hard to find me.

I shrugged on David's sweatshirt, pulling the too-long sleeves over my hands. There weren't many people whose clothes made me feel small. "Guess I'll go back in."

It sounded like a question.

"I'll come with you," David answered.

ॐ

Figuring the party might have escalated, I braced for mayhem: keg stands, people making out on kitchen counters, tragic dance moves. What we saw was much worse.

In the dining room, Meg and her friends were staring at themselves in the oversize mirror that filled most of one wall.

"It's so good," Ashley enthused, touching the thin strap of Meg's silky red top. My sister had undergone a wardrobe upgrade since I'd seen her last.

"You don't think half down?" Meg tilted her head to examine her elaborate updo, skimming delicate fingertips along her jawline.

Was that what they'd been doing this whole time — styling each other's hair like there was a pageant component to this party? One of them was even wearing a tiara in the folds of her intricate multipart bun. What kind of twisted private lives did these people lead?

"Depends which dress you wear," Not Ashley said. "If it's the green, you don't want to take away from the backless effect. Ooh, but if you go with the red, I have a necklace you can totally borrow." Her nose wrinkled. "A lot of people wear red to prom, though."

Tragically, we didn't hear the answer to this momentous question. One of Meg's friends caught sight of us in the mirror and did an SOS with her face: *Your ex. OMG. What should we DO?*

I didn't wait to see whether Meg was going to acknowledge David or freeze him out. Grabbing his hand, I dragged him out of there like the rug was on fire. We rounded the corner and ducked into a nearby room before I let go of his arm.

"Phew," he said, after a strained silence. "For a second there I was afraid that might be awkward."

"Yeah. Close one." I pretended to wipe the sweat off my brow.

"Uh, JoJo?" Laurie said from the doorway. "Can I see you in my office?"

David and I exchanged a look. "This office?" I asked, even though it was more of a den, and we were the ones inside the room.

Laurie nodded. "That works."

"I'll wait in the hall," David offered. Laurie gripped his hand as they traded places.

"We have a situation," he said as soon as we were alone. "It's H-man."

I raised my eyebrows.

"Hudson."

"I knew who you were talking about."

"Oh. Well, I need to ask you something." He paused so long I started to worry.

"Does he need an EpiPen?"

"Why would you think that?"

"I don't know! You were acting all serious. I thought maybe he had a reaction to peanuts or something and passed out."

"He did pass out, but not from allergies." Laurie's mouth pulled to one side. "I'm pretty sure. But that's not what I wanted to talk to you about."

I waved at him to go on.

"Do you think he's into me?"

"Hudson?"

Laurie nodded.

"Why?" Not that I doubted him; it was a depressingly plausible scenario, given that most people were at least a little bit into Laurie. Such were the perks of being beautiful, upbeat, and blessed with a public persona that had nothing to do with *Little Women*.

"He seemed kind of flirty. I told him I'm in a relationship."

"You are?" I was surprised Amy hadn't declared a day of mourning.

"Yeah, with myself."

"TMI, dude."

"*Spiritually*, Jo. I'm in my lone-wolf phase. Even if I wasn't, I'm not really into, you know." He tipped his head down as his brows crept up.

"Dudes?" I guessed, though Laurie had never explicitly stated a preference one way or the other.

"Blondes."

The joyful anticipation must have shown on my face, because he wagged a finger.

"You are not allowed to tell Amy, JoJo."

I stuck my tongue out. "You're no fun."

"I like myself better with two eyes. That haven't been scratched out. And speaking of perfect vision. Hudson got an eyeful of you and Big D gettin' your snuggle on." Laurie wrapped his arms around himself, wiggling like a cartoon bear.

It was a lot of information to process. (1) Hudson *had* seen me out there. (2) People thought David and I were hooking up in an Adirondack chair, which was . . . impractical, not that it would stop the rumors. (3) Laurie's weird shimmy.

"And that's when he got wasted?" I tried to imagine a heartbroken Hudson drowning his sorrows with the football bros.

"No, he was pretty faded before that. Little Man doesn't have the body mass to hold his liquor."

"Oh. Where is he now?"

"Basement." I must have looked worried, because Laurie rolled his eyes. "It's a home theater, JoJo. He's not chained up."

I was halfway to the door when Laurie called out, "Amy was right. You like the D."

Whirling on him, I held a finger to my lips. "Please don't say things like that out loud."

"Why, are you trying to pull both of them?"

"I have no idea what I'm doing. Except finding Hudson and making sure he gets home safe."

Laurie dropped a heavy arm over my shoulders. "Be careful. Strange guy, too much booze — things happen. You know what I'm saying, JoJo?"

I knew Laurie had a soft side, but it was touching that he was concerned about *me*. "I'm pretty sure I could take him in a fight."

"Totes," he agreed. "But you shouldn't have to."

❧

When I finally tracked Hudson down, in a separate basement room with a pool table and bar that screamed Middle-Aged Man Cave, he looked so happy to see me, I had to remind myself it was the beer talking. And that I was annoyed with him.

Even though he was cute and held on to me like a life raft as I led him up the stairs.

"Can we stop?" he asked when we reached the main floor. I thought he was woozy or about to puke, but he used the pause to work his fingers into my belt loops and press his face into the hollow at the base of my neck.

David cleared his throat. "Need some help?"

Hudson's sigh blew warm breath across my throat. "I thought we were alone."

"Nope," I told him. "Still at a party."

He adjusted his head to use my shoulder as a pillow. "We should go."

"Kind of tricky. My ride is drunk."

"That bastard." Hudson pressed a finger to the corner of my mouth, trying to lift my lips into a smile.

David grabbed his arm and hauled him off me, bending to keep Hudson's feet on the ground. After that, Hudson miraculously recovered the ability to walk.

"I'll follow you," David said as we stepped outside. I'd already taken the keys to the rental car from Hudson. When I unlocked the passenger door, he dropped like a rock.

"Seat belt," David told him.

Hudson blinked up at me with his long lashes. "Will you buckle me in, Jo?"

David yanked the shoulder strap across his chest, then fastened it with an aggressive *click*.

"Ow," Hudson whined.

David ignored him, holding his own keys out to me. "You want to drive the truck and I'll go with him?"

"That's okay. I'll see you there."

The streets were quiet, traffic lights glowing above empty intersections. Hudson took his seat belt off as soon as we were moving, slumping sideways to rest his cheek on my lap. I thought he'd fallen asleep, but when I said his name, he patted my thigh, leaving his hand there afterward.

"Would you like me better if I had arms like hams?"

I frowned down at him.

"Or I gave you the shirt off my back? 'Active Plumbing.' Kind of a *shitty* name." His fingertip traced the peeling letters on the front of my borrowed sweatshirt. "That was a joke, by the way."

"They sponsored one of our meets."

"See? There's so much about you I don't know. Like your running . . ."

"And my running?" I suggested, when his voice trailed off.

"So mysterious." His breath was warm through the fabric of my jeans. "How am I supposed to compete with these local boys?"

It was hard to tell whether he was fishing for a compliment or reaching the weepy stage of drunkenness. I patted his back.

"That feels nice." He arched his spine, like maybe this could transition to a one-handed massage. "I'm sorry, Jo."

"Did you drool on me?"

"The party." He sighed. "You and me. It didn't really go how I planned."

"No?"

"I wanted us to spend the night together." There was a very loud pause. "Not like that. Unless you wanted to."

"So this was a date?"

"I thought." It sounded the tiniest bit sulky.

"But then you ditched me," I reminded him.

"It was the peer pressure. Trying to fit in. I'm not strong like you."

I threw on the blinker, even though there was no one else on the road. David must have gotten caught at a red light.

"Talk to me, Jo. I want to get to know the real you. Tell me something nobody else knows."

Most days my brain felt like a hive buzzing with secrets, but I wasn't sure any of them would interest Hudson.

"Um, I got a really bad blister once, on the ball of my foot. My running shoes were shot but I kept putting off buying new ones." Because good running shoes are expensive, and I was hoping for a sale.

He shifted to look up at me. "Is . . . is that the secret?"

I shook my head. "I was afraid it was going to pop during a race, so I cut it open with my nail clippers and then poured rubbing alcohol over it."

Hudson sucked a breath through his teeth.

"Yeah. It hurt like a mother. But I kept it clean, and by the next race it was mostly healed. I got my best time of the season."

"And that is why sports are a no for me. I don't like pain."

"It's worth it for me. Cross-country is my ticket out."

"Like one day you're going to start running and just never stop?"

"No, like an athletic scholarship. So I can go to college out of state."

"You have a scholarship?" He sounded so impressed I was tempted to let him believe it.

"Nothing official yet. A few leads that might pan out, if I have a really good season next year." I felt the familiar squeeze of worry that I was falling behind, like a single choice could spoil everything. Going to a stupid party instead of working out, for example. "Anyway, that's my secret."

"Your family doesn't know?"

"Nope."

"You should do it. Definitely. Live free."

We lapsed into silence, in my case because I worried I'd said too much and in Hudson's because he was sleeping.

The motel was on the other side of town, still less than a ten-minute drive. I parked near a side door and cut the lights. "Here we are." I wiggled my leg to dislodge him.

"Too comfortable."

"Hudson. You can't fall asleep here." I probably *could* carry him if I had to, but there would be dragging involved. He mumbled something. I jostled him again. "What?"

He turned his face so that he was no longer speaking into my jeans. "Come with me. To my room."

"Uh, what?"

"You're too much of a good girl, aren't you? A good *little woman*."

"Did you just look at my boobs while making a *Little Women* reference?" RIP any hope of a normal dating experience.

Headlights swept across the dash as David's truck pulled into the next parking spot. I slid out from under Hudson (who turned out to be capable of sitting up on his own after all) and stomped around to the passenger side of the car. When I opened his door, Hudson staggered to his feet. He grabbed at me to steady himself. One of his hands conveniently landed on my ass.

That got David out of his truck in record time. "I can carry him."

Hudson sighed loudly. At the door, I tried to hand him his keys.

"Put them in my pocket." He spread his arms to give me easy access, ignoring the dark look from David.

I shoved the plastic fob in the front of his jeans without an ounce of playfulness. Fun 'n' flirty Jo had left the building. I was tired, disappointed, and borderline annoyed with both of them, even though I knew it wasn't fair in David's case.

"Sure you can't stay?" Hudson reached for my hair, like I was a cute puppy he wanted to pet.

I pulled away, conscious of David watching. "Go to bed. I'll see you later."

"I'm never angry with you. It takes two flints to make a fire: you are as cool and soft as snow."

–Little Women

CHAPTER NINETEEN

"Where to?" David asked after the door swung closed behind Hudson, who had managed to beep himself into the motel on the third try. Hopefully he'd find his room; if not, the hallway was probably carpeted.

"Home, I guess?" I knew he'd found a ride for Nathan and couldn't imagine any other reason David would want to go back to the party. "Unless you feel like knocking over a couple of banks."

He hesitated. "What about Meg?"

"Who?" I gave him my blankest stare before relenting and pulling out my phone. "I'll text her."

David tapped the steering wheel with the flat of his hand. "She doesn't always answer right away." This was true even if she was in the same room, and you yelled her name first. "You want to go somewhere else while we wait?"

"As opposed to loitering in this parking lot?" I pretended to weigh the options. "Is there an underground club scene I don't know about?"

"I was thinking more like DQ."

My ears perked up. Maybe the evening wasn't a total loss. "You would let me eat ice cream in your truck?"

He turned the key in the ignition. "Not a cone. Or a sundae."

"That would clearly be absurd. Even though I know for a fact you have wet wipes *and* napkins in your glove compartment."

David smiled, which (on top of the promise of sugar) boosted my mood.

"And now, the moment of truth." I used my fist as a microphone as the Dairy Queen sign appeared in the distance. "What flavor are you getting?"

"Royal New York Cheesecake. Obviously."

"You haven't even seen what the special is."

"I know what I like, Jo." He braked at a yellow light, coming to a full stop before glancing at me. "Why? What are you having?"

"Not sure."

"So Butterfinger."

"Maybe. Maybe not."

"Jo."

"Okay, fine. Now that you put the idea in my head." Where it had been dancing around since he'd said the magic letters

D and *Q*. "Don't you ever want to experiment with something new?"

"I already found my favorite. Why would I get a less awesome flavor?"

"But what if there's one you haven't tried you might like even more? You could be missing out."

"Or I could order something new and spend the whole time kicking myself for not sticking with what I know and love."

"You're a Blizzard monogamist."

"When you've had the best, why settle for less?"

Wait, was he talking about Meg? That was a depressing thought. On cue, my phone buzzed with a one-word reply: **No.**

Amazing she could spare the energy. I had follow-up questions. *How are you getting home? Don't you have a curfew? Did Mom say you could sleep over at someone's house? What do you even see in Ashley and Not Ashley?* But there was no point trying to understand my sister. "I guess Meg doesn't need a ride."

"Or a Blizzard." By David standards, it was a savage burn.

After I browbeat him into letting me pay, we pulled out of the drive-through. I held both cups so David could steer.

"I can take mine," he offered when we were back on the road.

Since he was the kind of driver who kept two hands on the wheel at all times, that would mean holding the Blizzard between his thighs. "Do you want to park somewhere and eat?"

"You don't mind?"

I shook my head. When was I ever in a hurry to get home?

On the next block, he pulled into a strip-mall lot between a nail salon and a dry cleaner.

"Maybe I should have switched them," I said as I handed him his. "Open your eyes to a whole new world of deliciousness."

"You're just trying to steal my superior dessert."

"Is it so hard to believe I could be doing something nice for once, out of the goodness of my heart?" I stuck a spoonful of candy-studded ice cream in my mouth. "Mmm. So good. You're missing out."

"Fine." He reached his spoon over like he was going to dip it into my cup, but I jerked it out of reach.

"You can't mix. Here." I loaded my spoon with ice cream before noticing his wary look. "What? I don't have cooties. We used to share jawbreakers all the time. It's no big deal."

Watching my spoon disappear between his lips, I realized I was full of it. This didn't feel anything like passing hard candy back and forth after riding our bikes to 7-Eleven. I hadn't given a second thought to David's mouth in those days, or to the fact that his tongue was touching the same place mine had been a few seconds before. It wasn't until later, as my classmates started coupling up and you heard rumors this person had kissed so-and-so, that things changed. When tween me imagined kissing someone — in a vague, movie-moment way — it was usually David. Which made sense, since he was the main guy in my life and (unlike most boys my age) not an immature jerk.

My actual first kiss was with a kid named Scott, at a Halloween party in eighth grade. By then kissing had become more of a skill to practice so you didn't embarrass yourself — like thumb wrestling — than an epic imaginary event with a sunset and orchestra. I wouldn't say I'd made out with a lot of people since, but enough to know everyone did it differently. Whether it was the darkness or the spoon swapping, I wondered what it would be like to kiss this David. A real kiss, not a middle-school lip smoosh. Would he be shy or—

"Earth to Jo."

I twitched violently. "Huh?"

"I lost you there for a second."

"Still here. Just really into my ice cream." I shoved the spoon into my mouth before I could say anything stupider.

"Do you want to taste mine?"

"Um. Sure. I mean, no. Thanks. I probably shouldn't." Was this spoon sharp enough to stab myself?

A car with a bum muffler passed our parking spot. The sputtering cough faded to silence before either of us spoke.

"What are you doing next Saturday?" David asked, eyes fixed straight ahead.

"That depends."

"On?"

"Whether the witness-protection program takes volunteers. Plan B is to dig a hole in the backyard and burn what's left of my dignity. Might as well go ahead and light it up before school tours." My hand shaped flames in the air. "Why? You want to hit DQ again? Maybe get a better Blizzard next time?" I took a big, gloating bite, waggling my brows.

He didn't laugh. "I was thinking about prom, actually. I thought maybe you'd want to go. With me."

A chunk of Butterfinger lodged in my throat. I covered my mouth with a napkin as I choked.

"Are you okay?" he asked.

I nodded, wheezing as I cranked the window open. It was like one of those scenes in a movie where a character is trapped in a room filling with water and they have to press their face to the ceiling for the last inches of oxygen.

"Are you going to jump?"

"I'm sweating. On your sweatshirt!" It sounded even dumber out loud.

"It's machine washable," he said quietly.

I exhaled, trying to get my heart rate under control. "You can't spring stuff like that on me."

"My bad."

"I thought we were just eating Blizzards!"

"I didn't mean for it to be a sneak attack."

"Yeah, well." I snorted, even though I knew it was unfair.

David said nothing. Hoping ice cream would cool my overheated brain, I shoved the spoon in my mouth. It tasted like aspirin.

"I don't even have a dress. Or shoes." Could I be more of a whiner? It wasn't like I cared about fashion. If David had asked me to prom six months ago — before my sister or Hudson entered the picture — everything would have been different.

"It's fine, Jo. Forget it."

It wasn't fine. David should have known I wasn't good in this type of situation. It was so much easier to express myself physically, but punch-and-run didn't seem like an option here.

"Meg took your tickets," I reminded him.

"We could get new ones. I think that's how capitalism works."

"That would be stupid. You could buy a pair of running shoes with that money."

"Okay. I get it."

Did he, though? It seemed unlikely, considering I had no idea what was going on with me. Was he asking me because he couldn't go with Meg? I didn't want to be David's second choice.

"So are you and Hudson . . . ?" David trailed off, leaving me to fill in the blank.

What was this, Night of a Thousand Questions? It wasn't *only* because of Hudson. Whatever was or would have been or might still happen with him had a built-in expiration date. That was part of the fun. Quick! Exciting! High-stakes, low-risk. The opposite of David, who was supposed to be safe and solid and permanent, especially now that we'd gotten past the mess with Meg. Except here he was trying to shake things up again, when we were barely back to normal. It was like he wanted to break my brain.

"I don't see Hudson as the prom type," I said lightly, dodging the real question.

"Not edgy enough for him."

"No—I mean, I have no idea." Add that to the list of things Hudson and I had never discussed. I clicked the button on my seat belt up and down. "Do you really want to go? Because I could find something to wear. That isn't plaid. If you're worried your life won't be complete without prom."

"Don't worry about it. I thought I'd ask. That's all."

As a friend? Someone conveniently located and also non-threatening? Or because I'd been giving off certain signals by climbing all over him tonight? If only there were a way to know without having to talk about it.

The phrase *mixed feelings* sounded like a gentle tie-dye effect, but to me it felt more like a cage match, panic and guilt and whatever else fighting for dominance. Life was easier when you had one emotion at a time — usually anger, in my case. I didn't like saying no to David. I didn't want to spoil our friendship. And I was too scared to dig deeper than that.

"I'll see you at the Night Before Not Christmas dinner, though, right?" Also known as School Tours Eve, though right now it was hard not to think of it as the day after prom. What an outstanding consolation prize! *Missed the big dance? How about an awkward semiprofessional dinner instead?* The only reason I brought it up was that I wanted David to reassure me we could fast-forward past the awkwardness of tonight, like it had never happened.

"My aunt's having a barbecue. We probably won't be back in time."

I forced a smile. "Lucky."

The spoon rattled in his empty cup as he wedged it into the console. "Yeah. That's me."

"She's got such a soft heart, it will melt like butter in the sun if any one looks sentimentally at her."

– *Little Women*

CHAPTER TWENTY

The purpose of staging a fake holiday dinner the night before school tours was to help everyone "get in the spirit." Mostly what I got from the experience was indigestion.

By now, Andrea and Hudson probably expected a certain degree of oddness from my family, but this would be kicking it to the next level. Were they ready to chow down on turkey and all the trimmings in late April? Listen to Bing Crosby on a warm spring evening? Drink cocoa and make popcorn garlands, even though it was closer to Easter than Christmas and the fake tree in the living room looked mangy enough without draping it in snack food?

None of that was my problem. I was responsible for vacuuming the downstairs, cleaning the guest bathroom, and peeling potatoes. That left just enough time for a quick run — or it would have, if I'd set off at the right time, or remembered to wear my watch. And if it hadn't turned out to be one of those days where you hit the perfect rhythm and running feels *right*, like your legs could carry you forever. The last thing I wanted was to turn around, so I kept telling myself *just a little farther*, which was how I ended up getting home late.

When I walked into the kitchen, pots were bubbling on every burner. Mom closed the oven door with a bang, sucking on the finger she must have burned poking at the turkey. There was so much steam in the air, condensation had formed on the inside of the windows. I unlatched the one behind the table, raising the bottom pane as far as it would go.

"Nice of you to join us," Amy scolded, like she was the grownup in the room.

Ignoring her, I crossed to where Mom was rolling out the store-bought piecrust so it would look homemade. "What can I do?"

She ran the back of her wrist across her forehead before glancing at me. "It would be nice if you put on something a little more festive."

એ~

I was so focused on speed I didn't realize there was someone in my room until I was whipping the towel off my wet hair after the world's quickest shower.

"What are you doing here?" I squawked. Hudson was stretched out on my bed with his legs crossed, flipping through my yearbook. Setting it aside, he smiled at me.

"Waiting for you. Can you do that thing with the towel

again?" He tossed his head, giving it the full shampoo commercial back-and-forth.

"In your dreams."

"Uh, yeah. I'm a teenage guy, sitting in a hot girl's room while she takes a shower. This is probably the high point of my existence." He sat up, swinging his legs to the floor as he inspected the dresser with its missing knobs and lopsided mirror half covered in cross-country ribbons and peeling stickers. "I have to say, I was hoping for more bras."

"Like confetti, just scattered all over the place?" I didn't add that he would have been even more bummed by my collection of cheap Target lingerie. "I'm just glad I was dressed."

"Really? I'm not."

I threw a balled-up pair of socks at him. Instead of lobbing them back at me, he held up his phone, hitting me with a series of flash bursts.

"Nice dress, though."

I shrugged, not wanting to admit that my mother had picked out the dark green maxi with a pattern of black chevrons. The color was sort of Christmassy, even if the lack of sleeves was not. For me that counted as making an effort.

"Can you look that way for a sec?" He gestured at the window.

"What? No. I haven't even brushed my hair."

"Trust me." Hudson crossed the room to stand in front of me. With a finger under my chin, he gently adjusted the angle of my profile. Then he drew the damp tangle of hair back from my face. "Perfect."

He took another series of shots at much closer range. I tried not to squint.

"These are going to be good," Hudson said, studying the screen.

"Why do you only take pictures of me when I'm scruffy and messed up?" At this distance, you could probably play connect-the-dots with my clogged pores. "These are not exactly glamour shots."

"First, that's not my aesthetic. If you're looking for soft focus and a feather boa, you're out of luck. Second, I'm trying to discover the real you. Not the yearbook version."

I made a skeptical noise as I turned to the dresser and started coiling my wet hair into a bun before it could soak the back of my dress. Hudson came to stand beside me, watching me root around for a bobby pin.

"It feels like we're running out of time."

Our eyes met in the mirror. I still had one arm raised to hold my hair in place. "Yeah."

His mouth twitched. "See? You're so stoic. I bet you won't even write to me. Out of sight, out of mind."

"What about you?" I gave my bun a quick pat to make sure it wouldn't unravel before turning to face him. "You're going to meet some lion tamer girl with a top hat and spangly leotard and forget all about this place."

"Wow. I mean, I wish. You do know it's not a circus?"

I lifted one shoulder, noticing the way Hudson's eyes fixed on my bare skin. Props to me for taking the extra twenty seconds to shave my pits. "Still more exciting than here."

"If the scent of animal urine gets you going." His fingers played with a spare hairpin, crossing and uncrossing the ends. "I'd rather stay here with you."

My heart said *Oh really?* Then my head smacked it back down. "No, you wouldn't. Trust me, it only gets worse. The suckage is real."

"We're both trapped. Maybe we should go on the lam. I hear Mexico is nice."

"You actually live in a cool place," I reminded him.

"On the rare occasions I get to be there."

I tried not to hear it as a complaint about his time here. "You'll go back soon, though, right? After the big cats."

"I guess." He straightened his glasses. "Too bad you can't come."

"Since I have to go to school and stuff." Among other hold-ups. Like the job I'd never applied for yet wasn't allowed to quit.

"Yeah." Hudson set down the now-V-shaped metal pin. "It would be fun, though. Hanging out in the city."

The sound of my mother's laughter carried up the stairs, followed by a raspier bark of amusement.

"Andrea brought wine," Hudson said, as if that explained our mothers' upbeat moods.

Both of us were quiet, listening to the murmur of voices from below. "What do you think they're talking about?"

"Their children, and how disappointing they are, because they don't realize how good they have it when plenty of people would kill for their opportunities." He shrugged. "If I had to guess."

That wasn't exactly my mother's party line. Her schtick was all about family and togetherness, because it wasn't like she could claim we were setting ourselves up for professional success. (In what, the bustling literary-reenactor industry?) Still, the underlying message was the same: *You don't appreciate how lucky you are!*

"What does Andrea have to complain about? You're here helping her, aren't you?"

"Right?" His face lit up. "And it's not like I had any choice. Apparently I'm not qualified to make up my own mind because I haven't had enough life experience." Sliding his fingers under his glasses, he rubbed both eyes.

I knew exactly how it felt to have your mother look at you like she wished you were a different person. One who fit in with her plans.

"That's better than my mom, who doesn't want me to go anywhere because she thinks you can learn everything you need from a single book."

"Why do they have to control everything? I just want a chance to do my own thing. Figure out who *I* am."

"Yes!" I grabbed his arm. "Working with family is a straight-up nightmare. They think they own you."

"And the pay sucks."

"Vacations are the worst. Want to get away? Too bad!"

Hudson laughed. *He* didn't mind the ocean of snark that lived inside me or get offended when I said something honest.

The door flew open, interrupting what could have been a moment.

"Mom says—" Amy broke off mid-complaint. "It's freaking Christmas and you're in here slutting it up?"

I spun her around and shoved her into the hall before she could say another word.

"Jo!" The closed door shook as she pounded it from the other side. "You're supposed to help. Mom said—"

"I *know*. I'll be right there." I waited until her heavy footsteps retreated before turning to face Hudson.

His expression was unusually serious. "Can I talk to you about something?"

"Okay?"

He reached for my hand. "I feel like things have been a little off with us. Since the party."

So we were an *us*. Good to know, even if our status wasn't something I'd been giving as much thought lately.

Everything about the last week had felt off to me, mostly because of what had happened *after* the party. On the surface, it wasn't as bad as the post-breakup era. David and I still acknowledged each other and made (very brief) eye contact, but the careful politeness felt like a lingering cold front. I kept having to remind myself not to touch him, which made me realize how physical I'd been with David before. On top of missing the ease of our friendship, I was starved for human contact—and worried about how I'd handled the prom invite.

Not that I was convinced David had been asking *romantically*. If I hadn't shut the conversation down after five seconds, maybe I'd know for sure. Either way, it didn't feel right to flirt with another guy in front of him, which was why I'd more or less ignored Hudson's attempts to erase the memory of his party foul by cozying up to me at rehearsals.

"I know I messed up." Hudson's fingers moved slowly up my arm. "I kind of got into it with my mom that day." He skimmed past my elbow to caress my shoulder. "Do you ever feel like you're going to explode? Like the pressure builds until you have to let it out?"

It sounded like he'd been reading my diary as well as the yearbook. Between the sympathy and the relief of being touched, I felt myself softening. "I thought you were bored. Wanted to hang with the cool kids for a change."

"You are the cool kids, Jo."

"Me and my multiple personalities?"

He was standing close enough for me to catch the amused twitch of his lips. "All of you."

My shoulder blades were pressed against the door, but I wouldn't have moved even if I could have. It felt unreal, this thing I'd dreamed about actually happening.

His hand slid to the back of my neck as he touched his mouth to mine.

There never was such a Christmas
dinner as they had that day.

– Little Women

CHAPTER
TWENTY-ONE

I was still a little dazed when I made it downstairs. Not because Hudson had cut off my oxygen supply (it wasn't that kind of kiss) but from the surprise. *This is what you wanted,* I reminded myself, trying on a smile.

"What's wrong with your face?" Amy scowled at me across the dinner table as she unfolded her napkin and dropped it on her lap. "It's creeping me out."

"I think Jo looks lovely." Mom offered a smile of her own as she deposited the tureen of green beans. "As do you, Amy dear."

My sister fluffed her hair at this totally spontaneous compliment that was definitely not to keep her from having a meltdown.

"Beth, too," Mom continued as she passed the platter of

turkey to her left, earning a huff of outrage from her youngest. "And Meg, of course."

Of course, because Meg was the beauty of the family, in the book and in real life. Although this Meg looked a little rough around the edges, what with the sunglasses indoors. Was our mother really so oblivious that she didn't recognize the signs of a hangover, or was she willfully ignoring the evidence of her eldest's post-prom partying?

"Very Anna Wintour," Andrea said, lifting her chin at my older sister.

Mom frowned. "Should we turn down the lights?" She glanced at the clunky chandelier, forgetting that if we set the dimmer any lower, it would flicker like a strobe.

"Must have been a rough night," I murmured.

"You know how slumber parties are." Mom shook her head fondly. "The next day is always a killer."

I pictured Meg and her loser friends crammed into a hotel room with gallons of cheap booze. Sometimes it really was like Mom lived in a different century.

"How was the music?" Beth asked. "My cousin plays bass in the band."

"Name-dropper," Amy fake coughed.

"We didn't go to *prom*." Behind the dark lenses, Meg was almost certainly rolling her eyes.

"Duh," Amy chimed in, like this was a fact everyone who was anyone already knew.

"What do you mean you didn't go?" I thought of the dresses,

the practice hairstyles, David's tickets. "You were in the bathroom getting ready for hours." I'd gone for an extra-long run to avoid the big reveal.

"It's called personal grooming, Jo. People do it every day, not just when there's a full moon." Meg lifted her sunglasses to give me a withering look.

I jerked back in my chair with a hiss of alarm. "What the hell is wrong with your eye?"

"And is it contagious?" Andrea added, leaning away.

The sunglasses dropped back into place. "I accidentally got some of my Natura Bisse Glyco Extreme Peel in there."

Only the knowledge that Meg had barely passed Spanish kept me from asking if she was speaking a foreign language. "Is that why you didn't go?"

She took a long sip of water before answering. "I never really cared about prom. That's not my scene."

"Then why did you steal David's tickets?"

"What are you even talking about, Jo? David doesn't dance, he doesn't have a tux, and he doesn't like parties. I did him a favor."

"You're a real humanitarian."

"He could have found someone else if he really wanted to go."

I felt a spasm of guilt, which immediately gave way to worry. Had he asked someone else? Why hadn't I considered that possibility?

Mom set down her fork and knife with an audible *clank*. "Let's talk about something else."

I couldn't remember the last time I'd been grateful for my mother's relentless cheerfulness.

"How was church?" Andrea asked, studying Beth over the rim of her wineglass.

Her interest surprised me. Maybe it was similar to Hudson's curiosity about small-town life—a phenomenon he'd heard about but never witnessed up close.

"Fabulous." Beth took a bite of potatoes, speaking through the mush. "We got the good band. Drums *and* mandolin."

"Our Beth is very musical," Mom informed the table at large. "I was saving this to tell you all over dessert, but we're adding something new to the show. An actual keyboard she can play onstage! Can't you just see it?"

Amy vibrated like a pressure cooker on the verge of blowing its top. "Where are you going to put a freaking piano?"

"It's not a piano, per se," Mom explained. "It'll be one of those small, portable ones."

"Are you talking about a synthesizer?" I couldn't keep the fear out of my voice. That was just what we needed: a bunch of electronic bleeps and bloops adding to the mood.

"We dressed it up. To look more old-fashioned." Mom made a vague swirling gesture that could have meant anything: tying on a bow, a sprinkle of glitter, cardboard and markers. "I was thinking we could do a sing-along at the end. Give the audience a chance to participate. What better way to spread the holiday feeling?"

I had a few ideas, starting with *wait until it's actually Christmas.*

"Indeed," said Andrea, tipping more green beans onto her

plate. I added that to my mental list of responses that could mean anything, or nothing. "Hudson was in a choir when he was young. He could have done something with his voice, if he'd kept at it. Talent without grit is fairly useless."

"Oh. Well." Mom looked torn between her usual impulse to agree and not wanting to dogpile on Hudson. "He's obviously creative in other ways."

"It's fascinating you tell people I'm not willing to put in the work when you're the one who crapped all over the idea of art school. Which is something I actually want to do." Like his mother, Hudson sounded casual on the surface, but the words hit the table like spattering grease, making everyone flinch.

It was the first I'd heard about his art-school ambitions.

"A BFA is for dilettantes and dabblers." Andrea didn't look at Hudson. I should have felt bad for him, except it was kind of a relief not to be the only dysfunctional family in the room. "Until you have a few miles under your belt, you won't have anything to say. At your age, it's a waste of time. And money."

"My father went to art school." Hudson addressed the words to me, but the whole table heard.

"It's like Laurie's father eloping with an Italian pianist." Mom smiled as if this made everything okay. Because that was definitely the cure for familial tension: comparing things to *Little Women*.

I shot her a skeptical look. "How do you figure?"

"That was a radical choice back then as far as society marriages were concerned.," Mom replied. "Artists didn't have the same cachet."

"Except we were never married," Andrea pointed out. "And he was barely an artist."

Even my mother needed a few blinks to recover from that one. "Well. There are different ways to be unconventional. I think everyone at this table has a bohemian bent, after their own fashion."

"My real masterpiece is my life. Just like in the book." Amy narrowed her eyes at Hudson, like she expected him to argue. "As anyone who has read it knows."

"She's the da Vinci of manipulation," I agreed.

Beth snickered. Amy rounded on her, nostrils flaring.

"Hypocritical, much? Book Beth is like a dark, diseased cloud hanging over everything. Nobody can have any fun while that little sicko is coughing and moaning in the corner." Amy pretended to gag.

"How rude of her to have a *terminal illness*," Beth said with heavy irony. "At least she didn't whine about it like certain parties who acted like the world was ending when they got busted bringing illegal fruit to school."

"Excuse you, Amy was *beaten*. In public. By a teacher!"

"Kinky," Hudson murmured.

Amy glared at him. "Like you'd know."

"Book Amy," I reminded everyone. "The lime scene."

"Don't do the crime if you can't do the time. Or should I say, the *limes*?" Beth winked at Mom, who looked like she was struggling not to crack a smile.

"It's not funny," Amy snapped. "All y'all are jealous Book Amy's life doesn't suck, but she can't help it if she's awesome.

Girlfriend knew how to work it." Dropping back into her seat, she gave an aggressive hair flip.

"Can I just point out that you're arguing about people who never existed?" I waited for some sign of agreement, but everyone was either angry, checked out, or taking notes. "None of those things actually happened to either of you. Obviously, since Beth is very much alive."

"Thank you," Beth said.

"You want to keep it real?" Amy pointed her fork at me. "I'm going to be a *teacher*. The awesome kind, who acts stuff out, with costumes *and* props. Either English or history. I haven't made up my mind."

"That's wonderful," Mom enthused. Probably she would have said the same thing if her youngest had announced plans to become a contract killer, but in this case I could tell she was genuinely excited.

"I'm really good at educating people about new things." Amy whirled to face Hudson. "Don't you think?"

"Sure," he said slowly, glancing around the table to see if the rest of us knew why he'd been singled out. "Are we sharing career goals right now?"

"Why?" Andrea asked. "Do you have some?"

Ouch. And also *ouch* for me, because how was it possible that even Amy had figured out what she wanted to do with her life? What was next, Meg announcing a full ride to an Ivy League college?

A buzzer sounded in the kitchen. Mom slid her chair away from the table. "That's the pie. Meg, can you give me a hand?"

All of us blinked at the empty chair where I would have sworn Meg had been sitting a second ago.

"I'll do it," Amy volunteered.

Beth leaped to her feet. "Let me."

They reached the doorway at the same time. After a few back-and-forth elbow jabs, the bottleneck gave way, sending them staggering into the next room.

"This should be good." Hudson could have been talking about the explosive potential of Amy and Beth working together, the fast-approaching nightmare of school tours (now with synthesizer sing-along), or the faux homemade dessert. It didn't really matter, since all of it was inevitable. Death, taxes, and the Christmas scene from *Little Women*.

Under the table, his leg pressed against mine. Maybe if I focused on the one thing in my life that was going okay, I could ignore the looming apocalypse. Grab a little happiness while I had the chance. Even Louisa May Alcott managed a few weeks' escape from her life of drudgery, if the rumors of a secret affair were to be believed. I wondered if Andrea knew about that.

"So, Jo." Andrea wiped her mouth with a Christmas napkin before setting it next to her plate. "Give us a preview of tomorrow. Is there anything in particular we should be looking for?"

Behind the sinking feeling there was a flicker of pleasure that Andrea had waited until everyone else left the room to ask. *The silly people are gone; we can speak freely.*

"We start with Christmas morning, for the little kids. The first scene in the book."

"'Christmas won't be Christmas without any presents.'"

Andrea delivered the line in her usual monotone. No melancholy falsetto for her.

"Yeah." I felt like a character in a war movie describing the ambush that slaughtered her platoon. "The whole presents-for-Marmee, giving-away-our-breakfast-to-the-Hummels bit."

Hudson looked puzzled.

"Where the baby dies on Beth's lap and then it's like, 'Hello, PTSD, my old friend'?" This was one of my (many) complaints about *Little Women*. Everybody acted like it was the original Hallmark movie, but some seriously disturbed business went down in that book. Dead pets, dead neighbors, Beth's undiagnosed mental illness, an entire freaking war — nobody ever mentioned those parts.

"Uh-huh." He didn't sound very certain.

"Then in the afternoon we do the play within the play." That part was significantly less familiar to most people, since it gets glossed over in the book.

"Interesting," Andrea said, adding another entry to my list of Ambiguous Comments. "Anything else?"

"There's the bus ride." That was probably the highlight of the day, especially when they got to escape this place and go back to school.

"Here we are," Mom announced, placing the pie at the center of the table.

"That looks delicious," Andrea said as Beth set down a stack of plates and spoons. Amy nudged it aside to deposit a half gallon of vanilla ice cream.

"It's just your basic apple pie, nothing fancy." Mom ducked her head modestly, like she was trying to downplay her mad baking skills for fear of making the rest of us feel bad.

Hudson tipped his head back as he sniffed. "I don't think we've ever had a pie that wasn't from Whole Foods."

Leaning across the table, Andrea patted his hand. "Both of your arms seem to be working."

Mom cleared her throat. "Guess what? Beth has offered to play for us if anyone wants to sing carols in the parlor after dinner."

It's a fricking living room. I didn't say it out loud, because — contrary to popular belief — I didn't share *every* critical thought that passed through my brain.

"Ah." The look on Andrea's face was a blend of *In what universe is that remotely appealing?* and unwilling curiosity. The kind people feel when they drive past the scene of an accident. "Regrettably, we'll need to head back to the motel."

My mother's face fell, like even she recognized the lack of sincerity.

"I want to make sure we're ready for the big day," Andrea added. "Tomorrow is *so* crucial. It's really the apotheosis of our time here."

Whatever that meant. It sounded a little like *apocalypse* to me, which would be accurate, but Mom perked up, thrilled as always by hyperbole.

"Very true," she agreed, dishing out pie. "Everyone should get to bed early tonight."

I had a brief, beautiful dream of escaping the musical portion of the evening, until Mom said, "We'll do a quick song or two as a family, then hit the hay."

Beth started humming "Deck the Halls," an impressive trick with a mouth full of pie and ice cream.

"Weren't you listening? She said *family*," Amy hissed at her stage sister.

Beth hummed louder. Not to be outdone, Amy launched into a weirdly aggressive rendition of "Silent Night."

As their voices climbed in volume, competing for dominance, Hudson leaned against me. "This is festive."

"Joy to the world," I grumbled, stabbing my pie.

Andrea poured the rest of the wine into her glass before raising it in a toast. "God bless us, every one."

It was excellent drill for their memories, a
harmless amusement, and employed many
hours which otherwise would have been idle,
lonely, or spent in less profitable society.

–Little Women

CHAPTER
TWENTY-TWO

For all the complaining I'd done about school tours over the years, there was one problem I'd never mentioned to another soul.

School tours were cursed.

Every year, something extra happened to make the day more of a disaster. In fourth grade my hamster, Clyde, got loose, never to be seen again. (*Probably got eaten,* Amy said, when I worried the buses were going to run him over.) My first period? Started the night before school tours, forcing me to perform with a maxi pad the size of a diaper. Eighth grade was the year I had a massive zit Mom swore no one would notice, so of course I heard people in the front row talking about the golf ball on my chin. Then there was the time Mom decided to spice things up by making shrimp scampi for dinner the night before — which was how we discovered my shellfish allergy. Nothing makes a show feel more endless than wondering if you're going to puke onstage. After that, Mom instituted the Christmas Dinner tradition, just to be on the safe side.

I wouldn't say it was a relief when I slept through my alarm and had ten minutes to throw on my costume and race to the barn, but at least I knew what shape that year's bonus stress was going to take.

Of course, that was assuming only one thing went wrong.

ᴄ◌

The other silver lining of waking up late was that I walked into the building and straight onto the stage, leaving no time to feel uncomfortable around David, or wonder if he knew that Meg had blown off prom. Maybe that was more of a gray lining.

The set for the first act consisted of a thrift-shop armchair with pink floral upholstery, a painted cardboard fireplace, and the newest addition, Beth's synthesizer. The latter was lightly camouflaged with a gathered floral "skirt" I recognized as one of our old sheets.

Powered by the Altoids I'd bummed off Mom as a combination breakfast/breath-freshener, I made it through the morning shows. Amy tried to steal my opening line, arguing that it would be more in character for Book Amy. I crooked an arm behind my back to flip her off as I recited the famous first sentence of *Little Women:*

"Christmas won't be Christmas without any presents."

Boiled down to its essence, the scene went like this:

JO: *This Christmas blows.*

MEG: *Remember when we were rich? Those were the days.*

BETH: *I've repressed all personal desires, except for my death wish.*

AMY: *I resent having to slum it with you losers.*

MEG: *Remember the war? Me neither. But it's happening, somewhere out there. (Gestures vaguely.)*

JO: *Let's not be selfish, because war.*

Then we all gathered around to listen to Marmee read a letter from Father.

That part hit a little too close to home. Our real dad wasn't off fighting a war, though listening to his descriptions of faculty meetings during our Skype calls sometimes made it sound that way. It still felt weird to playact *I miss my daddy*. I couldn't shake the worry that whatever I did would be wrong: too much emotion, or not enough.

Next came a quick pivot to the traditional Christmas-morning guilt trip, in which Marmee tells us about the poor German family with no food or firewood and wind whistling through the broken windows of their tragic hovel. After a few broad hints about how very hashtag-blessed we are by comparison, the March girls agree to give away their breakfast to those poor unfortunate souls. Since we didn't have a big enough cast to impersonate the suffering Hummel family, the teachers passed out individually wrapped mini muffins as the curtain closed on Beth playing "We Wish You a Merry Christmas."

Meg immediately took off, but Amy stuck around to peek

through the gap between curtain and wall. We'd been offstage two seconds, and she was already going through withdrawal. Out front, Mom was making a speech about how helping those less fortunate was something we should strive for all year, not just at the holidays.

Which this was not, but hey: details!

"That ought to shut them up for a few minutes," Amy muttered.

It was unclear whether she meant the muffins or the moralizing.

She was living in bad society . . . and was fast
brushing the innocent bloom from her nature by a
premature acquaintance with the darker side of life.

—Little Women

CHAPTER TWENTY-THREE

Meg was supposed to be dancing around our make-shift Maypole with a crown of flowers, but the streamers hung limp as the next wave of buses spewed high school students onto the yellowed grass. Probably she was doing something to her face before the afternoon performances. Of the two of us, I was way more in need of freshening up, but someone had to help prep the set for the next scene.

Backstage, David was straightening the cardboard "tower" we had wired to the front of a ladder, with fake stones drawn in black Magic Marker. This was the major set piece for the play the March sisters perform on Christmas afternoon. Luckily for us, it was *supposed* to look cheesy.

"Hey," I said.

"Hey," he echoed. It almost sounded teasing, which would have been enough encouragement for me to attempt a joke, if I'd been able to think of anything besides *How's it hanging?*

I was still drawing a blank when Mom hurried up to us. "Have you seen Meg?"

"You could ask Hudson." David bent to pick up a piece of tape that had fallen onto the stage.

I frowned at the top of his head. "Why?"

"I think he went off with them."

"Them who?" I looked from him to my mother.

"Her friends," she sighed.

"Is that why she's not pole dancing?"

"Jo, please." Mom held up a hand.

"Do you want me to go look for them?" David asked.

Mom pulled her watch out of a pocket. She never wore it on performance days due to the infamous Marmee-has-a-Fitbit incident. "We'll give her five minutes." She glanced at me. "You better get changed."

I did need time to squeeze into my villain pants; there was a lot of friction involved. Amy and Beth soon joined me in the dressing area, all of us scrambling to trade our life-size American Girl–doll dresses for the more flamboyant scene 2 costumes. When I emerged, David looked up from the prop table, blinking hard.

"Go ahead. Feast your eyes." Holding my arms out to the sides, I did a slow rotation.

"What are those pants even made of?"

"Pleather. The miracle fabric." I squatted a few times, knowing the farting sound would entertain him.

"Ooh la la," said Andrea's voice. "Very glam rock."

Hudson was there too, the pair of them taking in my puffy shirt, skintight pants, and long black curls—and also how close I was standing to David.

"It's my Captain Hook cosplay," I said, stepping away.

Hudson gave my legs another up-and-down glance, like he couldn't help himself. I flexed my quads.

"Do you know where Meg is?" There was an unfamiliar edge to David's question, like he blamed Hudson for her absence, even though Meg had no trouble disappearing without help.

He shrugged. "She was around here somewhere."

"Maybe she wanted to show her friends the bridge?" Mom said as she joined us.

Right. Because they would care so much about our DIY landscaping projects.

"I was at the bridge." Beth gave Mom a regretful shrug. "I didn't see her."

Amy edged slightly in front of Beth, spreading her elbows to take up more space. "Meg's probably in her room. That's where she always is."

"Did you text her?" Andrea asked.

"No phones on show day." Amy gave a virtuous little smile.

"I'll go," I sighed, before Mom could ask.

At the back door I passed Laurie, who was on his way in. "Uh, JoJo? Stage is that way."

"No Meg." Squinting against the sudden brightness, I stepped outside. Although I would never admit it to Amy, I had decided to follow her suggestion and check the house first.

"Meg!" I yelled as the screen door slammed behind me. She didn't answer, but that didn't mean she wasn't there. Sometimes you had to poke her to get a response.

I shouted her name again while pounding up the stairs. If she was asleep, might as well start the waking-up process now. The flower crown had been abandoned halfway to the second floor.

A muffled thump sounded as I stepped onto the landing. I paused to identify the source, but there was only silence.

"Meg," I said a third time, banging on her bedroom door. It popped open, because like every door, window, and person in this house, it was a little warped. My eyes flew to the unmade bed. That was where I expected to see my sister, so at first I didn't register the cluster of bodies splayed out on the floor.

My brain froze. What had I stumbled into—orgy? Drug den? Satanic cult? I flicked through the slideshow of potential horrors before registering that they were all lying around listening to whiny music on someone's phone. The most exciting thing in the room was the half-eaten bag of Cool Ranch Doritos.

"You're late." My annoyance at having to track Meg down was compounded by the fact that she hadn't acknowledged my presence. "Let's go."

Instead of springing up with an apology, my sister tipped

her head back against the bed. Ashley (or possibly Not Ashley; it was dim with the curtains drawn) giggled.

"Meggy," she whispered, "your sister's freaking out."

Meg yawned. Her hair was unbraided, and she'd shucked off her dress. Her legs were bare beneath the hem of her cotton slip. "I'm not coming."

"Uh, yes you are."

She extended a languid arm, her wrist limp. "I can't."

"You're not gushing blood, so get up." I grabbed her by the arm and tried to pull her upright. Meg flopped like a coat falling from a hanger.

"Oh my gosh!" Her friends fluttered around her, gasping and clucking while shooting me dirty looks.

"Go away," Meg mumbled against my stomach.

"What is wrong with you?" As if in answer, something rolled out from under the bed with a hollow rattle. I stared at the empty bottle, trying to sound out the label. It occurred to me that the too-sweet grapey scent filling the air wasn't from one of Meg's skin elixirs.

Another bottle joined the first. This one hadn't been drained completely. A trail of liquid fizzed onto the rug. "You're in here getting *drunk*?"

This provoked another round of laughter, like I was both slow on the uptake and hopelessly naïve. They thought my reaction was, *Oh no! Underage drinking!*

When what I really meant was: *Nobody gets to tap out in the middle of school tours. If I have to suffer, the rest of you better be right beside me in the trenches.* And, okay, maybe a sliver of my brain was scandalized. She was supposed to be Meg Freaking March, not a *Gossip Girl* reject.

"We don't have time for this." I spoke directly to my sister, ignoring her friends. "You need to get up, *now*."

Her chin tipped up, and her eyes drifted closed as she stuck out her tongue.

"I'm serious, Meg."

"Oooh, she's serious." Ashley pretended her hands were shaking with fear. These were the people my sister had chosen over David? How were we even related?

"Come on, Meg." I tried for sincerity this time, letting a pleading note enter my voice. "Mom's counting on you."

"I guess she'll just have to make the best of it."

It was one of our mother's favorite sayings, delivered with a sneer that left my usual level of rudeness in the shade.

"*Meg.*"

Rolling onto her stomach, my sister flipped me off. Downstairs, the grandfather clock chimed, distracting me from the giggling of Meg's friends. It was even later than I thought.

"Christopher freaking Columbus." Things were so bad, I was cursing in *Little Women*.

❧

In the space between my sister's bedroom and the barn, I made the leap from shock to resignation. Meg had crossed a line I'd never dreamed of putting a toe over, but there was no time to bitch and moan. We had a show to survive.

"Can we skip her parts?" I asked in a low voice as Mom, Amy, and Beth huddled up around me.

Amy frowned. "That won't make any sense."

Because the plot was so full of logic right now. "It's not like we have someone else who —" I broke off, glancing behind me. David must have been watching, because he immediately set down the fake chains he was showing to Laurie and hurried over.

"What do you need?" he asked.

Mom and I exchanged a look. Could we? *Should* we? She dipped her chin in the universal sign for *We'll make it work.* "The wings should fit."

"On it." Amy snapped her fingers.

"I'll help," Beth volunteered, following her.

Andrea ambled closer. "Everything okay?"

"Fine." My mother's spine was a steel pole. I flashed a thumbs-up, which probably didn't contribute much to Mission Pretend Everything's Normal. "We'll be on in two minutes," Mom added, with a smile that said *Go sit down.* She waited until Andrea was gone to exhale.

"Here goes nothing," she muttered.

Weird. I was pretty sure that was my line.

Public opinion is a giant which has
frightened stouter-hearted Jacks on
bigger bean-stalks than hers.

—Little Women

CHAPTER
TWENTY-FOUR

Y ou sure you don't mind?" I asked David. In one hand
I held a tub of body glitter; the other was pressed against
his bare chest.

"It's fine." He shivered. "A little cold." Goose bumps trailed
down his arms, following the path my fingers had taken while
painting his torso in iridescent swirls. In the last-minute scram-
ble to transform a towering distance runner into an ethereal
fairy messenger, the silver leotard had been a no-go for obvious
anatomical reasons, but we'd managed to strap him into the
gauzy wings and tie scarves to his belt loops in a makeshift
tutu. At Laurie's insistence ("sun's out, guns out, bro"), David
was going shirtless instead of attempting an undershirt-and-
wings combo.

"Kinda slimy, too." I added a glittery streak across his stomach. "Like snail trails."

His laugh vibrated under my hand. Our emergency truce might have been temporary in his mind, but I had no intention of letting David slip away again. He was stuck with me for good.

"Get a room," Amy whispered. "Or step aside and let a real artist take over."

"Dream on." No way was I letting another of my sisters get her dirty paws on David.

She held up a pair of scissors. "Do we need to shave him?"

He stilled beneath my hand, no doubt imagining the *snip* of Amy cutting off one of his nipples.

"No," David and I said in unison.

"It would be faster than you trying to rub off his chest hair."

"I'm handling it," I told her.

She snorted. "I'll say."

I sent her a death glare. "You don't send someone into battle without armor."

There was a beat of silence before David's huff of amusement, which made me choke out a laugh too, even though my head was about to explode from tension.

"Who needs the shield of righteousness when you can have this?" He did jazz hands in front of his torso.

"You both suck," Amy hissed, stamping her foot. "Just hurry up. This isn't a massage parlor."

Ignoring my sister, I circled a finger at David, who turned so I could do his back. It really gave a sense of scale when you had to cover the whole shoulder-to-shoulder expanse on some-one his size. We'd need to restock our supply of shimmery slime before the next show.

"This is like half of the prom experience right here," I murmured as I coated what would have been love handles on someone with a different BMI. "Body glitter and a floofy skirt."

There was a pause during which I worried I'd pushed too far in my rush to pretend everything was normal.

"Funnily enough, this is what I was planning to wear," he said after a beat, making me snort so hard I probably inhaled glitter.

David turned to face me, holding the wand out to one side. "What do you think?"

"Sparkly." I dabbed glitter on the end of his nose.

"How about my hair?"

"Good idea." Stretching onto my tiptoes, I dragged my fingers from the roots to the end, shaping spiky pastel tufts at his hairline.

"I meant, how does it look."

"Ah. Well, it looks awesome now." I punched him lightly in the shoulder, careful not to smudge the glitter. "Break a leg."

"And now," Mom's voice trumpeted from the stage, "a very special performance of an Operatic Tragedy, set in a gloomy wood. Written by Jo March."

From my vantage point backstage I heard a horrified, "An *opera*?"

"It's part of the play," hissed a voice I recognized as belonging to my English teacher, Ms. Reyes.

"Then why did she say it was an opera?"

"There's a play within the play, like a matryoshka. It's meta. Now zip it."

My palms were still tingling as David slipped around the curtain. It was either an allergic reaction to the body glitter or sympathetic nerves. All he had to do was introduce the major players. Since he'd seen this show a million times, that shouldn't be too hard, assuming he didn't choke under the pressure.

"Before we begin our dark and desolate tale," David said in a strained falsetto, "meet the heroes and knaves whose fates will play out upon our stage." On the synthesizer, Beth played a quick musical theme full of stormy chords and heavy reverb.

"First, the lovely Zara."

As Amy pranced onto the stage, twirling so the long sleeves of her satin gown fanned around her, Beth broke into a sprightly tune I recognized as "I Feel Pretty."

"Next up," David continued, briefly forgetting to speak in a high voice, "the handsome Roderigo, beloved of Zara."

That was Laurie's cue to jog out from behind the curtain, raising his clasped hands above his head like a boxing champ. His background music was "We Are the Champions," though you could hardly hear it over the squeals and catcalls from the students in the audience. They'd seen him in tights on the football field, but the effect was very different when paired with a ruffled shirt and the fake sword dangling at his hip.

"And now," David said, catching my eye, "let's give a boo and a hiss to Hugo, rival for Zara's affections!" Beth played "You're a

Mean One, Mr. Grinch" as I swaggered onto the stage, cupping my hands in a *bring it* gesture when the audience booed. After a fake bow, I snuck back behind the curtain, winking at David as I passed. He was killing it so far, beyond even the comedy gold of seeing someone so tall and gangly dressed like Tinker Bell.

"And last but not least," he finished, "the witchiest witch this side of a broomstick — Hagar!"

Beth plinked out the Wicked Witch theme from *The Wizard of Oz* before shuffling out in front of the curtain in her long black dress and ratty gray wig.

"This is so pathetic," Amy complained as we waited for Beth/Hagar to finish whatever she was doing to make the audience bust a gut.

"Her natural comedic timing?"

"She's showing off for her alleged girlfriend. Who probably doesn't exist."

"How do you figure?"

"Like a junior would date Barf. She's clearly delusional, hence why she's acting like the main character."

"Hate to break it to you, Princess Generica, but the witch is a much juicier part than the damsel in distress." I elbowed her. "Maybe you should switch. You'd make a very natural Hagar."

The curtains creaked open. The shabby living-room furniture had been replaced by a few potted plants and a flat cardboard tree, our nod to the "gloomy wood" setting. As Amy slipped out of sight to wait for her cue, I strode forward to address Beth, who was squatting near the front of the stage pretending to stir the contents of a plastic cauldron.

"What ho, minion." I waited for the laughter that always followed the word *ho* to die down before finishing the line. "I need thee!"

Hagar turned to the audience and rolled her eyes. "What a charmer. Calls me a ho, then asks for a favor. We'll see how well that works out for him." She threw her head back and cackled. And then cackled some more, until she choked on her own spit.

I seized the opening. "I require two potions — and a side of fries." My wink at the audience was accompanied by a saucy hip thrust. "The first will make the beauteous Zara fall madly in love with me. And the second?" I paused, stroking my chin. There hadn't been time to stick on the fake beard. "A foul poison to steal the life from that rogue Roderigo!"

At the mention of Roderigo, Beth clutched her heart and made kissy faces, earning another chorus of laughter from the audience.

"Well, witch?" I snapped my fingers at her. "I don't have all day."

Beth gave a phlegmy harrumph. "Keep your panties on — magic takes time." Turning to address the crowd, she added, "I'll give him a taste of his own medicine!"

While I pretended to clean my fingernails with a dagger, David flitted onto the stage in his fairy outfit to deliver two perfume bottles, one clear and the other black. Beth took them from him and held them out to me.

"Here you go, Your Greasiness. Two potions, hot and fresh for all your evil needs."

Clutching the potions, I exited stage right. The curtain

closed on the witch shrieking, "He's cursed! Cursed, I tell you! Cursed! Soon I will have my revenge! Ha-ha-ha!"

Backstage, David and I dragged Zara's "tower" into place. Amy tapped her foot as she watched us work, lunging for the bottom rung as soon as we'd lined up the legs with the masking-tape marks.

When the curtain opened, Amy's head was sticking through the hole in the cardboard that approximated Zara's window. She preened as the audience broke into spontaneous applause, though any reasonable person could see they were clapping for Laurie, who had strolled into view from stage left, ukulele in hand. He swept his red cloak over one shoulder before strumming a few notes.

Beth cranked up the synthesizer, and together they launched into Roderigo's serenade, for which Laurie had chosen to croon "Can You Feel the Love Tonight." Singing wasn't even in the top five in his arsenal of charms, but he knew how to sell a ballad. Amy wasn't the only one fanning herself as the last notes died away.

"Babe," Laurie said when the whistling and stomping of feet from the audience faded. "You know I love you. Run away with me?"

"Leave my home and my father and this lavishly appointed tower? That's quite a commitment." Amy wrapped a lock of hair around her finger. "Okay, fine, you talked me into it. Take me away, Roderigo!"

Since Laurie was almost as tall as our "tower," all Amy had to do was hold out her arms and wait. After setting down his ukulele, Laurie pushed his sleeves back and flexed a few times. That got such a big reaction, he did a few lunges as he crossed the stage.

"Oh, Roderigo!" Amy's smile was tight. Not even Laurie could upstage her without taking his life in his hands. "The hour grows late, and you walk so slowly. What if my father, Don Pedro, discovers us?"

"I'm coming, my dove! Fear not. Soon you will be in my big, beefy arms."

From backstage came the sound of a synthesized burlesque riff. Laurie added a little salsa to his hips.

"That's it," Amy snapped. "I'll rescue myself."

Laughter rippled through the crowd, rising in volume as Amy stuck a leg through the "window" of her tower and the whole contraption wobbled.

"Wait, my angel," Laurie cried, arms outstretched. "You might hurt yourself!"

The tower shook as she worked her other leg through the opening. "Ready or not, here I come!"

With a grunt and a twist, Amy dropped. She probably would have made it safely to the floor if Laurie hadn't panicked and tried to grab her on the way down. They ended up with his arms around her thighs, like figure skaters doing a lift. As he staggered back and forth, trying to regain his balance, Amy windmilled her arms, alternately beaming at the audience and hissing instructions at Laurie.

I assumed his athletic skills would save the day, but I hadn't factored in the ukulele. With a crunch of wood and twanging of strings, he crushed it underfoot, attempted to correct course, and then started falling to the side. When Amy grabbed hold of the tower to slow their descent, the top half ripped off, bringing the ladder with it.

Laurie hit the floor first. I winced in sympathy as Amy landed on top of him, followed by a slab of cardboard. We all jumped as the ladder crashed onto the stage, missing the two of them by inches.

"Oh no," Laurie groaned, sitting up and dusting himself off. "I injured myself in the fall!" He grabbed the collar of his shirt with both hands and ripped it down the middle. After pausing to let the audience feast their eyes, he patted his stomach like he might have sprained his abs.

"Let me see." Amy slapped his hands aside so she could inspect his pecs for herself. "Looks good to me." She waggled her brows at the audience.

"Get it, LB!" yelled a voice from the crowd, as laughter gave way to general applause.

⁓

Backstage, David and I exchanged a look of amazement.

What the, I mouthed.

I know, his eyebrows replied.

Somehow, our ragtag crew had pulled off the heist of the century. The audience thought we'd done all of that on purpose. While the hooting and whistling continued out front, I launched myself at David. Our stand-in fairy had saved the day, and for that he deserved a python squeeze. It was a little tricky with the wings, but I managed to maneuver my arms around his waist, getting a face full of sparkly chest hair.

"Too bad you weren't dressed like this on the bridge."

"I don't think the wings are functional, Jo."

"It's the glitter." I leaned back far enough to swipe at his ribs. "You're a lot less slippery this way. It's like when they put that scratchy stuff on the bottom of a bathtub."

"I'll keep that in mind next time someone jumps me." He ran his thumb over my forehead, the other arm still loosely around my side. "Speaking of glitter."

I shrugged at the evidence on his hand, and also smeared across the front of my pirate shirt. Iridescent stains seemed like a small problem compared to the disaster we'd just dodged.

"I'm sorry," I blurted. "About the other night."

"I asked; you said no. There's nothing to apologize for." He gave an abbreviated shrug. "Well, you didn't exactly *say* it, but I got the message."

I flicked him in the ribs. "I'm a good communicator."

"With your fists, yes." His eyes were laughing as he grabbed my hand to keep me from striking again. "It's okay, Jo. Words are hard."

"Hey," said Hudson's voice as he ducked behind the curtain. His smile faded when he realized I wasn't alone. "Oh. Sorry. My bad." He started to leave.

"Wait." Realizing how it must have looked (like the cover of a very strange romance novel), I stepped away from David's bare chest. "I was just thanking David for saving our butts."

I waited for Hudson to acknowledge the shocking success of the performance, though admittedly he didn't have the same frame of reference. Judging by the way he was staring at my rear end, his brain had gotten stuck on the word *butt*. I blamed the cheek-isolating properties of my fake leather pants. *A wedgie, but make it fashion!*

David cleared his throat.

"How's your sister?" Hudson asked, remembering I had a face.

"Fine." I hesitated, wondering what Mom was telling people. Food poisoning, maybe. Or a tragic exfoliating accident. "I mean, she will be. Probably."

"Jo," David said. It sounded like a warning.

Right. Because protecting poor little Meg was everyone's top priority. I'd filled him in between acts on the scene in Meg's bedroom, expecting him to share my outrage, but he mostly looked sad.

"You know Meg." I forced a closed-lip smile. "She's always flaking out on stuff."

"I was talking about Amy. Falling off the ladder like that." Hudson cocked his head, like he could smell a story. "What's up with Meg?"

"Amy's fine," I said, as if I'd only heard the first part. "She has a really hard head. All of her bones are extremely hard, actually." It was amazing my organs were intact.

"So Meg was supposed to be the fairy?" Hudson flapped his hands like wings. "That's why you were looking for her."

"Uh, Jo, shouldn't we go take our bows?" David reached for

my arm like he wanted to pull me away from this conversation. From the stage we heard Amy and Laurie belting the opening lyrics to "A Whole New World." Someone (it sounded like Beth) yelled, "All together now!" and the audience joined in.

I swallowed bile. "I'm not going out there."

"Did you find Meg or is she still MIA?" Hudson persisted.

"It's a family thing." David was trying to help, but he might as well have waved a red flag that said SECRETS! That plus the macho stare-down the two of them were doing almost made me reconsider the sing-along. Stand here and lie for Meg, or go out there and pretend to be a Disney princess? Choices!

It was all so stupid. Acting on top of acting, spinning the truth. By this time tomorrow, Mom would have reframed the entire incident as a heartwarming story about banding together to overcome adversity. And if I pointed out that there was a difference between adversity and choosing to be a truant and screwing over your family, she would tell me not to dwell on the negative.

I was sick of pretending. Hudson wasn't going to shriek and clutch his pearls over the fact that Meg and her brainless posse had been day drinking during a school field trip, like the world's stupidest criminals.

"Meg and her friends were off getting wasted."

David's mouth thinned to a disappointed line, but he didn't try to stop me.

"That's why she couldn't do the show. Our standards aren't high, but you do have to be conscious."

Hudson gave a low whistle. "Your mom must be pissed."

I shrugged. My mother wasn't like Andrea, ready to drop harsh truths at a moment's notice, especially where her eldest was concerned. At most, Mom would give Meg the greeting-card version of a lecture.

"Will she get kicked out?"

"Of the show?" As if. Nobody was getting out of here that easily.

"School," Hudson corrected, and a faint chill settled in my gut. Even if by some miracle the teachers hadn't noticed Meg's idiot friends skipping the show, they were bound to be suspicious when they giggled and stumbled onto the bus. Or threw up in the aisle. Mad as I was at Meg, I didn't want anything too terrible to happen to her.

A little community service, maybe.

"Where did they even get that stuff? Does Meg have a fake ID?" I couldn't help glancing at David, who shook his head. He didn't know either.

"Was it prosecco?" Hudson asked.

"Maybe?" I couldn't tell whether his slight wince meant it was extra strong or extra bad, like the Natty Light of wines. "Why?"

"Andrea brought it. She wanted to have a little celebration tonight, after the show."

"Like a cast party?" Once again, I heard the wind whistle through the bottomless canyon between what Andrea was used to (in this case, The Theater) and our world.

"Kind of an all-purpose thing. Thank you for having us. And, you know, goodbye."

"You're throwing yourselves a going-away party?" David shook his head.

"It sounds like maybe we should stick around," Hudson said with a little edge. "See how things play out."

"I don't think that's relevant." David crossed his arms, still doing that weird older-brother bit. Unless it was a protective-ex thing.

Either way, I'd had enough. I tossed my wig onto the prop table.

"Where are you going?" David called after me.

"Somewhere else."

"Both human nature and pastry are frail."

– Little Women

CHAPTER TWENTY-FIVE

When the last bus had departed in a cloud of dust, I decided it was safe to venture downstairs. A flicker of movement caught my eye as I passed the dining room. My mother stood at one end of the table, hands braced on the back of a chair. She was scowling at a white bakery box with the lid thrown open.

I took a tentative step toward her. "Mom?"

"They ate the flowers." Her gaze was fixed on a grocery-store sheet cake. It was the kind with piped white frosting and fancy rosettes — or, in this case, smudged patches where bare yellow cake peeked through smears of blue.

Slowly it dawned on me that I was looking at a crime scene. "Meg and her friends did this?"

"The little shits."

My eyes widened.

"Pretend I didn't say that. But honestly, how hard is it to cut yourself a piece with actual utensils?"

"You think they used their hands?" My gag reflex woke up and reported for duty.

She picked up a frosting-covered plastic fork from where it had been dropped on the tablecloth. "The cake knife is *right there*." Her shoulders sagged. "Though I grant you, touching it with their grubby hands would have been worse."

"Who busts into a cake before the party, anyway?" Outraged as I was, it felt like we might be focusing on the wrong thing. Crimes Against Dessert was more of a sideshow than the main event.

Mom rubbed her forehead. "The party. What should we tell Andrea?"

"Um, we could say it was rats?"

"I'm serious, Jo."

So was I, though on reflection I could see how a rodent infestation might not be the image she wanted to convey to a national-magazine audience. "Because Jo has that pet rat," I mumbled. "In the attic."

Her eyes squeezed shut. "Not now."

Wow. Things were really bad if my mother was turning her nose up at a *Little Women* reference.

"There's no point throwing a graduation party when your sister may not even get her diploma." Mom scraped a blob of frosting off the tablecloth with her finger, then wiped it on the unused spatula.

"I thought it was a thank-you-and-goodbye party?"

"That too."

Definitely the multitaskingest party ever planned. "What did you mean about Meg?"

"I left a message with the principal's office. I'll have to go in tomorrow to discuss our options. Academic *and* legal."

"Legal how?" It was hard to imagine Andrea suing for her stolen wine.

"I may be liable for contributing to the delinquency of minors. Since they were on our property, I'm technically responsible for providing them with alcohol." Mom rubbed her chest like she had heartburn.

"But you didn't give it to them. It wasn't even yours!"

"I don't know, Jo. It's a mess."

I wished we were still talking about the cake.

"Uh, Mom?"

"Yes, Jo?" Her sigh said *This better be good.*

"I sort of told Hudson. About Meg."

Her eyes closed briefly. "I suppose it was too much to hope they wouldn't find out. Not really the note I wanted to end on."

"Sorry."

"It's not your fault."

I couldn't tell whether she meant *You can't help being the way you are* or *This one's on Meg.*

"Andrea will understand." It sounded like Mom was trying to convince herself. "She knows what it's like to be the parent of a teenager. I'm sure Hudson's had his share of youthful indiscretions."

Were we already on the Meg Redemption Tour? *It wasn't so bad! All teenagers do unspeakable things to other people's cake!*

"You know the worst part?" Mom asked.

I shook my head, trying to put myself inside her head. Was the worst-case scenario a lawsuit? Losing the house? Shutting down the show?

"Things were going so well. That was a wonderful performance today." She smiled at me with real warmth. "You were so uninhibited and free."

In other words: *Congrats on sucking less than usual!* I couldn't even roll my eyes, because she might be going to jail. "What are we going to do?"

"I don't know." Mom dragged the bakery box across the place mat, reaching for the spatula with her other hand. "Right now, I'm going to eat cake."

She valued his esteem, she coveted his respect,
she wanted to be worthy of his friendship.

—Little Women

CHAPTER
TWENTY-SIX

For once my mother did the sensible thing and called off the party. She must have realized that celebrating your oldest daughter's delinquency sent the wrong message. The mangled cake moved to the refrigerator, and I thought that was the end of it until a can of Duncan Hines frosting appeared on the counter.

"We can patch the bare spots," Mom explained, like that solved everything. Instead of canceling it, she'd postponed the party until tomorrow. Maybe that was supposed to be enough time to whitewash Meg's crimes, too.

I didn't ask. For the rest of the evening, all four of us kept to our rooms, pressing pause on the messiness of life. You knew it had been an intense day when even Amy couldn't handle more drama.

When we (meaning Amy and me) got home from school Tuesday afternoon, I grabbed a garbage bag and headed outside. Trash pickup normally happened right after school tours, before wind or rain could make an even bigger mess, but snack-food wrappers hadn't seemed like the most pressing issue yesterday.

You might think Meg could have tackled cleanup duty, since Mom had let her stay home "sick" on the grounds that she was probably going to be suspended anyway. I knew better. My older sister wasn't going to lift a finger for anything more strenuous than dabbing goop under her eyes. But hey, at least this dirty job gave me an excuse to avoid my family.

I expected to do all the work by myself, and had already launched an internal monologue about my garbage martyr-dom, when I came around the side of the barn to find David with a plastic sack in one hand and a grabber stick in the other, plucking an empty Oreo package from the ground.

"Hey." I wasn't sure where we stood after yesterday's two steps forward, one step back. He'd texted (**everything ok?**) to which I'd sent back, **eh**. But he was here now, so maybe things were fine. We could avoid the whole subject of school tours — especially the part about Meg.

For a while we trudged along in companionable silence. It was a relief to dwell on more mundane annoyances, like why it was so hard for school-age kids to *not* litter. Short of uncontrollable muscle spasms, I couldn't come up with a reason for all the dropped snack wrappers and bottle caps. Were they like this in their own backyards? Maybe what we should really be performing was a musical about the life cycle of single-use plastics.

"Have you talked to her?" David asked.

"Who?" I replied, even though I knew.

"Meg."

"No. Why would I?" I almost smacked myself in the sternum with the nasty gloved hand but managed to lower my arm in time. The arrested motion looked weirdly diva-like, but neither of us cracked a joke.

"She's your sister."

"Yeah, well, it's not like Meg is up for sibling of the year. She doesn't tell me anything."

"I know, but—"

"It's supposed to go both ways. Not 'she does whatever she wants' and I have to pick up the slack. Everyone seems to forget that she's the older one. Why do I have to cater to Meg when *she* screwed up? Or is it too much to expect her to take responsibility?" With anyone else, I would have been yelling by now. Since it was David, my voice got tight and I could tell my face was flushed, but I kept the volume to a semi-normal level. "Why are you defending her? She was a total jerk to you."

He looked at his feet. The ground around us had been picked clean, so I knew it was an excuse to avoid meeting my eyes. "It's never only one person's fault."

"Are you sure?" Between the two of them, I would have assigned 99.99 percent of the blame to Meg.

"I'm just saying, I wish I'd talked to her when I had the

chance. As a friend. When I saw her getting caught up with those—"

"Flaming buttholes?"

"Basically." David rested the end of the grabber on the ground, like a walking stick. "I don't want her to mess up her life."

"You think I do?"

"No!" He rubbed his chin against his shoulder. "But you are really angry."

"And what, I'm not allowed to be pissed?" My brain coughed up a memory of the part in *Little Women* where Marmee tells Book Jo she has to learn to control her temper, as a womanly virtue. Which made me even angrier, first because I hated that part (what about justifiable rage when the world is deeply unfair, *Marmee*?) and second because it was infuriating to be confronted with yet more evidence of how deeply I'd been brainwashed by that book. "Maybe you should try getting mad some time. See how it feels. You might like it."

"I get mad."

"When? I've never seen it."

"While I'm watching the news. For example."

I stopped, propping the bag against my hip. "You *watch* the news—like on TV?"

"With my parents. *Sixty Minutes* is a good show."

My face contorted, caught between a frown and a laugh. "What about *Wheel of Fortune*? Do you like that one too?"

"I've solved a puzzle or two in my day. Though I'm more of

a *Jeopardy!* guy." He raised the grabber, clacking the ends like castanets before moving off in search of more trash. I followed a step behind.

"Is that where you got that grabber thingy, from an infomercial?"

"For your information, it's called a Grip 'n' Lift. Two-point-oh."

"That's not a no, David."

He bent to pick up a straw wrapper, pretending to be too absorbed in his task to hear me.

"Can I ask you a serious question?"

The line of his shoulders stiffened before he shrugged an *okay*.

"Do you keep your hard candies in a glass dish on the coffee table or just fill the pockets of your cardigan with Werther's?"

"Very funny, Jo. You wish you knew where I keep my stash."

"I want to point out that a normal teen would be talking about weed right now, not their old-man candy." I would have kept up the teasing, but despite his smile, David still looked a little tense around the eyebrows.

"What is it?" I asked, trying not to sigh.

"I'm not saying you can't get mad." He hesitated, like he was tiptoeing through the minefield of my anger-management issues and didn't know where to put his foot next.

"But?"

"But you might want to be more careful about it."

"Like pencil it in on my calendar ahead of time? Or put my

head under a pillow and whisper, 'I feel so angry right now,' so I don't bother anyone?"

He swallowed. "The thing about you, Jo, is that when you feel strongly about something, you have a tendency to . . . let it rip. And I love that you aren't afraid to tell people what you think. Except sometimes—"

"You wish I would shut the hell up? Keep it all inside and give myself an ulcer?"

"I don't care if you go off around me. You can say whatever you want. That's not the problem."

"You think I should be nicer to my mom? Because I know you're not talking about Amy."

"It's Hudson, okay?" He pressed his lips together like he hadn't meant to say the name. "I don't trust him. You might want to think twice before telling him things."

"Like about Meg?" I tried to sound calm, but I could feel my nostrils flare.

"Or anything. I just don't get a good feeling."

"Huh." I turned away to grab a torn Cheez-It wrapper. After a beat, David came up behind me.

"You're mad."

"Why would I be mad?" I slammed the foil pouch into the bag, not quite hard enough to puncture the side.

"Because you like him."

"It's not about whether I like him or not." A point on which my feelings were still a little up-and-down. "It's the part where you assume I'm delusional. Because, what, he couldn't possibly like me back?"

"That's not what I said. I know he seems cool and charming and all that, but you barely know him."

"I guess you're the expert on dating people who look good but secretly suck."

David winced but didn't lose his focus. "Does he even know the real you?"

"What's that supposed to mean?" *You're totally fake around him,* my inner voice translated. *If he knew who you really were, he'd be bored out of his mind.*

"If he hears you go on a rant about Meg, and stuff" — he paused long enough for me to catch the implication that I was likely to rage about a variety of subjects — "he might not get the full picture."

"Which is what?" My shoulders were so hunched, I'd curled in on myself like a shrimp.

"That you love your family, even though they can sometimes be a little —"

"Bizarre? Irrational? Embarrassing?"

"I was going to say eccentric. Or unconventional."

Because of course he would find a way to be nice about it. "Maybe *you* don't know me as well as you think. What if I really am a mean, nasty person full of angry thoughts?"

"You're not." No hesitation whatsoever, but my temper was too frayed to appreciate his confidence.

"Then why are you lecturing me? You think I don't get enough of that at home? That's basically what *Little Women* is — a long sermon about shutting up and being everyone's bitch."

"That's not *all* there is —"

I held up a hand to stop him. "You really want to go there? If you squeezed me, that book would come out my pores. I think I know what I'm talking about."

"Yeah. I know."

"Why do you say it like that?"

"You brought it up," he said lightly. "Again."

My eyes narrowed.

"I'm just pointing out that you talk about it a lot. *Little Women*," he added unnecessarily.

"Is that my fault?"

"Not completely, but." David shrugged.

"What?"

"You make choices too. You're a really strong person, Jo. Nobody could boss you around if you didn't let them. At least a little." He glanced at me and then away again, as if he sensed the explosion building.

"You think I chose this life?"

Instead of backing down, David set his jaw. "Isn't there some piece of you that likes it? Being the responsible one, the hard worker, the person everyone depends on." He pointed at his chest. "I love that about you, Jo. Your strength. How you never give up."

Blah blah blah, compliments that barely registered. I was stuck on the part where David — *my* David, the one who was always on my side — compared me to Jo March.

"So let me get this straight. You think I'm secretly a sap who gets off on taking care of her stupid family? Oh, and I should also try not to blab about my feelings, because repression is my friend. Great. Anything else you want to cherry-pick about my personality? Talks too much!" I made a biting motion with my hand, like I was using his grabber. "Always pissed off!" Another bite. "Mean to her sisters!" *Chomp, chomp, chomp.*

Instead of snapping back, David was silent for a long time, staring at the ground. "Isn't that what friends are supposed to do?"

"Make each other feel like crap when they're already having a terrible day?"

"I would expect you to tell me, if you thought I was doing something wrong." He tried to make eye contact, but I turned away.

"You're doing something wrong," I muttered.

"Okay. Sorry." He let out a long breath. "I was trying to help."

"Well, guess what? Maybe the person who needs a lecture is Meg. *I* didn't break all the rules and let everyone down."

"I know that, Jo. I didn't mean to upset you."

He sounded so glum I almost told him it was okay, but the urge to smooth things over wasn't quite strong enough to overcome the anger and hurt buzzing through me.

"Jo!" My mother's voice carried across the grass. It wasn't a panicked yell, like *the toilet is overflowing,* but there was a certain urgency.

"I better go," I told David. "Wouldn't want to be a bad daughter, too."

She had cherished her anger till it grew
strong, and took possession of her, as evil
thoughts and feelings always do.

−Little Women

CHAPTER TWENTY-SEVEN

Jerking her head at me to follow, Mom hurried toward the store.

"Why are we here?" I asked as she shut the door.

She rubbed her palms on the front of her jeans. "You know we have a separate credit card for the gift shop?"

I shrugged, meaning *sort of.* It was like dental insurance: not something I'd given a lot of thought.

"I realized I hadn't seen a bill for a couple of months, so I called account services and they said it was because I switched to paperless statements." She paused like this should mean something to me.

"Because it's more environmentally conscious?"

"*I* didn't change it. And they weren't going to my email."

"Someone hacked your account?" All I could picture was an Internet troll with a stockpile of gingham aprons in their basement lair.

"Not exactly." Mom beckoned me to follow her to the storeroom, which was really more of a closet with shelves and a tiny desk holding an old desktop computer she used for inventory. "Let me log in real quick."

I watched the screen flicker to life. After an eon or two, the system started booting.

"Can't you do this on your phone? I'm sure there's an app."

"I like it this way."

Of course you do. Only my mother could find a way to make using a computer old-fashioned.

"Bingo." She shot me a triumphant look, like it hadn't taken her four tries to remember the password.

I looked over her shoulder. "Is that the balance? Or the other thing—how much you're allowed to spend?"

"This is what we owe." She tapped the monitor.

"Is it usually that high?"

"No. I keep pretty narrow inventory margins."

What she didn't have to say: *because we can't afford to buy a ton of merchandise on credit, with no guarantee it will ever sell.* "What is all this?" I looked from the number on the screen to the sparsely filled shelves. Maybe the better question was *where is all this?*, since none of it seemed to have wound up here.

"You know how I've been letting your sister help select some of the stock?"

I shook my head. Probably I'd tuned this out as background noise.

"Well, I have. Meg took an interest, and I wanted to encourage that. As a possible career angle."

"Career?" I choked on the word. Did she mean here—managing the gift shop? That would be a one-quarter-time job at best. Which actually fit Meg's work ethic, but still. It wasn't much of a life.

"The relevant information here is that your sister has been using the store credit card to buy things."

"But not for the store." I was still struggling with the idea that our sad little gift shop had become a den of vice.

"No, Jo. Not for the store. For herself, apparently. And her friends."

"Like what?"

"Candles. Lotions. Clothes." She hesitated, like the worst was still to come. "Trips to the salon."

I pointed at the screen. "All that is Meg?"

"Not all of it, no. But more than we can afford."

"I can't believe she did this." Not just the lying and the stealing, but the effort involved. It was so unlike my sister to expend that much energy on anything besides her skin. A small part of me wondered what David would think when he heard. "We're in big trouble, aren't we?"

"It's not good." By Mom's standards, that was like the howl of a tornado siren.

"What are we going to do?" I braced myself, afraid she might say, *Drop out of school so you can do shows 24/7.*

"Tonight?" She tugged at the neck of her T-shirt. "We'll have to put on a brave face for the party. We need the publicity more than ever."

"I meant about the money."

"I'm hoping she can return some of this. Then we'll have to work out a payment plan. And pray we sell a lot of tickets this summer." She looked hopefully at me, like I might have a brilliant suggestion to offer.

And while there was a part of me that wanted to fix everything, it also felt like my hands — and legs — were tied.

We were all going to sink together.

"You are the gull, Jo, strong and wild,
fond of the storm and the wind, flying
far out to sea, and happy all alone."

−Little Women

CHAPTER TWENTY-EIGHT

T he party happened. That was the best you could say about it — and the worst.

Andrea offered to bring more wine, but no one felt much like toasting. Did prosecco even go with take-and-bake pizza? I'd probably never know.

What should have been the saving grace — cake — was more of a sad trombone. After slapping a piece onto a plate, I made eye contact with Hudson, tipping my head toward the door. He was trapped between my mother and his, listening to a conversation that veered between such exciting topics as sunburn remedies and the many uses of kale. I suspected he'd be grateful for an excuse to flee, but when the screen door swung open behind me, it wasn't Hudson who appeared.

"This cake is so sweet, it should be like eating sand," Andrea said, sinking into the empty rocking chair. (Because of course we had a rocking chair.) "And yet it doesn't crunch."

By Andrea's standards, it was a conversational slow pitch. I'd half expected her to hit me with a question about Meg right off the bat. Even something simple like *Where's your sister?* would have been tricky to answer. I had no idea whether Meg was staying in her room by choice, as a punishment, or because she'd spaced on the whole thing. It wasn't like the noise level would have tipped her off there was a "party" going on down-stairs. There were almost more ghosts than people here, since David hadn't shown up either. I told myself I was glad he wasn't there to silently judge me.

"It's like a hot-dog bun fell into a jar of marshmallow fluff." I was rewarded for this observation with a faint smile.

Andrea sank deeper into her chair, propping her feet on the porch railing. "People would kill for this much outdoor space in the city."

"Yeah, well. You probably have better things to do than sit and stare at the grass." I set down my plate, leaving half the cake untouched.

"Mmm." She rocked a few times, the boards of the porch creaking. "I worry about you, Jo."

Since I couldn't point out that there were people in this family whose situations were way more messed up than mine, I kept my mouth shut.

Andrea glanced at me, fingers steepled. "Do you know what I think Alcott was really writing about?"

I shook my head, pretty sure she was looking for something

other than Family and Growing Up and Making the Best of a Bad Situation — all the schmaltzy messages most people associated with *Little Women.*

"*Desire.* I don't mean in the sexual sense," she clarified, which made me approximately two percent less uncomfortable.

It was another of those *Andrea is not from around here* moments, listening to her throw around words like *sexual* and *desire* — as if those were topics people discussed in casual conversation. Maybe that was another thing you gave up to live in the city: first porches, then inhibitions.

"I'm talking emotional, creative, intellectual." Andrea tapped the arm of the rocking chair for emphasis. "Everything that gets forced out of the March sisters by nineteenth-century morality."

Like their breakfast, I thought, tempted to make a joke instead of guessing wrong. But how often did someone talk to me like this, one serious adult to another? It felt like a chance I couldn't waste. "You mean like Jo not getting to write the kind of books she wants?"

"That's the most egregious example, but it starts much earlier. Think about the messages those girls hear, over and over. Don't be angry. Don't move too fast or speak too loudly or have too much fun. Don't get dolled up for parties or spend money on yourself. Don't *want.*"

I swallowed, torn between excitement (because *finally* someone was singing my song) and a sour trickle of guilt. Though the queasiness might have had more to do with the cake.

"You don't agree?" Andrea spoke so suddenly I almost

jumped. Her green eyes locked on mine, like she didn't trust me not to fudge my answer.

"No," I said quickly. "I've thought about all that stuff too." Maybe not in the same words, but still. Frustration, resentment, having your choices taken away? Those were things I understood in my bones. And then being told by the one person who was supposed to be on your side that your feelings were wrong, and you should try harder, and also maybe you'd brought it on yourself.

"You know the worst part?" Andrea pulled her legs off the railing, twisting sideways in her chair. "Say you do everything they want, reduce yourself to a sacrificial lamb, what do you get?"

"Marriage?" I guessed.

"And cultlike worship from your dutiful daughters, as long as you raise them to be as servile as you are."

I'd never thought much about Marmee's role. To me, it was a story about four girls.

"It's like the scene yesterday. Let's all praise Marmee and shower her with gifts."

"It *was* Christmas." It felt disloyal not to point this out, especially since I wasn't sure whether we were talking about Book Marmee or my actual mom. The trick was to stay on Andrea's good side without completely selling my mother down the river.

Andrea's lips flattened. Either she found my argument weak or the cake was catching up with her, too. "Do you know what I liked about the second half of the show?"

I shook my head, not wanting to venture my first guess: *The part where Laurie took off his shirt?*

She leaned forward, hands clenched. "It was full of life. Pure appetite, grabbing and taking with no apologies. Those people weren't cut off from their feelings."

That was one way to describe it.

"And how do you get away with that, as a woman?" Andrea continued, undeterred by my silence. "By being a sexless old hag—or a man."

"Or you can be like Amy. Book Amy."

She gave a dismissive snort. "Selling yourself as a decorative object for some rich man's home buys you power for about five minutes, until your tits start to sag. That's not what I'd call freedom."

"So I can either be a witch or a dude?"

Andrea leaned back in her chair, regarding me steadily. "Some of us are capable of forging our own path."

I knew Andrea was talking about herself. At the same time, the look in her eyes said, *You're like me.* Warmth crept over my skin, as if the sun had come out from behind a cloud. It felt like an opening—a chance to say something and be listened to. A moment of truth.

"Sometimes I'm afraid I'll never get anywhere." I blinked hard to dry out my eyes. Fortunately, Andrea was staring into the distance, like she could see my future on the faded highway.

"It's not so much about the details right now. School and

work and rent." Her mouth twitched in distaste. "You need to figure out how to live first. *Who* you are as much as *where.*"

It would have been just my luck if she'd left it at that. The secret of the universe is . . . *psych! You're on your own.*

"Don't bury your feelings, Jo. Lock too much of yourself away and you forget those things were ever there. You become your own jailer." She reached out a hand, stopping short of touching me. "I'd hate to see someone like you shrivel and fade."

It was hard to believe she was taking the time to give *me* advice. More than that, Andrea was talking to me like I was special, a person with potential — not the shadow of a character from an old-time book.

"I'll lose my mind if I have to stay here forever." I slid a glance at Andrea to see how this confession had gone over.

Her expression remained serious, but I got the feeling she was pleased with me for admitting the truth. Maybe even a little proud. "Sometimes you have to rescue yourself from the tower, even if it means knocking it down." She stood, arching her back in a stretch. "We should go. I still have packing to do."

Oh. Right. This was an ending, not a beginning. The promise of something new and different waiting around the bend dissolved like fog burning off. Tomorrow everything would be back to normal. No more Hudson, or his mom.

She turned away before my face fell.

"It's fun to watch other people philander, but
I should feel like a fool doing it myself."

—Little Women

CHAPTER
TWENTY-NINE

My falling-asleep routine was simple: last sip of water, phone on the floor, lights off, scrunch myself down under the covers. It wasn't a process in the same way as Meg's skin-care regimen, but it did involve a conscious decision. Usually.

The night of the "party," I only realized I was sleeping when an insistent buzzing sound filtered into my dream, where it became the *beep-beep* of one of those motorized shopping carts backing up. Even dream me found that strange enough that a message pinged my conscious brain: *You are asleep.*

The buzzing stopped as I cracked an eye open. I must have passed out fully dressed, laptop still playing Netflix as background noise. The screen was dark now, unlike the phone positioned inches from my face. Not that I'd been waiting for anyone to text me a *good night* or *goodbye* or *I don't really think you're a horrible person.* As I reached for it, the buzzing started again. It took me a few tries to unlock.

I squinted at the first message, double-checking the time. Seven minutes ago: 12:42 a.m. I scrolled through the line of single words. **Hi. Hello. Jo. Hey. Yo.** Then a series of question marks, interspersed with waving hands, a cat . . . and the flamenco dancer?

After flicking to his most recent message, I sent back a question mark.

He responded with a car.

My mind felt like a computer in the middle of a major software update. Programs were still running, but not at their usual speed. Another text:

Look outside.

I dragged myself off the bed. When I yanked back the curtain, moonlight illuminated an empty yard. A flicker of movement caught my eye. Angling my head, I saw Hudson standing beneath Amy's window. He was doing something with his arms.

Wrong room, I texted. I opened my window and watched him jog across the grass.

"What are you doing?" I hissed down at him.

"Serenading you." Hudson did the thing with his arms again, which I now recognized as air guitar. He stopped fake playing to wave at me to join him.

Underneath the sleep haze, my heart lurched. Our earlier goodbye had been underwhelming: a hug in front of both of our mothers, followed by the classic *I'll text you.* It was such an obvious brush-off, I wondered if I'd imagined the weeks of flirting, the things we'd told each other, the freaking *kiss*. But now here he was, shaking everything up all over again.

I held up a finger, the universal sign for *I'll be down as soon as I deal with the taste of death in my mouth*. Then I closed the window and tried to figure out how to put myself back together. It helped that I was still dressed, although rumpled and clammy. In the bathroom I gargled with a blob of Colgate and splashed water over my face, ignoring the deep crease the sheets had engraved on my cheek.

David's warning flashed through my mind. I had no doubt he would disapprove. Then again, he already thought I was a mess, and also in denial about my life. Look at me, not being a Jo March after all!

I tiptoed down the stairs. An owl hooted as I stepped onto the porch. The familiar rental car was parked closer to the road than to our house, on the grass next to the long gravel driveway. Hudson leaned against the passenger door, turning the flashlight on his phone on and off like the beam from a lighthouse.

"Hey." He pushed off the car as I approached.

It wasn't that cold, but my body objected to being out of bed with a violent shiver. I shoved my hands in my pockets. "What's up?"

"I don't know. Couldn't sleep." His eyes slid to me and then away again, like he was unsure of himself. "Feels like I barely saw you tonight."

"You should have come out on the porch. Your mom could have grilled both of us."

"Pass." He ran a hand over his hair. The movement lifted the front of his shirt, revealing a strip of stomach. "I get enough of that at home."

At his sigh, I stopped my semi-creepy staring at Hudson's midriff to look him in the face. "You okay?"

"Just frustrated."

"Packing got you down?"

"You could say that." He shifted his weight, glancing at me and then away again. It felt like I was seeing a different side of Hudson: more serious, less above it all. "I didn't want to come here, when Andrea told me about it."

Was it really necessary to get me out of bed in the middle of the night to share that tidbit face-to-face? "You must be glad it's over. You got everything you need."

"You mean *Andrea* got what she wanted. It's never about me." A gust of wind whispered through the branches of the oak tree. "Do you ever think about just taking off?"

"Isn't that what you're doing?"

"But I don't want to."

"You just said—"

"I mean I'm tired of being my mother's little helper." He took a step toward me, though we weren't standing very far apart. "What about what *I* want?"

Any doubt about his meaning evaporated when his hand landed on my hip. He pulled, I leaned, or maybe it was both. I felt the thump of his heartbeat through the thin cotton of his T-shirt. The night air was cool against my skin, except for the places we were pressed together.

I'm kissing Hudson. Maybe my brain was still waking up, but it felt like the news reached me at a slight delay—a voicemail I had to play back before it made sense. I put a little more effort into it, in case I'd been phoning it in.

"We should have done this a long time ago," Hudson said against my throat. We had migrated back toward the car, which gave us something to lean on besides each other.

"Yeah. I could have just been like, 'Mom, hold my bonnet. It's on.'"

He choked on a laugh. I patted him on the shoulder, squeezing as I worked my palm down to his bicep. *This is Hudson's arm,* my brain said, still in preschool-teacher mode.

He tucked his face against my neck. "You feel good."

I murmured something inconclusive, burrowing closer to him. This part was nice.

"Here." He freed one arm to reach behind me for the door handle. "I brought snacks."

"The most romantic words in any language." I fell into the passenger seat, closing the door before the dome light could alert my family that I was out of bed.

The grocery bag at my feet was heavier than expected, the weight of something glass and sloshy tipping the whole thing sideways.

"Colt Forty-Five," I read, holding up what proved to be a forty-ounce bottle of malt liquor. "Interesting choice." Probably he was being ironic. It might have seemed funnier to me if Meg's escapades hadn't put me off the idea of drinking altogether. I handed the bottle to Hudson. He cracked open the cap and took a drink before offering it to me; I shook my head, pretending to be too busy checking out the rest of the provisions to get liquored up.

"What else do we have?" Bending, I rummaged through the bag. "Fritos. Chili Cheese, huh? Bold choice." Maybe he hadn't considered how that would taste on each other's tongues. More crinkling met my questing fingers.

"You don't have to do that—"

"Apparently I do if I want candy. You did bring candy?"

"Yes." He sounded strangely reluctant. Maybe he'd planned to keep the sweets for himself. *For the plane tomorrow,* said a small voice I chose to ignore.

"Aha!" I held up a pack of Twizzlers before tossing them to Hudson. He was welcome to hoard those if he wanted. The toe of my shoe made contact with another object. "Hold on." I frowned in concentration. The shape was vaguely familiar, small and square but with something round inside. "What are these, Peppermint Patties?" They felt like the mini ones they kept in a canister by the cash register. Hopefully I hadn't crushed them with my foot.

"Um," said Hudson.

They were not Peppermint Patties. I realized this as the package dangled between us, moonlight glinting off the wrapper. "You bought condoms?"

My voice sounded flat, the collision of surprise, embarrassment, and annoyance (some of us had *school* in a few hours) blurring into a pancake of uncertainty.

"Not that I'm assuming anything." He grabbed the package and tossed it into the back seat.

"So, what, you saw me in the plaid dress and the apron and were like, 'I'd tap that'?"

"No, like I said, I wasn't expecting to—"

"Get with one of the March sisters? Because you know they don't play that way. It's all about saving yourself for the wedding night. If you live that long."

"Yeah, but *you're* not like that."

"You mean sweet and virtuous? Depends who you ask." I stomped out all thoughts of David. There wasn't room for him in this car.

"I'm serious, Jo. You're just . . . *you*. Your own person. You make up your own mind. It's like Laurie said—" Hudson broke off with an almost-audible *oops*.

And it had been going so well. "You might as well tell me."

"It's embarrassing."

"Of course it is." I tilted my head back against the seat, squinting up at the closed sunroof.

"Not for you." Hudson hesitated. "He told me you were 'too much woman' for someone like me."

Maybe I should have been flattered. Two cute guys, talking about *me*! But I didn't like it. I was sick of being an object of public discussion, onstage or otherwise. Life would be so much easier if you could control exactly who got to look at you and when. Selective invisibility.

"What does that even mean?" I finally asked.

"I'm not completely sure."

"But you figured it might require personal protection." Despite being in the back seat, the condoms flashed between us like a neon sign. "In case I attacked you?"

"No! The condoms are because of Andrea."

"Your mom told you to bring condoms?"

He made a gagging sound. "Ugh, no. It's one of her things about 'raising a son.' Personal responsibility. Doing my part. Not expecting the woman to take care of everything."

"That . . . makes sense." It was a knee-jerk response, since most of my brain was busy thinking about how different *his* mother's rules of life were from mine. That was practical advice. Way more useful than twenty-seven variations on the theme of *It's always darkest before the dawn!*

"I usually have stuff with me. I just didn't expect to meet anyone out here."

That snagged my attention. "What did you think we'd be like? All prim and proper, knitting socks and feeding the hungry?"

"Not exactly."

"Go ahead. I can take it. You must have had a picture in your mind, from reading the book."

He suddenly got very busy ripping open the Twizzlers.

"Wait." I grabbed his arm. Clues I'd deliberately ignored snapped into focus. "You haven't read it, have you?"

"What? No! I mean, kind of."

I let the silence thicken before saying, "I hope you're not planning to take up a career in espionage."

"Fine. I read *about* it. And I watched the movie." He stuck a Twizzler between his lips, mumbling the rest around a mouthful of waxy candy. "Most of it."

Amy was right. I made a silent vow to take that fact to the grave. No doubt I would have caught on if I hadn't been so busy trying to impress Hudson. Or if I'd ever met anyone who wasn't at least mildly obsessed with the story of the March sisters. I grabbed a Twizzler for myself, waving it at him like a floppy pointer. "All this time, you didn't even know the whole story?"

It was a bold move, showing up here as a *Little Women* noob. The part where I'd been blabbing my feelings about the book at him for weeks, assuming he got what I was talking about, was less awesome.

"It's not that complicated, is it? Four daughters, some of them get married, one dies." He set the candy in the console between us. "Anyway, the book is the book and you're you. I'm more interested in your real life. That's the part I researched."

I whacked myself with the Twizzler. "You researched me?"

"No, I mean the area." He gestured vaguely at our house.

"Please tell me you didn't check TripAdvisor." Until I trained myself not to look, those reviews had haunted my nightmares.

"It was more like the socioeconomic context."

"Fancy." I was talking about his use of lingo, not my sad hometown. It was probably all the same mass of blandness to people like Hudson and Andrea. Appalachia, the Plains, the Upper Midwest—everything not New York or California. "Were you thinking wholesome farm people square dancing, or more like a *Dateline* special?"

"The second one," he said without hesitation. "A vanishing way of life in America's heartland. Small towns dying off in record numbers."

"Because of the meth labs and weird meat-processing plants?" I guessed. "And since no one has anything better to do on a Saturday night, we all get knocked up in high school and drive around in our pickup trucks with shotguns, like a country song?"

"Kind of?"

"That's why you thought we were going to have sex in your rental car. Or maybe a hayloft?"

"Turns out I'm kind of an idiot."

"Who knows nothing about *Little Women*."

He dipped his head at me before taking a long drink of beer. "I guess that's kind of cool."

Hudson jumped as I reached for the bottle, which he had braced between his thighs. I unscrewed the cap and took a long swig. *Watch me grab life with both hands!*

"Good thing your fans can't see you now."

"I don't have 'fans,'" I told him, wiping my mouth. "And even if I did, I wouldn't live my life based on what some randos think a fictional character would or wouldn't do." Maybe if I repeated it often enough, it would feel like the truth.

He reclined his seat, linking his hands behind his head in a way that gave me a great view of his arm muscles. "You know, if you're looking to break some rules, I'm your guy."

"Like if I want to jaywalk, you'll get wild in the streets with me 'cause you're such a rebel?"

"Yep. Whatever you want to do, I'm here for it."

For a few more hours. I shoved that thought down. "Should we give each other face tattoos?"

"What?"

"Kidding." I tilted my seat back to match his. "I have a better idea."

Often between ourselves and those nearest
and dearest to us there exists a reserve
which it is very hard to overcome.

—Little Women

CHAPTER THIRTY

When I snuck back into the house, the only light came from under the microwave, shining onto the empty stove. Halfway across the kitchen floor, the scent of pizza rolls clued me in that someone else had been here recently.

I flipped on the overhead light and almost choked on my tongue. A ghost was sitting at the table, staring at me. After a few seconds I realized it was Meg in one of her white sheet masks, looking like a disembodied skull. My heart started beating again.

"What are you, nocturnal now, Ghost Face?"

"Looks like I'm not the only one creeping around at night." She bit into a pizza roll, carefully maneuvering it through the mouth flap in the mask first. "You and David finally got your shit together. Congrats, I guess."

"I wasn't with David."

"You don't have to lie. It's not like it's a big surprise. I'm actually impressed you dragged him out after dark."

"I was with Hudson."

Meg's nose wrinkled, as best as I could tell through a layer of cotton. "I thought he left."

"Not until tomorrow."

"One for the road, huh? Classy."

Ouch. I had no idea whether my sister had always been this brutal or had picked it up from her friends. "You're not exactly in a position to judge."

"Like that ever stopped you from criticizing me. Guess I shouldn't have bothered feeling bad about the David thing."

I was still scrambling for a comeback when the timer on her phone went off. Meg was so deeply focused on peeling off her face mask, I was pretty sure she'd forgotten I was there. She raised her hands like a TV doctor getting ready to operate and then lovingly massaged the last droplets of moisture onto her neck and forehead. The limp wad of fabric hit the table with a damp thud.

That snapped me out of my trance. "This isn't about David."

"Sure. Because you definitely weren't crushing on each other behind my back."

"He doesn't think about me that way."

"Whatever, Jo. Figure out your own crap. I have enough

problems." She picked up a piece of pizza roll with the pad of her thumb and popped it into her mouth. I was pretty sure it had been touching the used-up face mask, but that wasn't the most disturbing part.

"You know we have real pizza in the refrigerator."

"I don't like cold pizza."

"You could have reheated it." I gestured at the toaster oven she'd used to cook the pizza rolls.

"Leftovers are disgusting."

"Seriously, Meg? What are you, a princess?" Who was too good for leftover pizza? I must have missed the warning signs that my older sister was becoming an entitled night-mare. Probably because Amy used up all the *I'm the worst* bandwidth.

"I'm sick of worrying about money all the time. I want to buy stuff like a normal person, without counting every stupid penny." She spoke the words to her plate, like she was having this conversation with her pizza rolls instead of me. "I never get to do what I want."

"What are you even talking about?" As far as I could tell, Meg's only burning ambition was to slather herself in goo.

"You don't know everything about me, Jo."

The *ha* whooshed out of me like I'd been punched. Talk about an understatement. For the first time in ages, I really looked at my sister instead of seeing the Meg I expected her to be: pretty and sleepy and out of touch. She had bags under her eyes and a reddish cluster of pimples on her chin, and her hair was greasy at the roots. On top of which she was eating off-brand pizza rolls by herself in the middle of the night, which didn't scream *living my best life*.

"Why don't you tell me what's going on, Mistress of the Dark? Unless it's something criminal, in which case, save it for your parole officer."

"Very funny. You wouldn't be laughing if *your* future was ruined."

Oh. I tried to shift gears to a more sympathetic attitude, but it wasn't like I'd had a lot of practice. "Can't you get your GED or something?"

"I'm not talking about *high school*. I want to be an aesthetician."

"Really?" I knew she liked taking care of herself, but other people?

"Yes, Jo. I give Mom and Amy facials all time."

That was . . . surprising. And a paper cut to my insides. Part of me had always suspected that the three of them celebrated when I was gone, like *Finally we can be happy without Jo spoiling our fun!*

"You're always running," Meg said, correctly interpreting my *Why don't I know about this?* expression. The implication was that I fled screaming while she chased me with a spray bottle and hot towels, when in fact no one had ever asked me if I wanted a facial. (Whatever that was.) Probably I would have said no, because it sounded like a waste of time and money and I didn't trust Meg to poke around my face, but that didn't keep me from feeling left out.

"Not that you care, but it's not going to happen now anyway."

"Because you got in trouble?"

This earned me an eye roll. "Yes, Jo. The most important qualification for doing pore extractions is your disciplinary record from high school."

"Is it . . . really expensive?" And was that why Meg had started stealing?

"It takes a *thousand* hours to get certified." She stared into my eyes, apparently waiting for my head to crack like an egg from the shock. I could tell this revelation had gotten a bigger response in the past, most likely from people named Ashley.

"Out of curiosity, how long do you think that is?" Knowing Meg, she'd assumed a smile and a cute outfit would be enough to get her what she wanted. Anything more demanding might as well be a one-armed hike up Everest, with a piano on her back.

"No one wants a facial from an old crone, okay, Jo? Trust me."

"And that's why you bought all that crap?" I was struggling to make the deductive leap from beauty-school wannabe to petty thief.

"I don't know. Why were you getting busy with Hudson in the middle of the night?"

"Making out with a guy is not the same as stealing your mom's credit card, sociopath."

"Whatever, Jo." She shoved her plate away. "I'm always going to be the bad guy to you because I went out with your precious David. Which is really unfair, considering you were never going to date him."

"That's not—you don't know," I sputtered, at a loss for how to defend myself.

"Did you even consider how much I hate driving?"

For someone who barely moved, Meg could be extremely hard to keep up with. "What does that have to do with it?"

"He lives right next door to us. And he has a truck. Not a great ride, but better than ours."

"You went out with David because you needed a *chauffeur*?"

Meg shrugged. "Ashley thinks he's nerd-cute."

"You used him *and* objectified him? That's great."

"Not my fault you missed your chance. This is so typical of you, Jo."

I shook my head like I disagreed, but inside all I could think was, *What chance?* And *Did I really miss it?*

"You complain nonstop, but you don't have the balls to do anything about it. 'Poor me, I hate my job.' Why don't you just quit if you're so miserable? It's the same thing, over and over. Mom lays a guilt trip on you, and you fall right back in line. Just like the book."

She wouldn't be saying that if she'd seen me in the car with Hudson. The March girls probably thought a hand job meant embroidering napkins. But I wasn't going to brag about how far I'd gone with him because (a) it was private and (b) I wasn't feeling proud, exactly.

Which didn't mean I was ashamed, like this was the 1800s and I was a fallen woman now that I'd done more than waltz with a dude. Maybe it was because I hadn't planned to get physical with Hudson, or maybe I was just tired. Whatever the reason, I felt a little flat inside. And I really wanted to wash my hands.

Meg sniffed at my lack of response. "Andrea was right about you."

"What did she say?" And when had the two of them talked? I'd never noticed Andrea paying particular attention to either of my sisters. It was one of the things I'd liked about her.

Meg's bottom lip jutted, and I knew I wouldn't get any more out of her. She'd always been like that: soft on the outside, but incredibly hard to move—like a king-size mattress.

"Well, at least I don't pretend nothing ever bothers me and then buy a bunch of stupid shit we can't afford. How is that taking a stand? Look at me, I screwed over my own mother! Oooh, I'm so brave. Now I'm going to mess up this cake!"

"It was my cake!"

"No, it was for all of us!" We were hiss-yelling at each other, not so carried away that we wanted to wake up Mom.

Meg leaned across the table. "I don't have to share or go without or give things away to a poor family with too many kids."

"Nobody's asking you to—"

"We're poor too! Doesn't anybody realize that?" She closed her eyes, nostrils flaring. "Mom's always saying we're partners in the business, so I gave myself a raise."

The fact that Mom used the terms *salary* and *allowance* interchangeably was a sore point for me, but I refused to be sidetracked. "How is that fair when you do less around here than any of us?"

"I'm the oldest. I have different needs. It's like when Beth gets to go on that beach vacation."

"You mean when Jo takes her to the seaside because Beth is *dying* and they hope it might cure her?"

"Whatever! Can we stop talking about freaking *Little Women* for one minute!"

It was like we'd switched roles. Or for once we were both reading from the same script. I wasn't sure I wanted to sympathize with Meg; it felt too much like admitting David was right. Before I could sort out my feelings, she pushed back her chair. I assumed she was about to slither out of the room, but she headed for the refrigerator instead.

"You won't have to worry about me much longer," Meg said as she poured herself a giant glass of milk.

"What the hell is that supposed to mean?" There had been too many visits from school counselors over the years for me to overlook what health-class videos referred to as "a cry for help." I pried the glass out of her hand and set it aside. "It's going to be okay, Meg. You know Mom never stays mad for long."

Tentatively, like I was netting a butterfly, I wrapped my arms around her.

"Ugh, get off me, Jo." She elbowed me in the ribs.

Surprise knocked me back a step, despite the lack of force. Meg had always been the weakest of the three of us, due to a combination of being small-boned and never exercising.

"I just want you to know I'm here for you. If you need to talk."

"Oh brother. You know who you sound like right now? *Amy.*"

I didn't know whether she meant the Amy sleeping upstairs or Book Amy, but I was offended either way. "You don't have to be mean. I'm trying to *help* you."

"Then stop acting like such a drama queen. I'm not going to off myself." She stuck a finger in her mouth, like my concern for her mental health was gag-worthy. "You can keep living that martyr lifestyle. I won't get in your way."

"Do martyrs have booty calls?" It would have been a more effective comeback if I hadn't been talking to an empty kitchen.

"I shall have to toil and moil all my days, with
only little bits of fun now and then, and
get old and ugly and sour, because I'm poor,
and can't enjoy my life as other girls do."

—Little Women

CHAPTER
THIRTY-ONE

The weeks between school tours and the start of the regular performance season were usually the calm before a storm—a brief respite from total immersion in *Little Women Live!* We ran a limited rehearsal schedule, supposedly to accommodate finals and term papers but really because it reduced the number of work hours for Laurie and Beth, saving us money on payroll. This year it felt like disaster had already made landfall, leaving everyone battered.

To Mom's relief, Meg would still get her diploma, assuming she passed all her classes, but she wasn't allowed to walk across the stage in her cap and gown (which had already been rented, no refunds allowed) or participate in any other graduation activities.

With Hudson gone and no idea how to patch things up

with David, I spent a lot of time going on long runs alone. Whenever possible, I made an excuse to miss family dinners, eating leftovers later at night. The menu was heavy on rice and beans, an unfortunate combo with the scratchy toilet paper Mom bought in bulk. It was anyone's guess which would kill us first: credit-card interest or hemorrhoids.

One evening I was headed for my room with a bowl of off-brand cornflakes when I stumbled across Amy in the darkened hallway. Literally — I braced the hand not holding my bowl against the wall, steadying myself from the impact. "What are you —"

"Shhhhh!"

I took a moment to assess the situation: light under a door-way, muffled speech, Amy being a creeper. She was eavesdropping on our mother. My initial theory was that Mom must be talking to Meg, but the rhythm of pauses made it clear this was a phone call. Also I knew Meg was in the tub, because the bathroom door had been locked for ages, and the whole upstairs smelled like lavender and eucalyptus.

"Who's she talking to?" I thought I was whispering. The attempt must not have been up to my sister's Super Spy standards, because she tugged me down the hall to my room and closed the door behind us.

"It's Dad." She opened her eyes so wide, I once again questioned whether Amy had learned human behavior from watching cartoons.

I licked milk off my hand. "And?"

She started to answer, then broke off, pinching the end of her nose. "It reeks in here. Are you trying to kill me?"

I kicked a pile of dirty running clothes toward my closet. "One, I didn't ask you to come into my room. And two, I sweat."

"Yeah, but do you Febreze?"

"Focus." I snapped my fingers in her face. "What's going on?"

She tipped her head back and shook out her hair. I recognized her Speech Incoming face. "They're talking about Meg." Pause, inhale, significant glance. "And her *troubles.*"

I was tempted to grab Amy's eyebrows and hold them still to stop the aerobics routine happening on her face. "You know about it?"

"Meg's life of crime? Duh."

Secrets never lasted long in this house, between the listening at doors and the pathological need to talk about our inner lives (while totally ignoring all the external issues). "So what's the deal?"

"Unknown. But something's definitely going down."

"Thanks, Captain Obvious."

Amy crossed her arms, expression smug.

"What?" She was probably faking, but there was a slim chance she'd uncovered valuable intel.

"I don't want to bore you. Since you already know everything."

What would it be like to have simple conversations with your family, instead of jumping through a flaming hoop every time you tried to ask a question?

"Fine." Amy sighed like she couldn't take any more of my

begging. "I'll tell you. Before she called Dad, Mom was on the phone with Aunt Joyce."

Okay, *that* was surprising. Our mother and her only sister had been on the outs as long as I could remember. Which was weird, considering they were both obsessed with old novels. Aunt Joyce was on the English faculty at a small liberal-arts college a few hours away. Her husband was also a literature professor, and four of their five kids were hard-core readers. The youngest, Jasper, was more like me: trying to lead a normal life despite being surrounded by book-loving freaks.

Amy dropped onto my bed. "It makes sense, when you think about it."

"What does?"

"Mom reaching out to Aunt Joyce." She stretched out full-length, punching my pillow a few times before folding it in half.

"Make yourself comfortable."

"Thanks." Her ability to selectively tune out sarcasm would have been impressive if it weren't so annoying. "Who else are you going to turn to when your life is in the crapper?" After a second or two she added an "ahem" to let me know I was missing my cue.

I shook my head.

"Your *sister,*" Amy supplied. "The beauty of the sisterly bond—"

"Nope. We're not doing a scene."

"Mom prolly hit up Auntie Joyce for some cash monies, okay? Since Meg is a kleptaholic now."

"Uh-huh." Several things about this theory struck me as

sketchy, beyond the non-words. First and foremost, I doubted our cousins had much money to spare. Amy must have read the doubt on my face, because she quickly changed the subject.

"I'm surprised David hasn't been around more. Now that your little city boy is gone."

"I don't see why that would matter." I managed to say this without an eye twitch, even though talking about the two of them together felt like bending a finger in the wrong direction.

"You might want to crack a window. The smell of BS is getting pretty strong."

"That's actual manure. It was mixed with the compost." I picked up the old pair of running shoes I used for yard work, carefully turning them over to inspect the treads. Probably I should have taken them off outside.

Amy launched herself off my bed, pulling the comforter halfway onto the floor. At the door she spun to stare at me. "I guess we'll see who really knows this family."

Another downside of spending your formative years onstage: no one could simply leave a room. It had to be An Exit.

"You can go through the world with your elbows out and your nose in the air, and call it independence, if you like. That's not my way."

– *Little Women*

CHAPTER THIRTY-TWO

Half the time when Mom announced a family meeting, it was code for *I need you to stuff these envelopes*. I could tell this one was serious because she was wearing a blazer. Or a blazer-like sweater. It had a collar, anyway.

Mom cleared her throat. "It's nice to have everyone together at the table again."

The three of us glanced at her with varying degrees of *yeah, right*. Meg's skin was back to its usual dewiness, so she must have found the strength to uncork one of her serums.

"As you probably guessed, I have an announcement to make, that concerns all of us."

My heart skipped a beat. Were we shutting down the show? I knew better than to ask. It was pretty much guaranteed I'd strike the wrong tone, since I wasn't even sure how *I* felt about the idea. Yes, it was everything I'd said I wanted, but Mom would be devastated. On the other hand, I might be able to get a real after-school job —

"Meg is leaving us." My mother's voice pulled the plug on my fantasy of honing my typing skills so I could work in an air-conditioned office all summer.

Amy leaped up from her chair, clasping her hands to her chest. "A wedding! How wonderful. And then you'll live just down the road with your husband and the twins!" She paused, apparently expecting applause. "You guys suck at improv."

"I'm not getting *married*." Meg's face twisted as if Amy had accused her of eating roadkill straight off the asphalt.

"She's going to spend some time with your father," Mom explained. Like that made everything crystal clear.

"You mean at Christmas, like always." Amy spoke slowly, in case Mom had forgotten how time worked. She was talking about the Christmas the rest of the world celebrated, in December, when the three of us made our annual trip to see Dad, not the theatrical version.

"I mean as soon as finals are over. We thought a change of scenery would do her good." Mom didn't look at Meg as she spoke.

"Wait." I held up a hand for silence, even though no one was saying anything. "Meg did everything wrong, and she gets to leave? How is that fair?"

"Lucky me." Meg's voice was flatter than a sheet of paper. "I get to hang out in Dad's stupid apartment watching documentaries and listening to jazz all summer."

Ignoring her, I turned to Mom. "So if I steal from you, can I go on a vacation?"

"Be reasonable, Jo. I need your *help* right now. Not ridiculous what-ifs." And there it was: the hint of anger, like I was the bad guy.

"Sorry, I thought being the problem child was the way to go if you wanted something."

"What I *want* is to stay here with my friends," Meg retorted.

"Right. Because they're so awesome."

"At least I have friends."

I scowled at her. "I have friends."

She made a show of looking around the kitchen, like they should be hanging out with us while we aired our dirty laundry. "I hope you're not talking about Hutton or whatever."

"It's Hudson."

"You know why he was interested in you, don't you?"

If Meg brought up the incident in the rental car in front of Mom and Amy, I was going to do things to her face no amount of moisturizer would fix. "Maybe he thought I could buy him stuff with my mom's credit card."

"That's a bit insensitive, Jo."

I stared at my mother. "But calling me a friendless loser is fine?"

"What about David?" Amy said, unable to resist sticking her nose into the argument.

"Yeah. Of course David is my friend." *Was* my friend. *Would* be my friend again. Hopefully. Once I figured out how to talk to him. Or enough time passed that we could pretend our argument never happened.

"I think maybe *he's* your Professor Bhaer." Amy toyed with the end of her braid, head cocked to one side in a pantomime of Deep Thoughts. "Not Hudson."

"There's no Professor Bhaer. Just like you're not really going to marry Laurie."

Amy gasped. "Rude!"

"LB's not even that rich." Meg addressed the comment to her cuticles, but it was still perfectly audible—which didn't stop Amy from throwing a napkin at me, like it was my fault.

Our mother clapped her hands. "Girls." She sounded tired. "If we could return to the main purpose of this meeting."

"Rewarding people for bad behavior?"

Meg stuck her tongue out at me.

Mom ignored both of us. "Sending Meg off for the summer is a big change, yes. But it's also an opportunity."

"For Meg," I muttered.

"For a fresh start," Mom corrected, unwavering in her belief that you could alter reality by giving it a cute nickname. "And she'll be working hard."

Amy and I looked from our mother to Meg, frowning. Had she met her eldest daughter?

"She has a job lined up on campus."

"A real job?" There had to be a catch. Like what Mom called a job was actually journaling every morning and yoga once a week.

Meg rolled her eyes. "No, it's a fake job."

"Good thing you have plenty of experience," I fired back.

"Your father and I came up with the arrangement, in consultation with Principal Henderson and Meg's counselor." The tightness around Mom's eyes conveyed what she wasn't saying: *It could have been a lot worse.* "Your sister will work as an office aide in the philosophy department twenty hours a week."

"But what about the show?" For once, the tremor in Amy's voice wasn't bad acting.

Mom squeezed her hand. "The show will go on. Your cousin has agreed to help out."

"Which cousin?" The calculating expression on Amy's face suggested she was running odds on who she could most easily push around when it came time to hog the spotlight.

"Adeline."

That explained why Mom had been talking to her sister. "We're allowed to dump our parts on someone else? Like it's just that simple?" I snapped my fingers.

"Will we call her New Meg, or just Addie? So many possibilities! She and David will be adorable together. *And* she's a natural blonde." Amy patted her head, as if those words related in any way whatsoever to her.

"I'm sitting right here," Meg reminded her.

"Not for long," Amy chirped.

Mom nodded as if Amy had made a useful observation. "Meg flies out next Sunday. That gives her a day to finish packing after school lets out."

I hadn't even thought about the plane ticket. "How much did that cost?"

"That's not for you to worry about," Mom said. "Your parents are in charge of the family finances."

Except when you forget and let your delinquent daughter go on a shopping spree.

"You could pull a Jo," Amy mused, smoothing her place mat. "That would cut costs."

"I'm not going to *run* all the way there," Meg scoffed.

"I'm talking about Book Jo. Duh. When she sells her hair so Marmee can have travel money?"

"Pretty sure selling your hair is not a thing in this century," I cut in, like a telegram from reality. "It's not like freaking plasma."

"Oh yes it is, Jo!" Amy yelled as if we were arguing about the fate of the world. "People pay a lot of money for human hair — *if* it's a nice color. Not boring brown."

"I'm not cutting my hair," Meg said. "They'd never pay me what it was worth."

Amy shrugged. "Probably smart. Somebody might use it for something weird."

"What are you picturing right now?" I asked, curious in spite of myself. "An Etsy shop with human-hair sweaters?"

"Spells and stuff." Amy shook her head. "Obviously." As if any of this made sense.

"Are we done here?" I asked Mom.

She glanced at the clock. "If no one has any questions —"

I was already on my feet, the familiar weight of their disappointment trailing me to the stairs.

"It seems as if I could do anything
when I'm in a passion; I get so savage, I
could hurt any one and enjoy it."

– Little Women

CHAPTER THIRTY-THREE

When I was a little kid, Mom used to send me outside to jump up and down or run around the house when I got angry. She called me her little firecracker, because my temper flared up and then burned out.

This flavor of anger was different. Sprawled out on my bed after the family meeting, I felt like the burned-out casing of a bottle rocket. Empty. Singed around the edges. Done. There was nothing to fight for, no way to change my fate.

The phone buzzed on my nightstand. I flopped in that direction. It was a text from Hudson. Underneath a picture of an empty parking lot with a small mound of trash and dead grass piled against a crumbling cement divider he'd written: **Wish you were here?**

Probably the joke was supposed to be that his current

situation sucked. This happened fairly often with Hudson, where I sort of got what he was talking about, even though part of me was left wondering if I'd missed a reference to something obscure and artsy.

Yes, I typed back.

What are you doing right now?

Thinking about murdering my sister. My fingers operated without permission from my conscious mind. Hopefully he wasn't expecting me to say something sexy.

Amy?

Meg.

The screen flashed with an incoming call.

"What did she do?" Hudson's voice said in my ear. He sounded halfway mad already, like he was just waiting for me to tell him why we were pissed. It made a nice change to have someone respect my emotions. Even the ugly ones.

"She's leaving." I gave him the quick and dirty version of events.

"And your mom expects you to stick around and take care of everything?"

"I know, right? It's like Amy stealing Jo's trip to Europe."

"Someone's going to Europe?"

There was an audible uptick in interest. It would put the story in a different category for Hudson if one of us was jetting off to a foreign country—more relevant to his interests. I'd forgotten that he wouldn't recognize the reference to Book Amy's multistage betrayal, possibly the bitterest pill in the whole book. Instead of going on the trip she's been promised for years,

Book Jo nurses Beth through her final illness, then keeps house for her grieving parents while Amy gets a months-long luxury vacation. The sparkler on top is that Amy comes home married to Laurie, who was supposed to be in love with Jo, except his attention span was too short.

"Forget it—just a book thing." I shook my head, not so much for Hudson's benefit (since he couldn't see me) but out of frustration with myself. "So how are things there?"

"We're actually heading back to New York tomorrow."

"Really?" I wondered whether he would have told me if I hadn't brought it up. Though I supposed his Instagram feed would have clued me in eventually.

"This place is tapped out, and so am I." He yawned the last word. "For once, Andrea agrees with me. We've got as much as we're going to get."

I told myself it was a compliment. *At least we're better than the animal hoarders!*

"I guess that's good? You can talk to your mom more about art school."

"What's the point? Andrea has me working so much I haven't had any time to focus on my portfolio, so there's no way I'll get accepted anywhere I'd actually want to go."

"That sucks."

"Yeah, and get this—my friend's uncle runs a gallery. Basically, if I want an internship, it's mine."

"And that would help you get into a good school?"

"Absolutely. The networking opportunities would be unbelievable. You'd think Andrea would be ecstatic, since she's all about hands-on experience."

"What did she say?"

"'If you want to order people's lunch and call it a job, you should at least get paid.' That's a direct quote."

"Ouch."

There was banging in the background, and then the muffled sound of Andrea's voice.

"Hold on." Bedsprings groaned, followed by the creak of a door. I wondered if he would tell Andrea who he was talking to, and how she would respond if so. A nod? *Tell her I said hello*? Or would she ask to speak to me herself?

Hudson must have had his hand over the phone, because I couldn't make out more than a few words of what either of them was saying, and then the sound of a door closing.

"You know what we should do?" His voice was low and intimate, speaking only to me.

"What?"

"Take a vacation from our mothers."

I made a noise like I agreed, even though my dreams didn't involve lounging by a pool. I would have been thrilled with Meg's supposed punishment: hanging out on a college campus, doing a job that didn't involve costumes or sappy dialogue or overhearing audience members say, *That's funny. I thought she'd be smaller.*

Still, I liked that he wanted to go somewhere with me, even if it was never going to happen.

After we hung up, I drifted across the floor to my dresser. Although I was as alone as I'd ever been, my head pounded with the pressure of too many voices talking at once. Andrea saying she worried about me. Meg telling me I never did anything but complain. David implying it was my choice to live this way. Hudson suggesting we run away together.

I leaned closer to the mirror, studying my face like it might hold the answers. Skin, so-so. A mouth that was on the large side. Brown eyes that could be bigger, but at least the lashes and brows were dark enough not to disappear. There were things I would have changed — not surgically, but if you could order a smaller forehead online, I might have been tempted.

As much as I fought against being lumped in with Jo March, some things bled through, including the sense that I was just okay-looking. Not the beauty of the family. Kinda plain, but what a lively personality! After all, no one had ever looked at me and said, *Are you nuts? That girl is much too pretty to be Jo March.*

I untwisted the rubber band from my ponytail. Basic brown, my hair fell almost to my elbows, thick and heavy with a hint of wave. I never left it down; having all that hair in my face was too annoying. For now, though, it was a relief to let go of the tightness around my skull.

If only there were a way to get some of this weight off my shoulders for good.

"You are a wilful child, and you've lost more
than you know by this piece of folly."

—Little Women

CHAPTER
THIRTY-FOUR

When I walked into the kitchen Wednesday evening, Amy and Mom were sitting at the table, heads bent together as they studied what appeared to be another press release. My sister was twirling a red pen between her fingers. Circles and slash marks dotted the page.

I wondered how they were selling the casting change. *New this summer: a different Meg!* Like we were Happy Meal prizes and someone out there would be desperate to collect the whole set.

This was probably a good time to tell them about some other changes, so they didn't have to send out back-to-back announcements. All I had to do was open my mouth and say—

"Holy crap!" Amy pointed at me. "Your one freaking beauty."

I pressed a hand to the back of my neck. It was weird to feel exposed skin. My eyes slid to my mother, trying to gauge her reaction. Right now, she seemed to be stuck on shocked. Maybe in a minute or two she'd work around to telling me I looked okay.

"I cut my hair." Not exactly news at this point, but no one else was saying anything. Maybe I should have put it in a press release.

"We're doing the hair scene?" Amy's face screwed up in thought, probably wondering how she could make Jo chopping off all her hair more Amy-centric.

"I hadn't planned on it." Mom's eyes were still wider than normal. "Jo?"

"Yeah?"

"Did you keep the hair?"

"What?"

"That they cut off," she explained, like that was the confusing part.

"Ooh, that would be dramatic." Amy rubbed her hands together. "We could glue it to a comb, and then in the middle of the scene, *snip*" — her fingers made a cutting motion — "it all falls down. The audience gasps!" She made a sound like a garbage disposal.

"I didn't keep the hair."

Amy shook her head, like this was yet another example of my constant failure to anticipate her theatrical genius. "What were you thinking?"

"I didn't do it for the show." It hadn't occurred to me that my family would assume my haircut was an homage to *Little*

Women Live! Which was probably foolish, but I had other things on my mind.

My sister settled back into her chair, studying me. "So, what, you wanted to be less attractive?"

"I like short hair. I've always wanted to try it." I shrugged. "Laurie likes it."

"No he doesn't!"

"He said so himself." What he'd actually said (after a double take), when I ran into him coming out of the Burrito Express next to the cheapo haircut place: *Whoa, JoJo! You make a hot dude!*

"These things happen in the life of a woman," Mom told Amy. She was getting on top of the narrative — figuring out an uplifting spin. "At some point we all experience the urge to do something radical to our hair. Especially after a breakup. You should have seen my bangs the summer before college!"

We were seconds away from busting out old photo albums. "I cut my hair for a reason."

Mom nodded, a sympathetic half smile curving her lips. "I understand, Jo. It was a symbolic gesture."

"No, it was a practical decision." I jerked my chin at Amy. "Like she said."

Amy laughed. "I never told you to do that to yourself. Do I *look* like someone with zero taste?"

Forcing myself not to get sucked into another round of Amy 'n' Jo Go to the Mats, I turned to our mother. "I sold it."

"Oh, Jo. You didn't have to do that." Mom's eyes welled up. "I told you, we're going to figure it out."

I shook my head, annoyed I couldn't pause to enjoy the swing of my newly shorn hair. The style was asymmetrical, a pixie cut on one side and closer to a bob on the other. I'd thought it was cool and even kind of cute until these two reacted like I was in a full-body cast with a face full of scabs. "*I needed the money.*"

"Am I the only one in this family who isn't a criminal?" Amy asked the ceiling, slapping the table for emphasis.

"I used it for a ticket. To New York." It turned out Amy was right: you could sell long hair that had never been chemically treated for hundreds of dollars — enough for a one-way trip on an airline I was pretty sure had been in business longer than a week. "Just like in the book."

I tacked on the last part in case that made it easier for them to swallow.

Mom put a hand to her throat. "I don't understand."

"Book Jo sold her hair to buy a ticket for Marmee, not herself!" Amy stabbed a finger at me, like we were in a courtroom and she'd just caught me in a lie.

"I guess I'm not exactly like her, then, am I?"

"That's for sure." I could see the calculation in my sister's eyes: *Was that enough of an insult?* It took her a couple of blinks to decide. "Because you're totally selfish."

"I'm allowed to think about myself. Someone has to."

Mom placed a hand on Amy's arm, silently telling her to zip it. "What's going on, Jo?" *You can tell me anything,* her tone said. *I won't get mad.* It would have been perfect if I'd been a three-year-old who'd broken her toy and then tried to hide it.

I squared my shoulders. "If Meg can leave, so can I."

"We can talk about next summer, possibly, but there's no way we can have both of you gone at the same time." Mom made a helpless gesture with her hand, like it was outside the realm of possibility. Not even worth discussing.

"We have more cousins." Apparently I needed to spell it out. "Jasper said he'd do it."

"*Jasper?*" If my sister's jaw dropped any lower, it would hit the table.

"Why not? He was a great Beth."

She looked from me to our mother. "Is this a trick question? Because my leg warmers could play Beth."

"I think it would be interesting," I countered. "A different angle on all the times Jo wishes she were a boy."

"Let's set all that aside for a moment." Mom made a sweeping motion with one arm. "You can't go to New York by yourself."

"I won't be alone. I'm going to stay with Andrea and Hudson."

"They invited you to visit? Now—with the summer season about to start?"

I couldn't tell who she felt more let down by, Andrea or me. It might have softened the blow to know the answer wasn't quite that clear-cut. If you added up all the times Andrea had said things like, *If there's ever anything I can do* or *Look me up when you're in the city,* the invitation was strongly implied. But I had a feeling that if I explained that to Mom, she would insist on calling Andrea. "She needs an assistant."

"What about Mr. Underfed?" Amy asked.

"Hudson doesn't want to work for his mom. He hasn't for a

long time." I didn't explicitly draw the parallel between his situation and mine, but Mom's flinch suggested it came through loud and clear. Which wasn't what I was trying to achieve. *It's not about you, Mom.* Somehow, I didn't think shouting that at her would help.

"It'll be a good experience," I said instead. "A great opportunity for . . . making connections. Networking."

Amy snorted. "Pretentious, party of one."

"I just want to go somewhere, see new things. Why is that so wrong?"

"There's more to life than *wanting.*" Mom shook her head sadly. "We have responsibilities to other people."

That was the difference between my mother and Andrea in a nutshell. Mom was stuck in *Little Women* mode, where desire was a thing to be shoved aside in favor of doing your duty—as defined by someone else. *Do this; don't do that.* Andrea understood that sometimes you had to be bold. Decide for yourself how to live.

I felt the ice inside me creeping from my heart up to my head. It helped shut out the devastated expression on Mom's face, and the guilt trying to sink its claws into me. Standing up for myself was not the same as being a jerk.

"I bought the ticket with my own money. I didn't steal from anyone."

"And yet you still managed to totally suck," Amy retorted.

"But Jo." Mom fixed me with a pleading look. "You're *Jo.*"

"No, I'm not. Not really."

"Been saying that for years," my sister huffed.

"It's just so sudden. Where did all of this come from?"

I stared at my mother. Had my lips been moving with no sound coming out? *This* was why I had to leave. They were never going to listen to me otherwise.

Amy threw herself on our mother, wrapping both arms around her shoulders. "Don't worry, Marmee. I'll never abandon you. I'll play all the parts if I have to."

Mom patted Amy's shoulder, but her smile was distracted. "You and Beth. Or rather . . . Liliana." The pause suggested I wasn't the only one who'd forgotten New Beth's real name.

Amy sat back. "I wouldn't count on *her.* You know how Beths are. Always one foot out the door."

Jo went prepared to bow down and adore
the mighty ones whom she had worshipped
with youthful enthusiasm afar off.

—Little Women

CHAPTER
THIRTY-FIVE

It's strange how quickly your entire life can change, once you make up your mind to do it. Things I thought were solid walls turned out to be more like shower curtains. If you pushed, they gave way.

And then, in a matter of days that feel more like minutes, you find yourself on a bus, and then a plane, and then wandering around the airport trying to follow the signs without looking like a stupid tourist when someone with a patch on their shirt that sort of looks official asks if you need a ride and you decide *okay, maybe this is how it's done,* and then they tell you "That'll be sixty dollars," which is way more than Google said it would cost to get to Williamsburg and puts a serious dent in your limited cash. It also turned out to be a normal car, not a yellow taxi like in the movies, but at least the driver was chatty and had pictures of his kids taped to the dashboard, which I felt lowered the odds of my corpse getting tossed into a river.

When we stopped in front of a nondescript building with a rusted fence and prominently placed dumpster, I reconsidered the odds of murder. It was a gray day, and every surface was covered in either asphalt, cement, or graffiti. It looked like the zombie apocalypse had rolled through and kept right on going, in search of someplace more hospitable.

The driver bent to peer through the car window. "This is one of those warehouse conversions, right? Must be nice."

I squinted at the building again, wondering what he was seeing that I wasn't. It looked like an old factory. The kind you'd see in a PBS documentary about oppressed workers going on strike — or dying in a fire due to unsafe conditions. Instead of old-time piano, the soundtrack was jackhammers and horns.

I couldn't sit in this stranger's car all day, so it was time to keep moving forward. Into the noise and grime. Grabbing my backpack with one hand, I reached for the door handle with the other. "Thanks for the ride."

The driver nodded, barely waiting until I'd closed the door to peel away from the curb.

My confidence felt like water I was holding in cupped hands, ready to trickle between my fingers and be lost forever. I glanced at the building in front of me, double-checking the address. I'd pictured Hudson living in a towering apartment complex with a shiny lobby. It definitely hadn't smelled this bad in my imaginary New York either. Exhaust fumes, rotting produce, a hint of grease — why had Hudson complained so much about the stench from a few big cats, if this was what he breathed in normally?

I checked my phone, reading his most recent text for the twentieth time. Hudson had said he was "just chillin'," which meant he was somewhere inside this one-fog-machine-short-of-a-horror-movie building. The prospect of seeing a familiar face gave me the strength to approach the cavelike doorway. There was a panel on the wall with names and apartment numbers. My thumb hovered over the silver button next to Andrea's. Was I ready? It was stupid to feel anxious about ringing a doorbell when I'd flown halfway across the country to get here. And yet my heart pounded harder than when the stylist had paused with the scissors around my ponytail to ask if I was sure, or the moment before I'd pressed *buy now* on my ticket to get here.

Andrea had always been intimidating. This was just my brain gearing up for another encounter. Holding my breath, I pressed the buzzer. Long seconds passed before there was an electronic click.

"Yes?"

The single word had a slightly robotic buzz, but I recognized the clipped inflection. "Andrea? It's Jo."

"Jo?"

"Jo Porter." I cleared my throat. "The Jo March one."

After another long pause, a buzzing sound emanated from the door. I grabbed for it a second too late. My face was hot as I pressed the intercom again. Before I could explain, the buzzing started again. (Had that been a judgmental silence?) I lunged for the door like it was a loose football. This time I managed to enter the building. Slow clap for the genius in the saggy leggings.

The lobby wasn't much more welcoming than the outside, though the bicycle leaning against the wall suggested human occupation. I assumed the 4D in their address meant Andrea and Hudson lived on the fourth floor. A metal railing that had once been blue (judging by the chipped remains of paint) lined the wide wooden stairs. When I reached the fourth floor, there were two doors painted the same blue as the railing. Both were completely blank. I was getting ready to eenie-meenie it when I spotted a familiar tote hanging from a hook outside the nearer door. The rumpled white bag was stamped with the word *GAGOSIAN* in all-caps black. I'd never worked up the nerve to ask *What's a Gagosian?*, but I did know one thing: the bag was Andrea's.

I knocked, then took a step back. Silence. Had I walked up the stairs too fast? Maybe I hadn't made enough noise. It felt like even my most basic life skills were a little iffy. I was debating whether to try again when I finally heard footsteps approaching from the other side.

The door opened. Andrea peered at me from the threshold, a slight tilt of the eyebrows the only clue to her thoughts. "This is a surprise," she said at last, stepping to one side.

I slipped past her before she could change her mind, then toed off my shoes and set them next to the rack inside the door. Had Hudson not told her I was coming? That was . . . awkward.

"What brings you to Brooklyn?" We were still standing in the dim hallway, as if Andrea thought I'd dropped by to say hello and wouldn't be staying long.

"Um." It didn't feel like the right moment to vomit out my whole plan: *I was thinking you could hire me to take over your son's job, since he hates working for you!* "You said I'd like it, so." I shrugged like that tied it all up with a bow. *Ta-da!*

"Hmmm." Andrea exhaled through her nose. "I'm afraid I'm in the middle of something."

"Sorry. You don't have to—" I broke off, not sure how to finish. *You don't have to entertain me? You don't have to let me stay?* Much as I would have liked to play it cool, I couldn't actually leave. I had nowhere to go. Continuing my streak of half-baked statements, I tipped my chin toward the rest of the apartment. "Is Hudson, ah?"

"I'll call him." Andrea didn't tell me to follow her, but she didn't tell me not to either, so I trailed her to the living room, a high-ceilinged space with windows along one wall and brick lining the other. This was more like my fantasy version of city life: colorful rugs, a leather sofa the same caramel shade as Andrea's favorite boots, mildly disturbing art. She gestured at a low-slung chair made of cowhide stretched over a metal frame. "Have a seat."

"Thanks."

A set of French doors opened onto another room. I caught a glimpse of a desk and bookshelves as Andrea disappeared inside what must be her office. She kicked one of the doors with her foot so that it swung most of the way closed. That meant I only heard two-thirds of her side of the conversation with Hudson. Some highlights:

"Obviously it wasn't a joke, because she's here."

"What do you think I mean? In our apartment." Pause. "Do I sound like I'm kidding?"

"I don't care where you are—you need to come home and fix this."

"I don't have time for this, Hudson."

"I suggest you hurry."

At the sound of returning footsteps, I pretended to be totally absorbed in reading something on my phone. I doubted Andrea was fooled. Then again, part of me wondered if she'd wanted me to hear. In case I hadn't picked up on the very subtle undertones of *you're not welcome.*

Stupidly, I'd expected her to be *more* interested in me now that I'd taken this huge step, not less. Hadn't Andrea told me to be bold? Here I was, striking out on my own, but she didn't seem impressed. I'd gone from *you remind me of myself* to a Jo-size inconvenience.

"He'll be here soon." As Andrea stepped back into the living room, her eyes locked on my backpack. "Where are you staying?"

"Oh. Well. I guess—I don't know." Nervous sweat dampened my armpits.

She held up a hand. "You can sort it out with Hudson."

"I like adventures, and I'm going to find some."

– Little Women

CHAPTER THIRTY-SIX

Two hours later, I heard a key in the lock. Hudson didn't exactly come running to find me; there was a stop in the kitchen first. The sound of the refrigerator door was followed by the click and hiss of a beverage being opened.

I turned off my phone as Hudson walked into the room. I'd texted Mom to let her know I was safe, then spent the rest of the time trying to distract myself with mindless games. Now the battery was almost dead, and I wasn't sure where to plug in my charger, or if I was even allowed to use their electricity.

"Hey." I stood, wishing I'd brushed my hair or splashed some water on my face. My alarm had gone off at four thirty in the morning. If I looked half as bad as I felt, this was not the glamorous reunion of my dreams.

To my relief, Hudson set down his soda to give me a hug.

At least one of us smelled good. I held on a little longer than normal. It had been a difficult day.

"I can't believe you're here." His smile crumpled around the edges, sending a mixed message: *I'm happy to see you* with a twist of *What are you doing here?*

"I said I was coming."

"Yeah, but I didn't think you were serious."

"That would be a really complicated joke." Complete with flight numbers and arrival times.

He shrugged this off. "We're always messing with each other."

I studied his face. Had he been skimming my messages while doing something else? Silly me, assuming something so important would at least capture Hudson's attention long enough to *read all the words.* "You really didn't know?"

He shook his head. My expression must have given some hint of the distress signal blaring in my brain, because Hudson draped an arm across my shoulders, pulling me to his side. "Don't worry about it. We'll figure it out."

As Andrea emerged from her office, Hudson released me, lowering his arm and stepping away.

"So glad you could join us," his mother said, not looking at me.

"I was all the way uptown."

"Doing what?"

"A friend was having a party."

"How nice for you." Her gaze flicked to me. "Maybe you can take Jo back with you."

Hudson laughed. "I'm not getting back on the train."

"Then you'll have to find some other way to entertain your guest."

Pretty sure the *guest* part was ironic.

"I don't mind. About the party." Especially since I wasn't convinced Andrea would let me in again if I left.

"You look pretty tired."

I chose to interpret Hudson's remark as sympathy, as opposed to dunking on my appearance. Plus, it was true. I was ready to fall over. The prospect of going to a party with a bunch of strangers made me want to crawl under a table and hide.

His phone chimed. He sent a quick reply before returning his attention to me. "You can sleep in the office. There's a pull-out bed."

"No, she can't." Andrea crossed her arms, giving Hudson a look my brain was too foggy to interpret.

"The couch is fine," I said quickly. Unless they didn't want me to sleep on their leather sofa, which did look pretty fancy. "Or the floor."

Jo had engaged to be as lively and amiable
as an absent mind, an aching head, and
a very decided disapproval of everybody
and everything would allow.

—Little Women

CHAPTER THIRTY-SEVEN

A ndrea left early the next morning, a yoga mat tucked under one arm. I cracked an eyelid as she crossed the living room at normal speed, making no effort to be quiet. The light through the bank of uncurtained windows glowed gray. It felt like I'd drifted off minutes ago, after lying awake for hours listening to unfamiliar noises and questioning my choices. Judging by the crick in my neck, I would have been better off on the floor than this stiff, too-short couch.

My stomach grumbled, the sound drowned out by the rattling whirr of a coffee grinder. I didn't want Andrea to realize I was awake. She'd sent a pretty clear message yesterday that having an extra body in her space wasn't her idea of a good time. My goal now was to make myself as unobtrusive as possible.

Like the most undemanding, self-sufficient future summer research assistant anyone could want.

When the door closed behind her, I rubbed my eyes. The apartment was silent. Hudson and I were alone, with no adult supervision, but all I could think about was sneaking into the kitchen to look for food. This wasn't exactly a sitting-down-for-family-dinner household, so there'd been no meal the night before — unless you counted the granola bar from my backpack I'd scarfed under cover of darkness.

Their small refrigerator would have been a bonanza if I'd been on a condiments-only diet. No wonder Hudson and Andrea were so thin. After easing the door closed, I settled on an iffy banana from the bowl on the counter, then buried the peel under a layer of trash.

By the time Hudson dragged himself out of bed, I was almost ready to brave the city on my own. He blinked sleepily at me, scratching his stomach with one hand.

"You want some breakfast?"

In my heart I pulled a Laurie, kissing my fingers and pointing them at the sky. My face played it cool. "I would kill for breakfast."

Mom always said I acted like the world was ending when my stomach was empty. Maybe everything would look brighter after a meal.

My relief at knowing people in New York ate solid food was short-lived. There was no secret pantry full of cereal boxes or even a loaf of bread. We were going out to eat. By that point,

I was almost too hungry to care. How expensive could breakfast be?

Answer: very, especially when the first three places we tried had an hour wait, and Hudson didn't want bagels because the "good deli" was too far away. We wound up at a tiny restaurant with maybe seven tables in all, which was probably why they had to charge twenty dollars for a bowl of oatmeal. It came with a bunch of weird toppings, but still. *Oatmeal*.

I ordered a sandwich. It was only a couple dollars more, and at least sounded like a meal. When the waiter (who must have been raking in the tips to pay for that many tattoos) had taken our menus and departed, Hudson regarded me over the rim of his coffee cup.

"You look different."

My fingers skimmed the back of my neck. "I cut off all my hair." It would have been a great moment for him to tell me he liked the new style.

He set down his coffee. "That's not it." A frown pinched the space between his brows as he flicked a glance at my clothes. "Maybe it's seeing you here. Out of context."

I had been dimly aware that my "look" didn't match the surroundings. Even *I* knew running shoes weren't a fashion statement, but I'd figured there would be a lot of walking — and I considered this pair lucky, since I'd worn them last year when I placed at regionals. They *usually* gave me a boost of confidence.

"Same old me." Aside from the missing hair. And the fact that I'd torpedoed my home life.

"I suppose you want to see the Statue of Liberty." Hudson flipped his knife over, sighing like he was already fried from our exhausting slate of tourist activities.

"I hadn't thought about it."

"Isn't that why you're here?"

I got the feeling there was a question behind the question, like *Please tell me you didn't fly here because you want to get married at seventeen and have my babies.* "I came for a job."

"You have a job?" He sat up a little straighter, like I'd suddenly become more interesting. I got a flash of the way he used to act toward me, when he was the outsider and I knew everything.

The waiter deposited a cutting board bearing the world's smallest sandwich in front of me. Hopefully it was more filling than it looked. "You know how you wanted to do that internship?"

"Uh-huh." He was scattering seeds over his bowl and didn't look up.

"I thought maybe *I* could help your mom."

Hudson went still. "You want to take my job?"

"Then you'd be free to do whatever you want." Logic that had seemed so simple when I was alone in my room landed like a pile of mush in this dank and crowded restaurant. Not unlike Hudson's breakfast.

"Yeah, no." He laughed as he reached for his coffee. "That's not going to work." Shaking his head, he took a bite of his oatmeal. "Did you really think you could just show up here and she would give you a job?"

You weren't there when it was just the two of us, I wanted to tell him. *We had a connection — an understanding.*

"Just for the summer." I took a long sip of water. It tasted funny, but at least it was free. "I'm pretty well qualified, if you think about it — for what she's working on now."

"But there's no way she'd pay you enough to live on. Rent is insane around here. Why do you think I haven't moved out?"

It definitely wasn't because of the home cooking. I shrugged, not wanting to admit I hadn't thought that part through. I'd envisioned myself staying with Andrea and Hudson at first — or maybe longer. Barring that, I'd imagined something like . . . a boardinghouse. The type of place Jo March stays during her time in New York. If our table had been bigger, I would have banged my head against it.

"I did not expect you to pull something like this." He sat back, totally relaxed as he scratched the underside of his chin. But then, there was nothing at stake for him. "You're kind of wild, aren't you? On the inside."

Subtext: *Even though you look super basic.* I forced the corners of my mouth to curve. "That's me."

ᘒ

Hudson showed me more of the neighborhood after we finished. Restaurant, restaurant, bar, restaurant, clothing store that looked like it sold used workwear only everything cost hundreds of dollars, another restaurant, and (for variety) one extremely sad playground. The exact same swings had probably been there when Hudson was a kid. Hopefully Andrea had kept him up-to-date on tetanus shots.

I tried to act interested, like I might one day need to know the best place for pho in this three-block radius or where they made a killer flat white. It was hard to do when my mind kept spinning from one obstacle to the next. Then there was the fact that slowly walking from one food place to the next while dodging crowds of people wouldn't have been my choice of activity even if I'd had money to blow on things like getting a fancier coffee ten minutes after paying for a normal one at a restaurant.

When Hudson suggested we go back to his place, I didn't argue. The rest of the day was spent playing video games and watching Netflix, which I could have done at home. Except that if this had been my house, I would have felt free to use the bathroom whenever I wanted or get a glass of water before my throat got scratchy with thirst.

Was this what having adventures felt like — ignoring basic physical needs?

"We'll go out later," Hudson told me, between episodes of a series he was already halfway through that he swore I'd be able to follow. Andrea must have been working, because she'd been in her office since we got back. Considering how many times he'd complained about his workload, I was surprised she didn't ask him to help. Maybe it was because I was there — though, really, who was more qualified than me to assist with a story about my family? I was like a walking fact-checker.

I wasn't sure how many hours had passed when Hudson closed his laptop and shifted toward me, placing a hand on my thigh. Was he tired of this show? Ready for a snack? It wasn't until he leaned over and kissed me that I caught on to his mood. *No snack,* I thought sadly, which only added to the lag between him kissing me and me kissing him back.

He was already pulling away when Andrea walked in. It should have been embarrassing to get busted by a parent, but I mostly felt relieved, even when she told Hudson she needed to speak with him. Sighing, he followed her out of the room.

Whatever his mom was saying to him — and I suspected it involved me — was less awkward than talking about how bad that kiss had been. *Fffft:* nothing. Like a match that doesn't strike. The most memorable part was trying to figure out which one of us had eaten something pickled for brunch. I definitely didn't remember that flavor from my sandwich.

Would we have tried again, if Andrea hadn't walked in? I got the feeling Hudson had kissed me the same way he'd picked up his gaming controller, more out of boredom than because he suddenly found me irresistible.

What am I doing here?

The question was like a scrap of litter blowing past the car window. I grabbed at it, straining to read the message. Because suddenly I knew I would have kissed Hudson again, and told myself it was what I wanted, when what I really craved was someone to be nice to me and make me feel like I belonged. How pathetic was that?

It was a weird sensation, like I was floating outside my life. Had I ever really been into Hudson, or was it always more about the *idea* of him? Or wanting *him* to like *me* and mistaking that for a crush? Sitting in this unfamiliar room, in this strange city, I heard David's voice say: *You barely know him.*

And even though Hudson wasn't the only reason I'd gotten on a plane, it was like pulling a Jenga block out of the tower and setting the whole thing wobbling. Had any of it been real? The attraction to him, the sense of connection with his mom, the idea that I could reinvent myself in their city with a bigger and more exciting life?

Hudson came back into the room. "I guess we're going out." He was annoyed. I read it in his voice, the way his mouth turned down at the corners, his refusal to meet my eyes. Andrea must have told him to take me somewhere, and I doubted it was because she cared about showing me the sights. Hudson was pissed because he had to get up and do something, and it was all my fault.

I suspected his mood had also been soured by the kiss. Either he blamed me for not being more fun, or he thought I'd rejected him and now his ego was bruised.

"Do you want to change?" It was obvious that what he really meant was *You should wear a better outfit.*

If he hadn't asked, I probably would have put on less sloppy clothes, but there was no way I was changing now. Which just proved that Hudson didn't know me very well either.

"I'm homely and awkward and odd and old, and you'd be ashamed of me, and we should quarrel."

-Little Women

CHAPTER
THIRTY-EIGHT

To me, New York was one big city. When Hudson talked about this neighborhood or that borough, it washed over me like noise. Especially now that my brain had gone numb around the edges.

We were going to visit some of his friends. My faint hope of spotting a few landmarks along the way vanished as we descended into the subway. That was a new experience, at least, even if it felt like being trapped inside my phone with the running playlist going.

The buildings were taller when we emerged, with wider streets and traffic whizzing past. I would have paused to take it all in, but Hudson wasn't giving off *let me be your tour guide* vibes, so I didn't stop to gawk. There were too many people to stand still anyway. I had no idea what I was hurrying past, but if you threw in a few giant floating cartoon characters and a marching band, it could totally have been the backdrop for the Thanksgiving Day parade, so that was cool.

Hudson's friend lived in a building with a uniformed doorman: another entry on my very short list of city experiences. Inside the apartment, the scene was more familiar. Yes, the furniture was flatter, and the light fixtures looked like they could double as weapons, but the teenagers draped across the low white sofas were hipper versions of what I would have seen at home. It wasn't quite a party, but it had the potential to go in that direction if another ten or twenty people showed up. And if someone turned up the music.

There were a few *hey*s and a couple of nods, but the mood (like the background music) was extremely low-key. Nobody yelled or bumped any part of their body against anyone else. Meg would have fit right in.

I waited for Hudson to explain the strange girl he'd shown up with, but no one seemed particularly curious. Maybe that would have required too much energy. We drifted toward the living room, across the shaggy white area rugs. I sat down at one end of a long sectional occupied by a trio of guys, leaving a space for Hudson.

Instead of sitting, he smiled at someone in the next room before taking off in that direction. It would have been rude to get up again, on top of which I didn't exactly get the feeling Hudson wanted me to follow. He probably would have looked at me if I was supposed to tag along. Or used his words.

"I'm Jo," I told the other occupants of the couch. They

looked up from the phone they were staring at long enough to introduce themselves as Jeremy, Paolo, and Lachlan.

"Are you a cousin or something?" asked the one with owlish round glasses. I thought he was Lachlan but wouldn't have sworn to it.

"I was going to say exchange student." This was from Probably Paolo, the roundest member of the trio.

The third boy rolled his eyes. "From where? She doesn't have an accent."

It wasn't surprising none of them guessed "girlfriend," since I wouldn't have been ditched sixty seconds after walking through the door if that were true. I wasn't sure how to explain myself without sounding like a lab rat. *I'm one of Andrea's subjects.* Maybe if she were a painter, that would be glamorous, but it wasn't like I'd been sitting for a portrait. Hudson was the one who'd taken all the pictures of me—though not since my arrival in New York.

"We met when he was on assignment," I finally said. "With his—Andrea."

That got their attention.

"You know Andrea?" Paolo (probably) asked.

"Yeah. She was doing a story about us—my family."

"Ohhh." Lachlan exchanged a look with the other two. "With the animals or . . . ?"

"The other one." I waited for one of them to say the word *Little* or *Women.*

Jeremy (most likely) coughed into his hand. "Hudson said he had a real good time out there." Lachlan kicked him.

"So Andrea's cool." Paolo adjusted the stubby ponytail that was almost as underdeveloped as his facial scruff. "She knows a lot of writers."

"Paolo thinks he's the next N. K. Jemisin," Jeremy explained, cementing my impression of him as the douchiest member of the group.

"What kind of stuff do you write?" I asked Paolo, feeling I would be on fairly solid ground talking about author life. Or at least the life of one particular author from a long time ago.

"I'm still gathering material." Paolo circled both arms. It looked like he was doggy-paddling on dry land. "Getting in touch with my muse."

Lachlan nodded agreement. "Same. I don't want to be derivative. I have to find my own voice."

"You're a writer too?"

"*Music.*" He sounded peeved I hadn't been able to tell by looking at him.

Probably I should have guessed Hudson's friends would be artsy types. Maybe one of these guys was Hudson's gallery connection. "Like — a singer?" I asked politely.

"I don't just stand in front of a microphone," Lachlan scoffed, like I'd suggested he was slinging fries at McDonald's. "I want to be a *producer.*"

"You don't have the hair to be a front man." Jeremy swept his bangs back from his forehead with one hand, apparently mocking his friend's hairline.

"We can't all work in banking like our daddy," Lachlan

countered. I tried to imagine Jeremy as one of the friendly tell-
ers at our credit union, though I had a dim sense they meant
something else by "banking."

Jeremy popped his collar. "At least one of us will have a
steady paycheck."

"Great," said Paolo. "You can pay for Hudson's share of
the gas. Since he bailed on us," he added, seeing my look of
confusion.

"Bailed on what?" I asked.

"Our road trip." Lachlan seemed surprised I didn't know
about an event of such global significance.

Paolo shook his head. "I still can't believe Andrea said no.
It's not like she was sitting at home when she was Hudson's age."

"Yeah, and she has the T-shirts to prove it." Lachlan leaned
toward me. "Andrea saw everyone who was anyone in concert."

"If my mom gave me her old clothes, I'd be wearing a cash-
mere twin set right now," Paolo reported sadly.

It took me a few seconds to catch up. "All those shirts
Hudson wears are his mother's?" No wonder he'd kept that
detail to himself. Sharing a closet with his mommy kind of
killed the cool factor.

"That's what this summer is about," Lachlan told me.
"Building our own collection of shirts."

Paolo seemed to realize this might not sound all that
impressive. "Not in the literal sense. It's about more than the
souvenirs."

"No, obviously. We're going for the music." Lachlan sketched a zigzagging line across the coffee table with one hand. "We have the whole route planned. From festival to festival, all over the country. It's a once-in-a-lifetime trip."

"Although you probably get a lot of concerts here," I pointed out. "Like, pretty much every band ever plays New York."

"It's not the same," Paolo assured me. "This is about the freedom of the open road. Little towns and diners with pie."

"Girls in bikini tops and cutoffs." That was Jeremy's unsurprising contribution.

A curl of embarrassment wormed its way from my stomach to my throat. Geographically, it was the reverse of what I'd told my family about needing to leave home, and yet the message was uncomfortably similar. Had I sounded like this much of a tool? I fought the urge to slap myself.

"Sucks to be Hudson." Jeremy glanced at his phone.

"I still think he'll talk her into it." Paolo looked up as Hudson approached, beer in hand. (*I'm fine, thanks for asking!*) "Hey, man. Any progress?"

"Not a good time to ask." His eyes slid to me.

I frowned at him. "I thought you wanted to do an internship. At a gallery."

"Eventually, yeah." He huffed a little, like he was being attacked. "I think I'm allowed to take a vacation. I just graduated."

That seemed to be the group mantra: *I'm totally passionate about my art/music/writing, but not quite yet.* From what I'd heard about Hudson's virtual "academy," which catered to kids whose parents were too important to stay in one place, it hadn't exactly been four years of hard labor. One of his assignments had been a photo essay on regional variations in Starbucks franchises, for a class on "urban planning." Poor Hudson, slumming with the norms.

"Just repeating what you told me." I added several spoonfuls of fake sweetness to my voice.

His three amigos glanced between us, clearly picking up on the tension.

"Jo's not really about the creative life." Hudson's tone was jokey, like we were all having a good time, but I could tell he was in a snit. He looked down at my feet—or, rather, my shoes. "She really likes running, though. In case you couldn't tell." His lip curled.

After a prickly silence, Jeremy said, "Dude." Even he was uncomfortable with that level of rudeness.

If Hudson were Amy, we could have settled this with a fist-fight. Since that wasn't an option, I stood up, dorky shoes and all. "I'm going to go pretend to use the bathroom."

"Down that hall." Paolo pointed. "Second door on the right."

"Thanks." I had no idea whether he lived here or was just being helpful.

I did some deep breathing in front of the bathroom mirror. At least I didn't look like I was about to lose it. That was one benefit to the slow-motion disaster that had been unfolding since I stepped off the plane: it wasn't all hitting me now, in this stranger's apartment. Very soon decisions would have to be made, but I wanted to be alone for that, so I kept my brain from straying any farther ahead than the next few minutes. As

I washed my hands, I studied the soap dispenser. It was heavy and marble, but the contents smelled like the generic white soap we used at home. Different lives, same suds.

A girl was waiting in the hall when I emerged, one of the few in this gang of lost boys. She had a pierced lip and a mustard-colored cardigan that looked like she'd knitted it herself.

"Avoid the hand towel," I told her, wiping the wetness I hadn't managed to shake off on the front of my jeans. I'd found it on the floor, a little too close to the toilet for comfort with this many teenage guys around.

She looked me in the eyes, and at least there was one person at this party who didn't default to a sneer. "Thanks."

I wandered down the hall, pretending to study the framed photographs. Laughter rose from the other end of the apartment, where all the people I didn't know had congregated. It reminded me of the party I'd taken Hudson to back home, when he'd gotten plastered while I hid in the yard. Except that I hadn't been alone that time, because David had been there.

The thought of David stopped me cold. I would have given a kidney to have him here with me now. Or however many organs I could spare and still be alive. I knew he would be *right* here, not wandering off in search of someone better. And we would make each other laugh, and he would be himself, not rude show-offy Party David.

What am I doing here? I asked myself again, before replacing it with a better question. *Why don't you leave?*

Following the sound of Hudson's voice, I approached the kitchen, planning to tell him I was taking off. The words were too low to make out, but his tone was teasing and playful, the way he'd been with me when we first met.

"Didn't you come with someone?" asked a second voice.

"Not like that. Please." Hudson snorted as if the girl had said something absurd. "She followed me here."

I stopped moving.

"Off the street?" She sounded skeptical.

"No, it's way worse than that. I told you how Andrea dragged me out to that shithole town in the middle of nowhere." There was a pause, the glug of liquid in a bottle. "It was Freak Show Central. And then this girl showed up at our apartment."

"She just randomly appeared — the one with the cool haircut?"

Freaking finally.

Hudson sighed. "We hooked up one time. There's literally nothing else to do out there."

If I hadn't been so busy dying on the inside, I would have stuck my head through the doorway and said, *Correction! We did not "hook up" in the technical sense! He's exaggerating!*

"Sucks to be you," she said.

"You have no idea. It was like being in a time warp."

Pretty much the whole point, asshole! Imagining Hudson's pouty expression made me want to puke. Or slap him. One of those.

"You want to *zhuvuh wa jubuluh*?" The second half of the question was unintelligible, probably because Hudson was whispering in her ear.

"Mmmm, no thanks. Sounds like your life is messy enough."

The girl with the lip ring stepped into the hall. I waited for her to alert Hudson to my presence. Maybe she'd think I really was a stalker.

"What a dick," she said, not whispering but also not trying to make a scene.

I nodded. My gaze strayed to the front door.

"You okay to get home?" she asked.

The word *home* lodged in my chest. The distance between here and there felt infinite, like I was shipwrecked on a speck of rock in the middle of the ocean, a million miles from everything and everyone I knew.

"Yeah."

Even though it was going to take a lot more than a map to get there.

"So we are to countenance things and people
which we detest, merely because we are
not belles and millionaires, are we?"

—*Little Women*

CHAPTER
THIRTY-NINE

I probably could have figured out the subway, but I
didn't want to go back underground. It wasn't that late, the
weather was nice, and even though the sun had set, there were
lights everywhere: on cars and buses, inside restaurants and
shops, shining down from streetlights and signs. After calling
up a map on my phone, I set off on foot, glad I was wearing
comfortable shoes. (*Suck it, Hudson.*)

It felt good to move at my own pace. I was happy to be outside, even if it didn't smell too fresh. City energy was different
from the rush of trees and wind and a big sky overhead, but I
could still feel it, buzzing up through the concrete.

When my phone rang, I was surprised Hudson had noticed
I was gone so soon. I was ready to send the call to voicemail
when I realized it wasn't his number.

"What is it?" I asked. "Is everything okay?"

"It's Beth," Amy choked out. Her breath hitched like she was mid-sob. "She's really sick. I don't think she's going to make it."

There were so many strange things happening at once. Hearing my sister's voice while walking down a busy street in the middle of New York. Imagining vibrant, healthy Beth dangerously ill. Amy caring that her nemesis was unwell. "Seriously?"

After several beats of silence, she replied in a normal voice, "If I say yes, are you coming home?"

"Is that why you're calling?"

"Maybe."

I detoured around a hot dog cart. "So Beth isn't sick?"

"Had you going for a second, didn't I?"

"Yes." I expected Amy to either hang up, having gotten what she wanted, or brag about her dramatic skillz, but she was silent for a long minute.

"Where are you right now?"

"No idea."

"Are you in a hostage situation? Say something like 'baseball' if you need help."

"And then what, you'll send in a team of commandos to rescue me?"

"If you can still be rude, I guess you're fine. Which, by the way, the commandos would have been hot, so your loss." The creak of a cabinet told me she was in the kitchen. "Way hotter than what's-his-nuts. Your little shrimp."

I didn't remind her of Hudson's name, which of course she knew. "He's not mine."

"Trouble in paradise?"

"You could say that." I was glad she couldn't see my face.

"Everything okay?"

"Define *okay*. Besides 'not getting abducted.'"

"Does this mean you're coming home?"

"I thought you'd be glad to get rid of me."

Packaging crinkled in the background; I pictured her digging a hand into the yellow bag of plain potato chips, and my mouth filled with the phantom taste of salt and grease. "It's not as awesome as I thought it would be. The only-child thing." Loud crunching accompanied this revelation.

"Things are different here, too. Not what I expected."

"I thought you sounded weird." More rustling. "Weird*er*."

By Amy standards, that was practically a valentine. "Have you talked to Meg?"

"She met some grad student. Sounds like he does all her work for her. But she's still pretty bored."

"That's good."

"Yeah. It would suck if she wasn't suffering a *little*."

I snorted, vaguely aware that if we'd been in the same room, I would never have given Amy the satisfaction of laughing at one of her jokes. "Meg's like a cat."

"Makes a mess and waits for someone else to clean it up?"

"Well, yeah, but that's not what I was talking about."

"Oh, the *napping*."

"I mean she always lands on her feet."

"Huh. I guess." She raised her voice to an earsplitting yell, not bothering to move the phone away from her mouth. "IN THE KITCHEN!"

"Is that Mom?"

"What's it to you?"

"Just—take care of her, okay?"

"Fix your own mistakes, loser." There was another voice in the background; I strained to make out the words, but Amy ended the call.

Which was probably just as well. I might have said something sappy otherwise.

"When people do one mean thing, they
are very likely to do another."

–*Little Women*

CHAPTER FORTY

A woman in a long skirt was leaving Andrea's building; I must have looked nonthreatening, because she held the door. One obstacle down.

I climbed the steps, first hoping the apartment would be empty, then realizing I had no way to get inside if Andrea wasn't home. When I got to their floor, I tried the doorknob first. Not because I'd gotten a *mi casa es su casa* feeling, but to avoid annoying Andrea any more than necessary. The knob turned. I slipped off my shoes and tiptoed inside.

The first thing I heard was my mother's voice.

After a heart-stopping moment when I thought she'd come to get me, I realized it was a recording. The flow of words paused and then resumed, repeating the same explanation. She was talking about the decision to start *Little Women Live!*

I'd never asked Mom about her thought process, partly because I didn't want to give her more of a platform for gushing about All Things Alcott. Even if I had, she wouldn't have answered me the way she was talking to Andrea. *You understand,* her recorded voice said. *I don't have to tell you.*

It sounded like she was speaking to a friend. Did Mom really think she and Andrea had that much in common, or was she just desperate for someone to listen?

I moved closer to the office, silent in my socks.

"Of course I tried my hand at writing," Mom's voice said. "I have a few unfinished novels tucked in a drawer."

I pictured my mother scribbling on loose sheets of paper with a leaky fountain pen for the full Jo March experience. Why didn't I know this about her?

"But that's not exactly a reliable source of income, is it?" If Andrea had responded to my mother's question, it wasn't audible in the recording. "At least not until you're established, and I had the girls to think about. It's such a balancing act."

"How so?" Andrea's voice prompted.

"I wanted them to see that it was possible to have dreams *and* a family. It hasn't always been easy, but I'm proud of that at least. That I found a way to put food on the table while doing work that meant something to me. It may not seem like much to them now, but when they're older, I hope they'll understand. I kept us together. They weren't spending fifty hours a week in day care while I shuffled papers around an office."

The recording cut off. A moment later, Andrea stepped out

of the office, empty glass in hand. If she was surprised to see me, her expression gave nothing away. I waited for her to ask why Hudson wasn't with me, but she seemed to expect me to speak first.

"I walked home."

A flash of interest lit her eyes, reminding me of before — when she'd been curious about me. The walk *had* been interesting, both for the scenery and the thoughts churning around my brain. Like the moment I'd realized I would be crossing a bridge. Who knew? And this was a real one, huge and functional, unlike other bridges I had known. I was imagining the conversation we could have about it when Andrea's expression shuttered.

"A long way," she said, moving toward the kitchen.

"Are you transcribing?" I lobbed the question at her back before she could disappear.

"Checking a few quotes for accuracy. Hudson did the transcription." She glanced at me over her shoulder. "Part of his job."

I was trying to decide which word she'd leaned on harder, *his* or *job*, when she went on.

"You do realize that if I wanted to replace him, I could snap my fingers and have a hundred qualified applicants tomorrow? People who have put in the time — trained researchers hungry for the work? Not just a teenager with mommy issues."

My mouth opened, but I couldn't find any words.

"Yes, Hudson told me." She shook her head. "I know you've

led a sheltered life, but out here in the real world, no one's going to give you special treatment because of who you happen to be named after."

My throat ached as I swallowed. "That's not why." *I thought we were the same kind of person. I thought you liked me.*

"I've never understood women who use a man to get what they want."

It took me a second to realize she was talking about Hudson; the word *man* had thrown me. "I wasn't *using* anyone."

Andrea switched the glass to her other hand, leaning against the wall. "No? You came all this way because of your sincere attachment to my son?" She made a show of looking around, like I was the one who'd ditched him.

I couldn't decide whether this was more of an insult to me or to Hudson. "I didn't say that. We were just . . . talking."

"Did you think that would skew the story to your advantage?"

Was she seriously suggesting I'd made out with Hudson for better media coverage?

"I don't care about the story. It was never about that. I'm not . . . that place." I couldn't even bring myself to say the name. "I *left.*"

She studied me. "So maybe you weren't angling for a rave review at all."

"What?"

"If what you really wanted was an exit strategy, that would be one way to make it happen." Andrea must have seen the confusion on my face. "Subconscious sabotage," she explained. "If there's no more show, you're free to go, preserving the illusion that your hands are clean when you run off to college to do sports."

Two things were immediately clear: Hudson had told his mother about my secret dream of a cross-country scholarship, and Andrea thought athletes were stupid.

"I didn't sabotage anything. They can keep doing the show without me. I'm just trying to *forge my own path*."

Andrea's "hmmm" sounded skeptical. There was no sign she recognized that I was quoting her words to me. "And yet you haven't exactly liberated yourself."

"Yes, I have!" It might not have seemed like much to her, but getting on a plane for New York City wasn't a small thing in my world.

"Open your eyes, Jo. You traded one mother for another." She gestured at herself. "If that's not playing it safe, I don't know what is."

Right. Because Andrea was so very maternal.

"The worst part is, you're still letting that book control you."

"What? No I'm not."

She sighed like I was a toddler whose antics had stopped being cute. "You're really more of a Louisa May than a Jo, aren't you? Destined to stay in the same small orbit. And I'm afraid Hudson is a Laurie. Charming, but fickle. He's not for you."

Not that charming, I thought as she pushed off the wall and walked into the kitchen. I heard the tap run, followed by the thunk of the glass in the sink.

I was still standing where she'd left me, trying to recover from the body blow, when she emerged.

"Running away is for children. You have unfinished business at home. I suggest you sort it out."

It didn't sound like a suggestion. This was more like the bad fairy at a royal christening: *Guess what, you're cursed. Deal with it.* I wondered what had happened to *the world is as big as you make it.* Striking out on your own. Filling a passport by the time you're twenty-three.

"I'm going out." Grabbing her keys and wallet from the table in the hall, Andrea left me alone.

She began to see that character is a better
possession than money, rank, intellect, or beauty.

—Little Women

CHAPTER FORTY-ONE

Maybe this was Andrea's version of a time-out, since apparently I'd adopted her as a mother figure. Mean Mommy dropped her truth bombs and then took off so I could reflect on the error of my ways. I'd have to be a lot dumber than she thought I was to miss the *run along home* theme. Did she really care about my unresolved family issues, or just want me out of her hair?

Something else niggled at me, now that it was too late to argue. I was a loser for being trapped in that *Little Women* life, but when Andrea used the book to diss me, it was a brilliant insight? It felt like whatever was convenient for her became true, at least temporarily.

None of that changed the fact that I needed to leave, and there wasn't anywhere to go but home. Now that I'd accepted this reality, the longing to be back in a familiar place was growing stronger by the minute. It would be a relief to feel more welcome than a migraine, despite the humiliation of my big adventure only lasting two days.

I would have headed straight to the airport if not for the small detail that I didn't have a ticket home. My brilliant plan had been to use some of my earnings (ha!) to pay for my return trip. Unless I could find a fare that cost less than my remaining bank balance, I was going to have to ask one of my parents for help.

Definitely looking forward to that conversation. *Hi, it's me, your selfish jerk of a daughter. No, the other one. Can you give me a lot of money you don't have because it turns out I'm an idiot?*

That was tomorrow's nightmare. I still had to get through tonight first. Pretending to be asleep so I didn't have to talk to anyone was probably my best strategy. It took about three minutes to gather my things. In the kitchen I downed some water, carefully washing the glass and putting it back in the cabinet afterward. There was a surprisingly fine line between "polite guest" and "hiding forensic evidence."

Wandering back into the living room, I took a last look around. Here was a place I would never see again. I tried to picture a different me coming to work here every day for a less hostile Andrea, while dating a not-two-faced version of Hudson.

The door to Andrea's office was ajar. I drifted in that direction, curious to see where the great reporter did her work. The light spilling in from the living room showed a cluttered desk and a rolling stool. I took another step inside, fumbling for the wall switch.

The first thing I noticed was the couch, clearly the kind that folded out into an actual bed. That must be where favored guests spent the night. Then my gaze landed on the whiteboard next to the desk.

No wonder Andrea hadn't wanted me to sleep in here.

The board was covered in black-and-white photos. Some I remembered Hudson taking; others were new to me. What they all had in common was that we looked like crap. Amy on the floor with her dress hiked up, flipping me the bird. Meg sprawled across a bed with her friends. Mom with lipstick on her teeth, smiling too big.

Me dripping with pond scum.

Leaning over a giant trash can as if about to dig through it.

Glaring like I was about to cut someone, with a bonnet dangling off the back of my head.

We looked pathetic. A pathetic family.

I heard Hudson's voice: *It was a total freak show.* He'd certainly framed it that way.

My brain grasped at excuses. Maybe these were the rejects, the pictures so bad they couldn't be used. Only why put them on display? Especially right next to the desk, where all Andrea had to do was glance to the side for inspiration. Was this how she saw us too?

Tearing my gaze from the pictures, I grabbed the nearest handful of loose papers from her desk. They were printed with double-spaced type on one side, ballpoint scribbles and strike-throughs littering the lines. On the back of one page was a list of handwritten phrases:

Brittle Women

Middling Women

Illicit Women

Too March, or Not Enough?

Little Women Live! Or Do They?

Louisa, May I?

March Madness

And then, circled in red pen: *Belittled Women.*

I sifted through more pages, needing to know what kind of story went with *those* pictures and *that* headline. Near the bottom of the stack, I found these words:

Like the proverbial preacher's daughter, the modern-day March girls are desperate to prove they are more than their reputation. Forget Alcott's prim and proper little women. Conventional morality is a distant dream for these hard-partying, sexually adventurous sisters. Onstage, they simper. Behind-the-scenes, acts of rebellion range from talking back to petty larceny. Even the most fevered work of fan fiction would shy away from the image of Jo March indulging in casual hook-ups in the front seat of a car.

"No effing way," I said to the empty room. How dare that little weasel tell his mom about our make-out session. And *I* was supposedly using *him?*

It went on. Quotes I was sure had been taken out of context, things I'd said to Hudson when we were alone. Like the pictures, the story was slanted to show my family in the worst possible light. And some of those images were from the very first day, as if they'd already had an angle in mind.

The bad snapshots of me were embarrassing, but the thing that made me want to vomit all over Andrea's desk was that the worst lines came straight from my mouth. She might have twisted the context, but they weren't lies. I'd said those things. All the cozy chats, when I thought Andrea and I were bonding? She'd been collecting ammunition.

I'll lose my mind if I have to stay here forever.

That quote was set off on its own, italicized and underlined.

My mother was going to read this story. Mom, who thought this article was our lucky break. Whose voice I'd just heard in the recording telling Andrea that the thing in her life she was most proud of was *Little Women Live!*

I had to do something, stop it from coming out. Without realizing, I'd crumpled a page in my fist.

As if I could pull an Amy and burn it all to ash. And then Andrea would turn on her computer and print another copy, because this wasn't the 1800s. For the first time in my life, I almost wished we were living in Alcott's world.

"Forgive me, dear, I can't help seeing that you are
very lonely, and sometimes there is a hungry
look in your eyes that goes to my heart."

—Little Women

CHAPTER FORTY-TWO

I bought a ticket on a bus leaving New York at a few minutes to midnight. It was less a strategic plan than the flailing of a person who'd just felt a bug crawl across her bare skin and was obeying a primal urge to flee. *Get home,* said every throb of my pulse. Or maybe it was *Get away*. In either case, this was the soonest I could start moving in the right direction, so I handed over my debit card and emptied my account. That left me with slightly less than five dollars' cash. It was going to be a long, hungry trip.

I didn't call my mother to tell her I was coming home. There was no way I could have kept the secret of *why* I was leaving, and this felt like something I needed to tell her in person. Maybe I'd have an idea by then of how to make it better. The trip to Chicago was supposed to be twenty hours long, which should give me plenty of time to think.

When we changed buses for the second time somewhere in Ohio, I was dizzy from tiredness and bad smells, many of which came from me. Though at least I wasn't the person who thought coleslaw was a reasonable snack on public transportation. After I spent my last dollars on Cheetos and Oreos, I paced up and down the sidewalk, wishing I had someone to talk to. Not one of my fellow passengers but someone who knew me well enough to care whether I was about to be murdered in this desolate parking lot.

The only problem was that the list of people I could stand talking to right now was depressingly short. I didn't want to call Meg and say, *Guess what? I screwed up too!* Amy would make a scene, shrieking the house down. Which left . . .

Oh, who was I kidding? I wanted to call David. He would talk me down and tell me everything was going to be okay. *This might be too much even for David,* a small voice whispered. Not to mention that I'd have to start the conversation by saying, *Hey, guess what? Turns out you were right about Hudson!*

I put my phone back in my pocket. Then I took it out again and sent him a quick text:

Coming home.

❧

I finally managed to fall asleep with my face pillowed on my backpack, which was propped against the window. The first thing I did on waking was check my phone, partly to see the time but mostly to know if David had replied.

343

Nothing. No missed calls or messages of any kind. That might have something to do with the *No Service* message at the top of my screen. Or it could mean he didn't want to talk to me. Which, fair enough. My battery was low, so I powered down the phone. Even if I'd managed to get through to David *and* he'd been willing to talk to me, this wouldn't have been the right moment, unless I wanted to treat the entire bus to the emotional equivalent of coleslaw fumes.

It was typical of my amazing timing that only now, separated from him by miles of featureless terrain, technological failures, and too many pigheaded mistakes to count, could I find the words I wanted to say to David.

I wish you were here.

I would go to twenty proms with you.

You're my Butterfinger Blizzard.

⤨

When we reached Chicago, it was late evening. Stifling a yawn, I climbed down the stairs. Most of the other passengers had luggage to collect, but I shouldered my backpack and moved away from the bus, looking for an information kiosk or ticket window. Once I knew how much a ticket south would cost, I could figure out how to pay. And then get out of this station, which didn't exactly give off a Safe Place for Teen Girls to Hang Out Alone vibe. Though to be honest, my more pressing concern was the aroma coming from the snack bar, which made me want to gnaw off my own arm.

"Jo."

I froze. Then I spun so fast I nearly took out an innocent

bystander with my backpack. "David? What—what are you doing here?"

"I came to get you." He held up his keys.

"You drove to Chicago?" That was hours and hours on the road, and his truck was loud at highway speeds. Not to mention the cost of gas, and how scary it must have been to drive through city traffic alone.

He shrugged like it was no big deal—something anyone would have done. But it really wasn't.

"I'm a mess." I looked down, not wanting him to see the mini breakdown playing out on my face. *I wish you weren't seeing me like this, but I'm so freaking glad you're here.*

He gave me one of his stealth David smiles. "At least you're not covered in killer pond amoebas."

My laugh sounded disturbingly like a sob. He took a step toward me, looking worried, and I threw myself at him, pressing my face into his neck as his arms came around me. We stayed that way a long time. He didn't squirm or stiffen, even though we were standing in the middle of a bus station with people all around. I got the feeling David would hold on as long as I needed.

"I'm just really happy to see you," I whispered, as if that explained it all. Pulling back, I took a deep breath. "Sorry for attacking you."

"I'm used to it." His gaze moved over my face. I was pretty sure he wasn't staring into my eyes because he'd been captivated by their beauty. "Are you okay?"

"Tired." I ran a finger under my lashes, hiding the evidence of tears. Then my stomach growled so loudly we were both startled.

"Um," said David. "Food?"

Ten minutes later, we piled into his truck with two cheeseburger value meals and extra fries. I'd gone for coffee instead of Coke, because I didn't want bubbles coming between me and the caffeine.

"I'll pay you back," I told him, for at least the third time.

"I'm not worried about it." He slid his drink into the cup holder. "I know where you live."

"Yeah, but how are you here?" Mom would have said I must have *sent the intention out into the universe,* but I knew that wasn't it, because my imagination wasn't this good. Assuming magical thinking was like the lottery, and you had to actually buy a ticket in order to win.

"Amy got the ball rolling. She knew something was up, so she called Meg, who said your dad had all of you on his family-locator app, which is how they figured out you were heading this way, even though you weren't answering your phone. Your dot was moving so slowly, we figured it had to be a bus." He shrugged like it was no big deal. "Pretty much all of them stop here, so I came to find you."

"Have you been here a long time?"

"Eh." He waved this off. "I'm used to it."

"Bus stations?"

"Waiting for you." Another blink-and-you-missed-it smile, this one sending my heart into my throat.

We finished our meals in silence (other than the feral

animal noises of me inhaling my burger), because I needed time to absorb the news that my sisters had banded together to help me. Sitting in this truck in a grungy parking lot in a strange city with ketchup on my face and a series of small explosions happening in my brain: it was the most comfortable I'd been in days. Maybe longer than that.

"Do you want to talk about it now or get on the road?" David asked, after gathering up all the trash and tossing it in a dumpster.

"Let's drive." It would be way better if he had to keep his eyes on the highway so I couldn't see the disappointment on his face when he found out what I'd done.

It haunted her, not delightfully, as a new
dress should, but dreadfully, like the ghost
of a folly that was not easily laid.

–Little Women

CHAPTER FORTY-THREE

I waited until his phone had navigated us onto the interstate to tell the story of my brief and depressing New York interlude. Some parts I skimmed over, like the ambiguous status of my relationship with Hudson before it crashed and burned. Where I didn't hold back was in describing what Andrea had written, or my role as her major source. David swore under his breath several times, but when I finished, he was silent.

"Do you hate me?" I asked.

He shook his head. "Hudson's the one I want to fire out of a cannon. Not that I ever liked the guy."

"Because you're smart."

"Yeah, well." He huffed at that. "He wasn't trying to get on my good side."

The cheeseburger felt like a boulder in my stomach. "I should have listened to you instead of having a hissy fit."

"No, that's on me. I handled it all wrong. It's not like I was an objective bystander."

"But you were right. I just didn't want to hear it."

He reached across the seat, offering me his hand. I took it and held on tight.

⁓

"Jo." David's hand was warm on my shoulder, gently shaking me awake. I had the feeling he'd been holding on to me for a while, keeping me from tumbling off the seat while I used his leg as a pillow.

I squeezed my eyes shut. It was too soon. "Are we there?"

"Just stopping for gas. I thought you might want to—"

"Totally." I yanked my toiletries from the backpack and made a break for it. In the bathroom, I splashed water on my face and brushed my teeth, then reapplied deodorant. I thought about changing but didn't want to strip down to my underwear in a gas station, and there was really no point slapping on a clean T-shirt if I couldn't ditch this nasty bra for something less funky.

When I got back to the truck, David was already behind the wheel.

"Want me to drive?" I asked.

"I'm fine. You can sleep if you want. Or, if you want something to eat, I got stuff." He nodded at the plastic bag on the seat between us. I wasn't exactly hungry, but if I was going to stay awake and keep David company, I might need an energy boost.

Chex Mix, cranberry juice, and two bags of peanut M&M's. It was exactly what I would have chosen for myself. A tide of emotion started to fill me up inside. David knew my favorites, just like I knew the Junior Mints were for him. One way or another, it was going to burst. I might cry or —

He grunted in surprise as I half climbed onto his lap, wrapping my arms around his neck. Maybe I meant to press my face against his for the feeling of skin on skin, or maybe I was going for a cheek kiss, but somehow my mouth brushed the edge of his lips and then corrected course and suddenly we were full-on kissing.

This was what I needed to tell David. Not *sorry* or *thank you* or even *I missed you,* though all those were true, but how I felt about him deep down, without all the words getting in the way.

Kissing someone I trusted with every fiber of my being should have felt like less of a plunge than making out with a pretentious stranger. And yet to me kissing David was a flying leap. I'd been tiptoeing around the edge of this cliff for ages: a few steps forward, then pulling back again out of fear. Which seemed stupid now that my whole body was soaring and weightless with the thrill of finally taking that last step.

Seriously, what a rush. *I could jump out of this plane all day.*

Our kiss slowed but didn't stop. I adjusted myself so I had my knees on either side of him, the steering wheel poking me in the back. A car door slammed, and I remembered there was a world outside this truck.

"Oops." I slid off his lap. "Didn't mean to do that."

His forehead creased. "Really?"

"Well, not now . . . at this gas station. Sorry."

His exhale was half laughter. "Don't apologize. Except to the snack mix." He tugged the flattened bag from under my leg.

"I'll still eat it."

David nodded, like that was the burning question hanging over us. *Cheese dust: yay or nay?* He gazed steadily at me, daring me not to look away. Were we doing this? It seemed like we were.

"So . . . it's okay?" Probably in the top ten most romantic speeches of all time. Go, me.

"Yep." The corner of his mouth twitched. There must have been a string running from there to my heart, because my insides leaped in response.

How weird to feel this shimmering happiness when the rest of my life was in the crapper. "Took me long enough."

"Better late than never."

"I could have at least showered before I climbed you like a tree."

"You can throw yourself at me whenever you want, Jo."

This time, I moved the snack bag out of the way.

❦

"I was afraid you thought I was too much like Laurie," David said, many miles later.

"Um." The wheels in my brain spun so hard they were probably smoking. "Because . . . you both do sports?"

"Book Laurie. The boy next door." He cleared his throat. "More of a brother."

"Nope. It was the part where you dated my sister. That bugged the crap out of me." Which should have been a clue that

I didn't think of David in a brotherly way, if I hadn't assumed I was annoyed with Meg for her general Megness. I'd been so busy calling my family on their BS, I'd skipped right past my own steaming pile of nonsense.

"By that point I figured I was permanently friend-zoned with you, so there wasn't anything to lose." He glanced at me before returning his eyes to the road. "It won't be a problem, for you and Meg? If the two of us—"

"What do you mean, *if?*" I poked him in the side. "This is happening. And no. It's not going to be an issue. Not because I'm pissed at her either. I got over that." *Around the time I realized I was a total dickhead too.*

He hesitated, frowning at the darkness beyond the windshield. "That's not why you changed your mind—about me?"

"Like a twisted jealousy revenge plot from one of Amy's melodramas?" It would have been easier to keep teasing, but it felt like we were in full-disclosure mode, so I made an effort to open up. "You were never an option. In my head. I assumed you were too nice, or you knew us too well, and we'd probably scared you off ages ago. But when you started going out with Meg it was like, 'Wait, why not me?' So maybe it is a little bit because of her—making me reevaluate the possibilities."

"Only then you were with Hudson."

I flopped back against the headrest, cringing. "If Meg and I are competing in anything, it's who can be the bigger dumbass. Or do more damage to the family business."

David's hand closed around mine. "At least you know what to expect. With the article."

"Yeah." It was better than being blindsided, though that only helped so much. I was still sitting inside a dunk tank, waiting for the drop. Between the article and what she'd said to my face, Andrea had hit me from all sides. *Am I out of control or too naïve? Make up your freaking mind, lady.*

What made her think she had the right to tell my story, like she knew better? It was the same as every *Little Women* fanatic who assumed I was a clone of Jo March. When would it be my turn to say, *No, THIS is who I am?* Or *I'm still figuring it out—check back in ten years?* Instead they wanted me to stay in my box and shut up. Like a good little woman.

I thought of Book Jo, and of Alcott. In both cases, their choices had been constrained by other people's expectations. Was that what I was supposed to do too—suck it up in silence? Let someone else decide the plot of my life?

Ahead of us, the sky was beginning to lighten, color seeping back into the world as the sun peeked over the horizon.

The first faint glimmer of an idea started to take shape.

"I almost wish I hadn't any conscience,
it's so inconvenient."

-Little Women

CHAPTER
FORTY-FOUR

Amy stood on the porch with her arms crossed, staring through the windshield of David's truck as he pulled in behind our house. The screen door slammed as Mom joined her.

This was not going to be pleasant.

"I hope I'm not permanently grounded."

"I'll help you sneak out the window," David promised, squeezing my hand.

He was being discreet, keeping the handholding out of sight below the dashboard, but that wasn't my style.

"Wha—" he grunted as I yanked him toward me, grabbing his face with both hands so I could kiss him for real. None of this peck-and-run business.

"You said I could jump you anytime."

It took him a few seconds to find his voice. "Sure you don't want me to come in?"

"Better not." I didn't want to subject him to the drama, which might make him second-guess any further association with this family.

As I slid out of the passenger seat, I could still sort of feel the pressure of his hand holding mine, which was the next best thing to having him there—like a night-light in a dark room.

"Well, well, well," my sister said as I started up the steps. "Look who came crawling back."

Mom put a hand on her shoulder. "Amy." Like that was going to shut her up.

"I thought you were dead in an alley. Or chopped up in someone's freezer." Without warning, my sister launched herself at me. I didn't have time to take up a defensive stance before she was crushing me in a hug that would probably leave bruises. "FYI, Beth already knows all your lines," she said in my ear. "She's ready to rock. You're going to have to fight her if you want to be Jo opening weekend. Not that it's that great of a part."

With an epic hair toss, she stormed into the house.

"At least she's speaking to me." I didn't quite sell the joke, but Mom gave me a gentle half smile anyway.

The silence felt clammy, like my post–bus trip skin. I wanted to give my mother the chance to lay into me, but it seemed like maybe she was waiting for me to apologize first.

Then she opened her arms, and I stepped into a hug much

softer than the one from Amy. This was like being wrapped in a blanket and held safe and sound. I exhaled like I'd finally set down something heavy.

"Let's go inside," Mom said. I nodded against her shoulder. She stroked the back of my head before letting go to lead the way into the house.

"Tea?" she offered as I collapsed into a chair. She was already filling the kettle.

Home is the place where you don't have to worry about dehydration. My thoughts were blurring around the edges from exhaustion.

"I talked to Andrea." Mom had her back to me as she switched on the burner. After pulling two mugs from the cabinet, she turned to face me. "She said you weren't there."

"I left in kind of a hurry. I thought I'd be home before you knew I was gone."

She nodded, like she wasn't totally surprised. "I called David, and he said he was driving to get you."

We really didn't deserve him.

The familiar movements of my mother making tea soothed me into a trance, even when the kettle whistled. When she joined me at the table, the steam rising from the cups smelled like peppermint.

Mom wrapped both hands around her mug. "Tell me."

It was an invitation, not an order, but I still felt like the starting pistol had gone off and I was frozen in place. Pulling out my phone, I opened the pictures I'd taken in Andrea's office. "I found the article. A draft of it, anyway. It's . . . really bad."

For once I hoped my mother would take the sunshine-and-rainbows view. If anyone could find the silver lining in getting dragged by a major magazine, it would be Mom.

As she squinted at my phone, her face was like a time-lapse of a balloon deflating. "Bitchy much?"

"I'm sorry. I didn't think about how it would sound—"

"Not you. *Her*. This is what you call fair and accurate reporting? Andrea makes us sound like Little Asylum on the Prairie." She set the phone on the table, face-down. "I could have said 'puppies are cute' and she would have passed it off as the ravings of a madwoman."

"Sorry," I said again. Maybe if I stacked up enough apologies they would build a dam tall enough to hold back the sea of regret.

Mom sighed. "I'm not even completely surprised."

"You're not?"

"I've known people like Andrea before." She blew on her tea. "Very clever, but not someone you want to rely on when the chips are down. All that glitters, et cetera."

"But I thought she was the opposite of glitter. A straight talker. Like she had nothing to hide." One of the few people I knew who wasn't faking it. Kind of like I'd thought Hudson couldn't be a jerk because he was borderline nerdy. Or how I'd convinced myself I knew the score when in fact I was clueless about plenty of things.

"And yet." Mom tipped her head at my phone.

It was embarrassing to remember how hard I'd tried to

impress Andrea, like she was a queen who could tap me with her sword of sophistication and declare that I was cool. Did you really have to choose between succeeding in life and treating other people like dirt? If that was adulthood, it sounded like a bad bargain.

"I shouldn't have gone out there." *And spent all my money for nothing.*

Mom covered my hand with hers. "You took a chance. That's not a bad thing. I'm the grownup. I should have known better than to ignore my instincts. When you want something badly enough, it's easy to fool yourself into believing it's possible."

Ouch. But also: truth. I tried my tea again. Either it had reached a drinkable temperature, or I'd singed the inside of my mouth so badly I could no longer tell. "I heard what you said. About why you started *Little Women Live!*" I pinched a crumb off the tablecloth. "I always thought that was why you and Dad split up."

"Really?" Mom's mouth made an O of dismay as she shook her head. "We were already separated. I knew I needed something to do, for money and for my sanity. Speaking of taking chances." She turned her mug in circles. "You know, Alcott grappled with the same questions. How to live, and where, and with whom. Whether to follow your passion or devote your energies to a life of service. She was still working through a lot of that when she wrote the character of Jo. I'm not sure she ever entirely made peace with her situation."

"What about you?"

"Am I happy with my choices?"

I shook my head, filing that under TMI. "How did you decide what you wanted?"

"Oh, I blame Great-Aunt Helen."

"For dying?" Seemed a bit harsh, but then I was seeing a new side of Mom this morning.

"For leaving me this place. It was so exactly like Jo inheriting Plumfield, I figured it had to be a sign."

A bit of a leap considering this wasn't exactly an estate with a manor house and apple orchards, but I knew better than to get bogged down in the details. Besides, that wasn't the part that snagged my attention. "Does that mean *you're* the Jo?"

Mom gave me one of her Marmee smiles, the kind that said, *I'm about to hit you with some serious wisdom.* "I like to think that there's a Jo inside all of us."

Speaking of signs from the universe, this one was letting me know my mother would still be too much for me sometimes. "Even Andrea?"

"It's buried pretty deep in some cases. Subterranean." She walked to the pantry and returned with a box of chocolate marshmallow cookies. Sliding off the cellophane wrapper, she set the tray between us. "I'm sorry you felt trapped, Jo. As a mother, you spend so many years tied up in your kids' lives, you think they'll always be that close to you. Peas in a pod. And then suddenly they're grown up and you wonder, 'Wait, what scene are we doing now? I think I missed a cue.'" She flicked crumbs off her fingers. "You used to love it, you know."

"What?"

"Being onstage. You had zero fear."

"I also had extremely tragic bangs, according to the pictures. And a lot of missing teeth. Things change."

"As they should." Mom took another cookie. "Biting into apples was a real struggle for you." Her face took on a thoughtful expression as she chewed. "I guess that's one good thing to come out of all this."

"Me having a full set of teeth?"

She slanted me an amused look. "Getting things out in the open. Clearing the air."

It was a classic Mom-ism. *Our business is hosed, but at least we had this talk!*

"I'm sorry for stomping all over your dream."

"What, the show?" She waved this off with a partially eaten cookie. "That's not what matters. Why do you think I love that book so much, Jo?"

"Um." Had it suddenly gotten hot in here, or was I walking over a bed of coals? I should really know this answer. "The Christmas scene?"

"Because it's about a *family*. A family that loves each other, through thick and thin. And speaking of family." She winked at me like I was in on the joke, but I had no idea where she was going. "I'm happy about you and David. He's always been like the son I never had."

Before I could explain how incredibly wrong that sounded, Amy burst into the room. "Who called it?" She pointed at herself with both thumbs. "This girl!"

"Congratulations, Great Detective. It's not like it's a secret."

"I'm not talking about the kissy-kissy business." She

puckered her lips like a fish. "Even Meg saw that coming. No, this goes way deeper."

"I have no idea what you're talking about." But as usual it sounded inadvertently dirty.

"Do I seriously have to spell it out? The elephant in the room? You're totally horning in on my territory." Amy moved to the middle of the kitchen, possibly imagining a spotlight shining onto the linoleum. "Pop quiz. Which Little Woman is supposed to snake her sister's boyfriend? Is it Jo? No! Boyfriend stealing is one-hundred percent Book Amy's bag. It's one of the things she's most famous for."

"If by *famous* you mean *hated*," I said, "then yes."

"Whatever. I know the truth. What's next, you're going to fall into a pond and have to be rescued by the cute neighbor?"

"Um." Probably it was a lucky guess. Unless she had the grounds under drone surveillance.

"Don't bother denying it. You want to be me."

"How cunning of you to see through my diabolical plan."

"Furthermore, I think we can all agree that it's my turn to have a breakdown. It's not fair if Meg and Jo get to fall apart and I don't."

"Maybe you're already a disaster?"

"You wish."

"Do I, though?"

"Girls," Mom said, then paused for a wistful sigh. "It's like old times, isn't it? Good to have you back, Jo."

"Actually," I said, "while we're on the subject of Amy being a mess—"

"That's *hot mess* to you."

"Sure. You know how you've been whining for years about doing some of the other Alcott stories? The PG-13 ones?"

"You mean like what Jo really wanted to write until Professor Boring shut her down? Possible subject of my future master's thesis, hashtag watch-this-space?"

"Uh-huh. Do you think we could pull something like that off?"

Amy glanced over both shoulders, like I might be talking to someone else. "Are you asking me for real?"

I nodded. "If it's okay with Mom."

She was biting her lip, but I could tell she didn't want to be the one to destroy this historic moment of her daughters almost agreeing. "What did you have in mind, Jo?"

I wasn't sure it would still make sense now that I wasn't delirious from bus travel and cabbage fumes, but I pressed on. "Instead of being humiliated by all the . . . stuff Andrea says about us in the article, maybe we should own it. Play it to the hilt. Total melodrama."

Amy nodded slowly. "Get our freak on." Because of course she'd been listening the whole time.

"Definitely do not put that in the press release."

"You mean instead of *Little Women*?" Mom held one hand to her chest, like she'd been stabbed in the heart.

"It could be an extra thing. Part of the rotation. Or a special performance." I shrugged. "I haven't figured out the details. It was more of an attitude."

"We'd be laughing it off," Mom said slowly. "In on the joke."

"Especially if we do get people coming here after they read the story." I spread my hands. The salesperson schtick didn't come naturally to me, but I was committed to doing whatever it took. "Publicity is publicity."

"And it wouldn't be a complete departure." The excitement in Mom's voice told me the idea was starting to take hold. "We'd be showing them another side of Alcott. Keeping it in the family."

Amy held up a finger. "Once again, you people should really try listening to me for a change. Speaking of which, I have an announcement."

I'd been home for less than an hour, so I limited myself to a very small eye roll. "Go ahead."

"If I get to go full gothic, maybe I won't freak out and take up a life of crime. Or abandon my family for a doomed romance with a scrawny loser."

"He did turn out to be a bit of a scrub, didn't he? Hudson," Mom added, seeing our baffled expressions.

"We got that part." I glanced at Amy to see if she knew what was going on.

"I think it's from her *Hot Jamz of the Nineties* CD," my sister said, squeezing the words out of the corner of her mouth. "She listens to it when she's sewing."

"Your mother knows many things, girls." Mom tapped her temple. "It's not all *Little Women* up here."

These hearts of ours are curious and
contrary things, and time and nature
work their will in spite of us.

—Little Women

CHAPTER FORTY-FIVE

"I, Rosamond Vivian, will never succumb to your evil wiles, Phillip Tempest!" Amy staggered across the barn floor, one arm crooked over her forehead. She was wearing a long red wig we'd found in the clearance bin at a party store, left over from someone's Little Mermaid Halloween costume, and a white gown with a dragging train.

"You can run, my little rosebud, but you can't hide! Not in a convent or on an island, in Paris or Germany, as a seamstress or a governess." Laurie had one leg up on a prop boulder, the better to show off the fit of his breeches, as he twirled his gigantic fake mustache. He'd given the lines a distinctly *Green Eggs and Ham* rhythm, but the bulging thighs distracted from the Seussness.

"Even if I have you committed to a hideous lunatic asylum"
—he aimed a massive wink at the audience—"I will find you.
You know I love the chase!"

"Why can't you let me be, you brute? I am yours no longer!"
Amy/Rosamond angled herself so the giant fan I'd turned on in
the wings blew her wig back over her shoulders.

"Oh, really? What do you say to this, my dove?" The sound
of Velcro ripping open was like a fanfare of trumpets, announcing Laurie's regularly scheduled chest-baring.

"Don't tempt me with your earthly pleasures, you beast! I
would rather have dignity than a bigamous relationship with a
smooth-talking murderer!"

Offstage, David cued the thunder-and-lightning sound
effects while I hauled the curtain closed on a tableau of Amy
pretending to fight off Laurie's embrace. The applause was
hearty enough to be audible backstage, where David and I were
hauling a canoe into place for the next scene.

Ticket sales had been rising steadily since the publication
of Andrea's story. There was the expected flurry of distant family members sharing the link on Facebook (because apparently no one bothered to read the actual article), but it spread
beyond that. Meg called one night to let us know that she'd
heard people talking about the story in a coffee shop.

"They thought it sounded cool." By Meg standards, it was
practically cheerleading.

I'd always known my mother wasn't the only *Little Women*
fanatic out there, but I figured there were at most a few dozen

others scattered around the country. Despite the scathing tone, Andrea's article had kicked over a surprisingly big rock, sending legions of Alcott obsessives scurrying out of the dark.

It had also put us on the radar of the Irony Tourism crowd. They seemed to especially like the melodramas, and the souvenirs we'd printed with some of the choicer lines from Andrea's muckraking. SEETHING WITH REPRESSED DESIRE was my personal favorite, while Beth preferred the BETH'S DEATH WATCH design, with the timepiece logo. Amy was planning a Weekly Volcano Weekend later in the summer, where we would perform nothing but sensation stories.

I still felt the occasional stab of humiliation when I thought of Hudson, or my embarrassing trip to New York. Mom assured me time would take the edge off the overwhelming sense of regret, especially as I made new and more mortifying mistakes. *Something to look forward to!*

It helped to focus on the positive. Laurie loved his sideline as the Hot Villain du jour, and Beth was all about her new roles as scheming abbess, wisecracking maid, and nasty nurse. Amy told everyone who would listen how her brilliant idea had saved the day. I still played Book Jo occasionally, but I'd also stepped in as Meg a few times, which made the scene where she marries David's character a lot less awkward.

Not that I was looking to settle down to a life of jam-making and popping out twins. It was just nice to know I could still be myself, whatever they called me onstage.

"Here you are, home at last," Amy said one evening, barging into my room without knocking.

"I've been back for weeks," I pointed out as she flounced to the window. "And I was only gone for like two days."

"You know you could have asked us for help. Meg still had the store credit-card number memorized. She totally would have bought you a plane ticket home."

"I guess that possibility didn't cross my mind."

"Well, next time maybe it should. Not that you're allowed to do something like that again. Also Mom canceled the card, so that part isn't an option."

"Good to know."

"In the end, Jo learned a valuable lesson." Amy clasped her hands in front of her, addressing an unseen audience. "Never again would she choose the wicked lures of a small man from a big city over the loving embrace of her family."

"Okay. I get it." Hopefully sitting through this performance was enough of a concession, and she wouldn't expect applause.

"Humbled and grateful, Jo was content to spend the rest of her days ensconced in her childhood abode, cheerfully doing her beloved younger sister's share of the household chores."

"Nice try, loser." I threw a pillow at her back.

"I'm kidding. Geez. And people accuse me of being dramatic!" Still laughing, she ran off to be a weirdo somewhere else.

❧

Unlike Amy, I wasn't ready to sum up the last few months like a smug narrator with an agenda. What lesson had I learned —things that seem terrible can turn out okay? Change is good? Sometimes people who act cool are full of themselves?

Book Marmee would know. Ditto for Mr. March, when he could be bothered to show up. Those two had unwavering moral certainty about everything. It was part of what made them so annoying.

I still wasn't sure what I wanted to do with my life after next year, or how I would pay for it, but here and there I'd glimpsed possible next steps, like arrows spray-painted on the grass of a cross-country course. Dad was enjoying his one-on-one time with Meg so much, he wanted each of us to come for a longer visit. Since there were also a lot of schools back east, and some of them had scholarships for runners, David suggested we make it a road trip, in case he decided to transfer after next year.

For now, he'd signed up for classes at community college, which was a lot cheaper than the big state schools. And also conveniently located half an hour from our houses. He didn't come right out and say so, but I took that as solid evidence I hadn't scared him off yet.

"I don't get how you put up with us," I said to him on one of our long runs, after the last show of the day. The heat had softened to something almost bearable as afternoon eased into twilight. The hint of a breeze ruffled the long grass on either side of the road.

"Why?"

"Because we're a mess. Our baggage has baggage."

"I don't know, Jo. Easy isn't everything."

"Who you callin' easy?" I rammed him with my shoulder before speeding ahead, cackling.

Some things hadn't changed.

That was okay, because I didn't need to torch my old life, like Book Amy flame-broiling her sister's manuscript. All I wanted was to know that there were options. That I wouldn't be stuck treading the same sad loop forever.

Which was maybe a matter of perspective.

Like how on one hand, David and I were pounding down the old, familiar road we'd run yesterday, and the day before. We knew where we were going, because the choice was either toward town or away. But if you lifted your eyes to the horizon instead of staring at the dirt, the path stretched on and on ahead, daring you to run as far and as fast as you could go.

THE END

MEET
THE CAST OF
LITTLE WOMEN LIVE!

(in alphabetical order)

By Amy Porter

AMY:

Teen phenom Amy Porter has always had a flair for the dramatic. As the youngest member of the *Little Women Live!* cast, this child prodigy practically grew up onstage. Amy loves the spotlight, and the spotlight loves her. Her hobbies include art, having lots of friends, being an amazing daughter, and fully embodying the most criminally underappreciated character in the history of books, the one and only AMY MARCH, a fierce feminist icon with a killer sense of style. Words that coincidentally also apply to Amy Porter. Amy is the driving force behind the spectacular new theatrical experience known as Weekly Volcano Weekend (trademark pending).

BETH:

What can you say about Beth? We get a new one every year. The clock is already ticking.

JO:

Jo Porter wants everyone to know she's super into running. Pro tip: don't get her started.

LAURIE:

Superstar in the making Leo "LB" Benitez is well known to fans of sports, great acting, charisma for days, and totally owning the role of LAURIE, a.k.a. everyone's favorite Hot Boy Next Door — and future husband of the *best* March sister. His wardrobe malfunction is your lucky day.

MARMEE:

Abigail Porter is our mom and our MARMEE, the creative visionary behind *Little Women Live!* and a devoted parent on- and offstage, doing her best to raise her girls to be upstanding young women. Which is more of an uphill battle in some cases than others. Love you, Mom!

MEG:

Many will be surprised to learn that our MEG is the oldest of the Porter girls, because she takes such amazing care of her skin. It also helps that she isn't always scowling, unlike certain cast members who spend a lot of time *running around* in the sun.

MR. BROOKE:

Joining the cast for the first time this year in a supporting role as LAURIE'S TUTOR (and secret love interest for one — or more! — of the neighbor girls), local tall person David Vang-Gilligan is a longtime friend of the show. He's a man of few words, but you know what they say: It's the quiet ones you have to watch.

ACKNOWLEDGMENTS

Thank you to everyone who laughed at the (completely absurd) idea of a family of *Little Women* reenactors.

I remember talking about this story with a gathering of writer friends in the before times (it was your housewarming party, Dot Hutchison!) and trying to explain the Beth auditions, and how the book-burning scene turned into a full-on brawl, complete with *Highlander* reference. I expected crickets, but you fools got it, which (for better or worse) encouraged me to carry on. You know who you are, KS/MO peeps, unless you had too many Bellinis that night.

Mom, thanks for cackling so loudly while reading an early draft that it disturbed Dad's *NCIS* reruns. That remains my #1 marketing testimonial. And Dad, I'm so grateful for the magical day we spent together at the Kansas Book Festival, talking about this and many other stories.

Hats off to the members of Team B and my fellow 2020 debuts, especially Rebecca Coffindaffer, for general support and valiant assistance with the Great Title Search. So many Alcott puns, so little space on the spine!

My agent, Bridget Smith, helped shape the Silly Putty of this pitch into a book. I am grateful for her narrative insights, unflappable composure, and all the business-y stuff I gladly leave in her capable hands. Cheers also to the rest of the JABberwocky fam. Here's to many more together!

At this point I would dedicate a special song to my editor Lily Kessinger, but I am still recovering from the shock of learning that she was unfamiliar with the immortal classic "Careless Whisper." This book may be short one Wham! joke as a result, but in every other way it has grown immeasurably thanks to your editorial guidance. One might almost say that when I felt unsure, you took my hand and led me to the dance floor. With the dance floor being a keyboard. (I could go on.) Working on a second book together has been a joy both professionally and personally, and it brightens my day every time your name appears in my inbox.

To everyone else at Clarion and HarperCollins who had a hand in making this book a reality, especially designers Natalie Sousa and Samira Iravani, keen-eyed copyeditor Karen Sherman, publicist Sammy Brown, and production editor Erika West, thank you. I'm also thrilled to have another glorious cover by Monique Aimee, once again perfectly attuned to the mood of the story.

A belated shout-out to Emma Mills, Mary O'Connell, and Miranda Asebedo, who were kind enough to blurb my first book. And to Megan Bannen, Sarah Henning, Raquel Vasquez Gilliland, and Jessica Spotswood, who said nice things about this one, you're the best! The same goes for all the talented members of the book community who play such an invaluable role in connecting readers with stories. Your efforts are deeply appreciated, especially by those of us who couldn't create a cute aesthetic if our lives depended on it.

Thank you to the human and feline superstars of the Raven Bookstore in Lawrence, Kansas; to Darci Falin for letting me borrow the likeness of Finn the Dog (a.k.a. @mamaswiddleguy on Instagram); and to Julie Tollefson for an early beta read.

I could thank Miranda Asebedo and Megan Bannen for a great many things, from hot tips for sheet-pan dinners to the privilege of getting to read their amazing work early. There is also this: The two of you make me feel like a real writer and remind me what that means. When I would otherwise have floundered in a dark sea of doubt (and probably also sharks), you kept me afloat. Thank you for letting me play the triangle in our underground band.

Much love as always to the entire extended Henry/Howlett/Sellet clan. One day I'll find a book to dedicate to you, bros. Sharks, sorcery, fart jokes, spaceships: it'll have it all.

Professor Freddy Bear, who bravely attended the movie with a bunch of sniffling women of varying sizes, has my undying gratitude for resurrecting this file from the depths of my laptop when it appeared all hope was lost. And to our brave and brilliant Gillian, I'm grateful every day that we can laugh about the ridiculousness of life as we write our own mother-daughter story. If I ever force you into show biz, it's because you're such a star. Nar-nar.

It's soothing to imagine a future in which someone might be reading these words unaware of the strange and often bleak state of the world during the years in which it was written. This book was a welcome escape for me when so many other avenues were closed, both as a chance to play make-believe and because Jo feels everything so fiercely. I hope her stubborn, snarky, and ultimately hopeful story is weirdly cathartic for you, too.